Scottish Tales

Scottish Tales

Anna Blair

Richard Drew Publishing, Glasgow

First published 1987 by
Richard Drew Publishing Ltd
6 Clairmont Gardens
Glasgow G3 7LW
Scotland

British Library Cataloguing in Publication Data

Blair, Anna
    Scottish tales.
    I. Title
    823′914[F]   PR6052.I.3427

    ISBN 0-86267-186-8

Designed by James W. Murray

Set in Century Old Style by John Swain and Son Ltd., Glasgow
Printed and bound by Cox & Wyman Ltd., Reading

. . . .

To Evelyn and John
for long friendship
and shared interests
and for the first push
towards print.

. . . .

Contents

Introduction

The tourist pamphlet makes passing reference to a long-gone local character, a moss-grown headstone tantalises with the hint of tragedy, a line in a song presumes a knowledge of some famous infamy or romance of long ago, and there's a drifting shame in the mind that cannot really quite remember the stories behind them. Why *was* The Bonnie Earl of Moray laid on the Green? What was the Gowrie Conspiracy, or the tale of Sweetheart Abbey? Who was John o'Groats?

This book was written, not only to bring those hazy, half-forgotten tales into focus again, but to record others so little known that details of them are tucked away only in yellowing books or in the memories of the very old. Nevertheless they have seemed to me to be worth retelling before they are lost entirely.

The collection is of some fifty stories originating from places as far apart as the Border lands and Orkney, Galloway and Lewis and many inland towns and hamlets in between. They vary in type, with tales of love and battle, smuggling and adventure, of kings, rebels, kirk and commerce. They differ too in tone and period and, in recomposing them, I have tried to be faithful to accent and vocabulary and to match style to the spirit of each tale.

The search for stories has taken me all over Scotland and it has been surprising to find that in spite of the torrent of 'received' speech and pronunciation pouring through radio and television, the accents of storytellers in different areas is still very marked and local words remain in regular usage. To convey meanings of words peculiar to certain districts I have added a glossary of terms as employed in the text. The *style* of speech can be suggested only by idiom and turn of phrase. It is interesting to note in passing that until the Scottish gentry took to the 'good life' of the South along with their transplanted king, James VI and I, or sent their sons there for education, the use of the Scottish vernacular was common to all classes of Scots, and one must suppose that the form of it used around Edinburgh and Fife was also the language of the Court before 1603.

The sources have been as varied as the stories themselves. References in ancient gazetteers and local histories have led to productive visits to villages and towns to follow up clues: ballads have been traced to the old tales which inspired them and chance encounters have thrown up anecdotes and lore passed on to people by their grandparents. The earliest of the stories is *The Dream of Fergus,* a lowland legend of the 6th century, and the latest are those belonging to the eighteen-hundreds, with tales from almost every era between. They are not, nor ever were, aimed at any particular age group . . . or even at Scots alone for, although they are our enriching heritage, they must surely reveal to visitors something of the traditions which make us what we are.

A. Blair. GIFFNOCK *1987*

The Fortune of Willie Guthrie

Archibald Guthrie had a busy little curio-shop in that part of the Edinburgh of the 1850s where middling-to-bien merchants had their establishments.

He himself was prosperous if not fabulously wealthy . . . and generous. The stamp of that was probably his wife's jewel-case, perhaps not the envy of the richest woman in Scotland but with some pieces in it well worth insuring. There were the gold studs he had brought her from London and a fine silver-link bracelet he had found in York, a string of excellent matching Spey pearls sold from a laird's home in Grantown and a ruby ring that she wore with her best cramasie velvet gown. All were good pieces, but young Willie Guthrie, their only son, had known all his life that her beautiful pearl and diamond gold-set brooch was his mother's most cherished possession . . . worth a king's ransom.

Archibald's business had not always been the flourishing concern his son Willie knew. It had started on a stall down the Grassmarket with selections of ornaments, pewter dishes, tea and snuff-boxes. But he had had a good eye and the wives of scholars and ministers with taste but not too many bawbees had found that they could beautify their sparse homes modestly and with refined restraint. Archibald had always conducted his business with strict integrity and when he had taken over a small shop he had kept to the same code. The business expanded and by the time Willie had come into it the boy had never known anything but comfort.

But, although he had grown up in easy surroundings, when he became part of the business it was Archibald's plan for him that he should have no more than a message-boy's pay and start the way he had done himself. But small allowance and prospects were not much to Willie's taste and before he had been a month at work he had deliberately overpriced small items. The first time he had made the sale and pocketed the extra, the second time the customer had turned away and bought his gee-gaw instead from the Guthries' rival, Sam Hay, at his establishment further down the street.

'That's no way for a Guthrie to dae business, Willie, and you'll oblige me by no tryin' such tricks again here,' Archibald scolded him sharply.

Willie was a handsome young man with waving fair hair, a fine moustache and perfect white teeth which he showed in an irresistible smile. One of those captivated by that smile was Nansie, the lissom daughter of Sam Hay of the other curio-shop. Nansie was eighteen and quite certain that in Willie she had found her bonnie lad. Willie was likewise overwhelmed by Nansie with her glossy hair and floating walk. Knowing that their fathers were rivals, and taking no account of the common sense of the two men, they expected opposition and took to a highly romantic and secret wooing.

Nansie too, was used to the good things of life. It grued Willie that he had so little money to spend on her and for several nights he lay awake on his bed wondering where to lay hands on the siller to hire carriages and buy her presents that would impress her. It did not take him very long to think on his mother's jewellery and in particular the pearl and diamond brooch.

It was an easy-enough matter to take it from her velvet jewel-case one evening when only he and a little servant lass were in the house. And there was no shame in him when the lass was dismissed in protesting tears. Willie planned to sell the brooch at the far end of the town or maybe when he was away on some other errand for his father to another town.

He had the brooch in his pocket two days later when he and Nansie were walking hand in hand in a quiet part of the Meadows. They stopped at a bench and he drew his handkerchief out with a flourish to dust the seat for his lady and to his dismay the brooch came with it and fell to the ground.

'My, Willie! Have you really bought this for me? It's a fine brooch.' She held it against her collar. 'Thank you, thank you.' And she looked round to see that no one was nearby, and kissed him shyly.

'You ken my father's close-fisted Nansie. I saved a long time for this,' he lied self-righteously, wondering uneasily if she had any idea how valuable it was.

So Willie did not, after all, have the money from selling the brooch to line his pockets and spoil Nansie. But by now the thought had occurred to him that his father and Sam Hay, both canny business men, might find a match between himself and Nansie a fine thing. Maybe in time the two shops might be his. All the same the brooch must never come to light.

'Mind Nansie. It's a secret between the two of us. Just you wear it when I'm alone wi' you . . . just a kind of love-charm.'

Nansie sighed in ecstasy and promised. And she fairly danced home that day at Willie's new idea that their fathers would be pleased to see them wed. She was to speak to hers before Willie came asking for her hand.

She would have to confess to walking with Willie and she expected to have to plead some with her father, but she had always wound him round her pinkie before and almost looked forward to the wheedling. But Sam Hay's answer when it came, horrified her.

'You shouldnae have been stravaiging on your own wi' that young man, and he'd no business to take you. That was shameful Nansie. All the same if it had been some other laddie we might just have overlooked it, but Willie Guthrie's no' for you my girl. His father's rivals wi' me but he's an honest man. Willie Guthrie's no more like Archibald than a bee's like a bulldog. He's a cheat, no' the lad for my lassie, and no Hay tocher-gift will go to him or any like him. It's only a token gift, you ken that, but it's worth a bit and my father and my grandfather gave them wi' their girls when they were wed, for sign the young man was welcome. But Willie Guthrie's no' welcome to me.' Sam waved his hand and dismissed Willie for ever. 'Besides I have other plans for you. There's young Jamie there, a grand hard worker and as honest a lad as ever I met. He's maybe nobody yet Nansie, but mind, I've no sons to follow me. He'll make you a better man than ten Willie Guthries.'

Jamie Scott, new to Edinburgh from the Borders, was Sam Hay's assistant, steady and quiet, with a shrewd eye for worthwhile porcelain and pictures and small furniture, and more than half in love with Nansie already.

There were stormy scenes with her father and tearful scenes with Willie, whose ardour had cooled considerably when his notion of a joint business came to grief. Willie wrote the brooch off to bitter experience, Nansie had to wrap it away in memory of her dashing lover and prepare to wed the plain Jamie with the shy smile. Not to be outdone Willie offered for a plump unbraw girl whose father was a rich city merchant only to find out too late that she was one of six children, five of them sons in the business.

In a month Sam Hay had given Jamie a fine gold watch and chain for a tocher; in two, Nansie and the Border lad were wed. In a year he was Sam's partner and she was contentedly nursing a little daughter; and in another she was loving Jamie as she had never known how to love Willie Guthrie. Sam had two years to enjoy the baby, Lilias, before he died and the business passed into Jamie's hands.

Over the years while Lilias grew from winning child to comely woman Willie's diamond and pearl brooch lay in the bottom of the drawer containing the rings, bracelets, jades and necklaces that were some of the jewels that Jamie lavished on Nansie. Sometimes she looked at it a mite wryly and wished that her husband had been a poor man so that she could have shown her love for him by selling it to set him up in trade. But Jamie was not a poor man. Not in money matters. But he thought himself the most stricken of men when his lovely Nansie died on Lilias's tenth birthday.

While that was the story of Jamie Scott's life with his lost Nansie, Willie Guthrie was still moodily working for his father. For a long time Archibald was a disappointed man. He had never been able to trust his son, never made him either a partner or a confidential assistant. Only his little grandson Robin was of any comfort to him. Willie chafed with resentment that he was allowed to sell customers only the lowest-priced of their wares. He still had a fair conceit of himself, had Willie though, and was sure that if he could lay his hands on even a hundred pounds he could start from next to nothing and by clever deals soon be upsides with his father. It was just that wee bit of capital that eluded him.

Archibald, almost blind now, was turning more and more to

rely on his grandson, Robin, grown into a worthy young man, as
honest as clear water, with none of his father's shiftiness but with
an integrity to match Archibald's own. Quietly old Guthrie made
Robin his partner.

Willie was never one to bother the kirk much, but Robin
enjoyed the walk there with his grandfather of a Sabbath morning.
He had lots to thank God for and when he first caught a grown-up
glimpse of Lilias Scott, in a gown the very blue of a summer sky,
sitting in a nearby pew with her father he decided, there and then,
that before he was done he would have a lot more to thank Him for.

He bowed to Lilias at the kirk steps that morning. Then for a
month he walked her home after sermon time and for another he
sat in the Scott's parlour of a Saturday night. And then he asked
Jamie Scott if could he wed her.

'Aye, if she'll tak' you, Robin Guthrie, for you're a well-doing
lad like your grandsire.' Jamie said nothing about Willie.

Willie himself had no particular hindrance to put in their way.
He supposed there was a kind of queer justice in a match between
his son and Nansie's lassie. He shrugged a cool acceptance when
the family met to drink their gude-health.

'Don't forget we've to give Robin's father a tocher,' Lilias
reminded her father of the family tradition. And at the mention of
the dowry-gift Willie's eyes gleamed.

Jamie and Lilias spent a sentimental evening looking over the
jewellery he had given her mother. While he had had a rare
knowledge of porcelain and old woods, Jamie had never been
much interested professionally in gems and settings. He had
trusted a jeweller friend's judgement and good faith, willingly paid
the bills and given them to Nansie with love. He looked at them
now. There was the gold pin he had bought when they'd been a
year wed, the bracelet when Lilias was born, the pendant with a
clear drop-crystal when they had lost a bairn. He minded all of
them, clips, chains and earrings, but there was one brooch there
among them that he'd no minding of at all . . . a birthday maybe or
after some illness . . . since he could not put a memory to it
maybe that should be the thing to give Willie Guthrie. It would be
worth a fair bit for he'd never been a man to stint on quality. Aye
that would answer fine for the gift.

Jamie smiled with goodwill as he gave over the tocher. Lilias and Robin smiled at one another with love, Archibald, blind as he was, smiled that he had lived to share this day, Willie Guthrie smiled with satisfaction as his hand closed once again over his mother's precious diamond and pearl circle. For it was to free him at last from being for ever tagled by honest men too scrupulous for fortune-making.

And maybe, somewhere, Willie's long dead mother smiled as she remembered the moment Archibald had pinned it to her dress in the unprosperous days just after they were wed. With his down-to-earth honesty, not willing to deceive her, he had whispered, 'It's no more nor glass and bead, mind, Jinnet, but I thought it was bonnie . . . maybe someday you'll get better.'

The True Story of James Macpherson

If the Laird of Invereshie House near Kincraig had known that his lad Jamie, that he sired by a flash-eyed gypsy girl from the hills, was to be his only son, he might have been brave enough to marry her instead of cravenly sending her back to her own people and keeping the boy to raise by his own hand, at Invereshie.

Jamie had the dark, proud handsomeness of his mother, and her free spirit, and the laird, who had delighted in those in the mother, gloried in them in the boy. He did not heed the sage from over the hill when the old man twice warned him against making the lad too reckless, for he had foreseen ill-fate attending on the son of the house of Invereshie. If anything the father increased his efforts so that if harm awaited his boy he would be the stronger to defeat it.

Jamie was a steering infant and a fearless child. By the time he was seven years old his father had had the smith make him a double-handed sword heavy enough for a lad of twelve and taught him to whirl and thrust it like a warrior. The laird took him up frowning peaks till he could climb the juts like a goat, and had him wade, guddle and swim the rivers so that he could cross safely in all but the wildest spates. He rode hard and fast, and knew every gulley and short-cut path between his own glen and any of a dozen others. By the time he was a youth he was headstrong, adventurous and a match for anyone or any situation that confronted him. And yet for all his skills he had never any real desire to hurt or terrify.

The laird saw with satisfaction that, along with the traditions of his own line, he had nourished in his son the strengths and love of freedom of his mother's people. What he had not accounted for in those gypsy hill-folk was the other side of their nature, the poetry and music in their souls, just as marked a characteristic as their aptness with sword and the fleetness of their limbs. It took a priest in the Feshie valley to see and foster that in Jamie Macpherson. The priest met him a time or two during his green years, neither battling with river or rock-face or slashing at imaginary foes with his sword, but sitting absorbing the beauty of the riverside, the arcing silver of leaping fish, or lying on his back in the heather watching wheeling birds in the sky. And he heard Jamie whistle slow Highland lamentations and blithe jigs as he wandered the moors. It was the good Father who showed him how to put his long thoughts into verse, who taught him to play the violin and had the laird provide the boy with the best instrument the old fiddle-maker could make for him. It was the priest too who, like the sage, warned Jamie that gifted, dauntless, though he was, his fearless spirit could be his downfall. But the boy was young and would not tremble at any such prospect.

The Laird was ailing now and, looking to the future, was sadder than ever that this young man was not his heir. But he was not: and when Invereshie died, the inheritance passed to Jamie's cousin, Donald Macpherson. Jamie would not have been human if he had not resented society dictating that nephew and not son became the new Laird. But he had another inheritance that was not of great house and lands, and so, burdened with little more than the huge two-handed sword which had been his father's last gift, and his precious fiddle, he set off into the hills to taste the life of his mother's gypsy people.

And it was much to his liking. His mother had never lost her girl-love for Jamie's father and now that he was dead she lavished it on the boy, teaching him all she knew of the wisdom and passionate poetry of the wild. The authority he had of his gentry rearing combined with the guidance of a strong-willed mother made a powerful mix and in a year or two he was a leader among her people. He entertained them with poetry and song by night, had twenty-seven men ever at his heels by day, a piper at his side and another thirty ready to come at his call.

Jamie and his men were thirled to no master but they were neither brigands nor thieves. They were, rather, astute judges of horse-flesh and made their living buying animals in the Highlands and driving them to the Lowlands to sell. Other men who travelled the country, sleeping in empty barns or farm outbuildings, might have been unwelcome sorners but Jamie and his band were well-received and none ever thought to turn them out if they had helped themselves to a night's hospitality. They were untroublesome and, more than that, brought a night's entertainment and even protection with them. So Jamie Macpherson was a popular man wherever he went . . . until he fell foul of Alexander Duff, the Laird of Braco.

Macpherson and his merry men had that day been south with a selling of horses and had taken a day and a half to ride back up into the Highlands, arriving at the Balloch hill near the borders of Banffshire, as dusk was falling. They had settled themselves into a barn there and Jamie went to the house to tell the farmer that he and his company would be spending the night on his steading.

When he swung open the door he happened on a scene he never afterwards forgot. A girl was crouched in a corner trying to fend off a man who had waited his chance of her farmer father being from home to come and molest her. She was in tears and holding the remnants of her bodice together when Jamie strode across the room, grasped him by the collar and breeches and propelled him out through the doorway.

In a moment the yard was a-whirl with arms, legs and staves in a melee, Jamie's twenty-seven against the party Alexander Duff of Braco had called from behind dykes and tussocks to his assistance. Macpherson's gypsies were too much for Duff's men and soon they were in furious retreat; fled into the dusk.

But from that night Alexander Duff was set to be revenged on Jamie Macpherson. From the comforting of Mary Gordon after her attack, protection and gratitude became love, and by the time, a day or two later, that Jamie left the farm it was under the promise that he would be back to woo her.

Resentment by now had taken Duff to lay before the Sheriff of Banffshire a complaint that the gypsy James Macpherson had made an unprovoked attack on a douce respectable laird and his party. The Sheriff, much impressed by Duff's well-put-on airs outlawed Jamie since he was a roving tinkler with no fixed home in which he could be found and arrested.

He might in fact have been easily enough found at his old home at Invereshie, or calling like any other country lad on his lass Mary Gordon. His cousin Donald was proving to be more friend than usurping Laird, a kindred spirit almost as much at home in wild country as Jamie himself. It was common enough practice in the late 1600s for lairds to make cattle-thieving forages against neighbours and Donald found in the outlawed James, and his gypsies, a band of braves unbeatable in either defending Invereshie beasts or helping themselves to those on other lands.

For a few months they exulted in the two-way forage and chase, until it came to the sharp ears of Alexander Duff that his enemy was roaming the Invereshie lands. The Sheriff of Banffshire who had outlawed the gypsy made new efforts to catch him for the added crime of sheep-lifting. Jamie was safe now only in the remotest shielings. Farmers, shepherds and cottars who welcomed him under their roof were warned not to harbour him and three times he found he was putting families in danger by taking shelter for himself and his men among them.

When James Macpherson's mother died the next spring, it seemed to him that perhaps it was time for another stage in life, after having lived half, so far, as his father's lad and half his mother's. Now he would be his own man and, God willing, Mary

Gordon's. But it would not be in Scotland. They would emigrate and start new lives in America where there was wild country to be tamed. . . .

It might have been possible for them to slip quietly away among others taking to the sailing ships. But that was not Jamie Macpherson's way. He was not by nature a skulker in sheds or corners or a slipper-away quietly, and the reckless demon that the priest had seen in him long ago drove him now, before he would take Mary off over the seas with him, to gather his tribe of twenty-seven round him and make a farewell march out of outlawry to the St. Rufus Fair in Banff. One of his men carried his sword and he played his fiddle through the streets to the cheers of the crowds, made three rounds of the fair and was ready to march out of town and back to Mary Gordon's place to marry her and prepare for their departure. It was a brave flaunt of defiance at Alexander Duff's tame sheriff, who was by now apoplectic that the gypsy was still evading him and made even angrier by Laird Braco's contempt that as Banff's law officer he had not laid hands on Macpherson long since. But Jamie's time had come. As the braw straggle skirled their way to the outskirts of the town the Sheriff's men, leaning from an upstairs window, dropped plaids on the company and took a handful of them in a blind fankle of wool and fringe.

Donald, the piper and most of the gypsies escaped but Jamie was held.

There was a hasty trial and, before the townsfolk had organised themselves in his support, he was sentenced to death and left in jail to receive Mary on two tearful visits, to give her his only legacy, to contemplate his end and make his peace.

Laird Donald fought manfully for a reprieve and had high hopes of its arrival before noon on the day of the gibbeting. Indeed news had reached Banff that the rider was even now only a few miles from the town. Time was being marked by the clock at the jail and alert citizens might have noticed that shortly after Alexander Duff went into the jail the hands had been put forward thirty minutes and the prisoner brought out half-an-hour early to take his last walk.

Jamie stepped out into a bleak November day of snell wind and sleet, into a street packed with mutinous citizens. He had parted from his sword but he still carried jauntily his fine fiddle. He lifted a hand in farewell to Mary and when she would have clung to him he put her gently away.

'You cannae help me noo Mary, but keep you safe my papers.'

Then he put the fiddle to his chin and played a defiant rant all the way to the gallows. He leapt up on to the platform there and wilder and wilder sang out the fiddle in the music he had been composing these last days in the jail. The bow flew faster and faster and the crowd grew still, silenced by the eerie magic of his play. A last drawing of bow across strings and half-gypsy Jamie looked out over the heads of the crowd. He held out the violin.

'Who'll tak' my fiddle?'

There was no response to the offer. It was as if they thought there might be wizardry in a fiddle that played so wild.

'Will none tak' it?'

Silence again. He held the violin above his head, lifted his knee and brought down the fiddle to crash it across his thigh. Then he threw it into the crowd and beckoned the hangman to his work.

Jamie's body had dangled there no more than fifteen minutes when the horseman carrying his reprieve clattered into Banff. The Laird of Braco was hounded from the town and never dared set foot there again. Mary Gordon, already half-crazed with horror at the death of her lover was quite crushed at the reprieve-man's coming. She left the town and wandered for a long time in the hills like a wanting-woman and none who gave her shelter in these months could prise from her the manuscript of her man's music which was all Jamie had been able to leave her.

When time brought healing, she was proud to let it be copied and to hear men playing the haunting, wild music of Macphersons's final rant.

There were two legacies, then, of James Macpherson, the tune that bears his name and the broken fiddle-neck they cherish as heirloom in the family of Cluny Macpherson, kinsfolk of Donald Macpherson. Aye, and a third; the memory of a daring Highland outlaw with a sword no other man could lift, but without innocent blood on his hands and with music in his soul.

They were proud men in past days in the Highlands. And none prouder than the clan chiefs with eyes like eagles looking out from above the pinch-bridge of great beaks to the mountains and firths and to the effete Lowlands, and they were wary against invading authority. They scorned the petty ways of townsmen with their barter and scrabbling for money.

When clan ways eventually fell apart, the chiefs dwindled into lairds, as the clansmen dwindled into trousers, and almost all that remained of their fierce spirit was their pride and their scorn for trade.

Lairds lived in bien mansions now, instead of gaunt keeps and their lady-wives had gone soft and wanted tight roofs, new windows and fancy carvings on their mantel-shelves.

And so it was that some two hundred years ago one of these half-chief half-laird men owed a substantial debt to a Lowland cabinet-maker and joiner who had done work for him but whom he despised for his fascination with the columns of his ledgers. The tradesman had widened the laird's eaves and put stout arched doors at his entrance, bossed and studded like a targe. Then he had had the grovelling temerity to send a man, post haste, for settlement. The pride of the chief's wild forebears swept over him and he had the courier chased from his house. The poor man did not stop running until he was into Stirling and halfway home to the town. Another messenger, and then a third, suffered the same fate, the last one having jouked a whipping only because he was young and fleet of foot.

The chief drew bristling eyebrows together and growled to his lady that he would pay the scoundrel when he chose and not on the whim of money-grabbing collectors. For such men had no pride.

The tradesman was irked by the unbalance in his books and made the journey north himself as soon as ever the weather was fit. The laird, at his window, saw him coming across the moor and called his steward to give him instructions. . . .

The traveller studied and re-admired his handiwork as he waited a little nervously at the front entrance, but he was surprised at the courteous welcome he received. To be sure he was sent from the fine new front entrance he had built to the servants' rear door; but no matter, he was taken in, led down to the kitchen and warmed with a stoup of thick broth. He did not state his business . . . that was between himself and the laird, man to man. The chief was not at home, he was told, but he was welcome to stay over until the master returned next evening. This treatment was so kindly that the visitor began to wonder if his messengers, having been given money to make the journey, had not been bothered to come at all, or if they had played him false in any other way.

He was taken up the back stairs to a turreted room, barely furnished, but with a comfortable-enough bed, a small ingle and a clear view of the rear 'green' from the window. As he prepared for bed there was some commotion out in the yard and he stood by the window to watch the figures moving briskly about the back area. There was a gnarled black tree, a sturdy stool and, lying between them, a coil of rope. Then, startled, for he had been reared after all in the douce ways of the city, he saw a man's figure hoisted roughly on to the stool, an end of the rope thrown round a branch above, a noose slipped over his head and round his throat. Then the cutty-stool was kicked away, the victim's body jerked once, and hung dangling there, gently turning round and round while the mesmerised spectator stood rooted at the window until he was chilled to the marrow.

He lay rigidly awake all night and his face next morning was sheep-grey as he supped his porridge, hovered over by the great broody woman who ruled the kitchen.

'Was that some murdering blackguard of a Highland cattle-thief I saw gallused there last night?' he ventured at last.

'Never, never that,' said the woman shortly and turned to her swee at the fire. 'Jist some impudent wee town merchant that had the shame to dun and pother the master for some footlin' debt he had-it the laird owed him. And the master good enough to give him the honour of cuttin' a bit plank for his front door-place here. There's nae pride in city folk . . . except for the likes of yoursel' of course.' It was a long speech for the housekeeper and she said no more.

In ten minutes time the visitor was moving hurriedly south over the moor again mentally putting a line through the debt in his big book. A pair of satisfied eyes watched him out of sight and then the chief came down from his armour-room with a sword his sires had used proudly in old battles. He went out into his back yard. There he cut down the bundle of rags from the gibbet, took it back to where it belonged and re-erected it there on the empty scarecrow stake in the minister's adjoining glebe. Then he too struck off that debt, mentally of course, for he disdained to keep books like any small-souled Lowlander.

· The Sceptic and the Merwoman of Uist ·

There's so many a tale of mermaids and mermen round the Scottish coast that it must seem to even your hardest-headed sceptic that there is some queer knuckle of truth behind them.

Neil Macdonald of South Uist once saw a mermaid. And he would have told you so quite firmly if you had been living at that time, which was some years before the great '45.

Anyway Neil was not a gullible youth, nor fey, for he was man-enough later to wander throughout two months with the fugitive Charlie, to prop up the adventure with Flora Macdonald and at the end to go into exile with the Prince to France. He was the sire, too, of a son by his French wife . . . a son who became a marshall in the army of Napoleon Bonaparte. So Neil, it can be reckoned, was no dreamer of dreams or credulous Uist ninny.

Well, when he was a lad, he was walking along the shore one day to his small boat drawn up on the sand, when he met two younger boys scrambling along through sea-weed and pebbles, blethering excitedly that they had just that moment seen a merwoman in the water beyond the boat. Neil laughed at them, ruffled their hair and offered them a sail in his boat to cool their heads. But today they did not jump at the offer. They had seen a mermaid. No doubt of it. Neil shook his head, went back with them and was shaken to see, floating vertically, her breasts on the level of the water, a woman nursing a child. But she was not the beautiful sea-creature of fables. Her skin and heavy hair were coarse, her face flat, grey and unbonnie. He thought at first that he was seeing perhaps a dead woman with a baby sucking at an empty breast and was preparing to fetch the boat to go out to bring in the corp.

"Tis but an ill woman needs our help. You find Father James and I will go for her,' said Neil, not to alarm the small boys.

'No, Neil Macdonald. 'Tis a merwoman, did we not see her tail?'

'The more do we need the priest if she's an unchancy being like that,' said Neil firmly and sent them off to the Father's hut, not far back from the shore. If there was time for some last rite, it was but Christian to bring it.

Before Father James had come back, Neil had pushed off in the little boat; there was a quick thrash in the sea and he could have sworn he saw as fish a tail as he'd ever seen twitching on a line. Then the merwoman was gone and only a white frill of a wake behind her.

The priest was back with the lads while Neil still stood there scratching his head and in danger of toppling into the water. Father James listened gravely to the boys and did not show the disbelief that Neil thought would have to be overcome before the good man would hear them out. The priest took a piece of driftwood and drew with it on the sand . . . the flat head, the mane of hair, the high breast.

'With skin the grey of a dark sky?' he asked.

'Indeed.'

'Coarse, like drowned?'

'Aye.'

'Then you have seen here what I have seen only in the warm waters of Spain or maybe the south of Ireland in a fine summer. You have seen a sea-cow, a dugong, and each of you will remember it to your dying day.'

Many a one Neil Macdonald told of the mermaid he had seen that morning; his little French son for sure, and maybe he told Betty Burke to cheer her on her way across to Skye. But only the priest and the young boys knew the meaning of the twinkle in his eye when he spoke of the merwoman of Uist.

But, come to think of it, it was maybe just as strange a thing to see a dugong in these cold Hebridean waters as to see a mermaid.

Ninian MacSkimming's Come-Uppance

Matthew Gilmour was a Glasgow man, middle of everything . . . age, height, colouring and income. It was said of him that, when he was slandered, defeated in argument or otherwise done down by one or more of his acquaintances, he turned the other cheek only long enough to search the horizon for a way of bettering his tormentors.

There had been the time that he had buttered the knobs of one group's walking canes because they had scorned his new snuff-coloured waistcoat, then watched from a corner in the coffee-house when they went to the stick-stand and had all five of their canes slipping and slithering among their legs. Another time someone who called Mistress Gilmour bun-faced, had his shoe-lacings tied together under the coffee-house table and his lum hat tacked to the bonnet rack. Matthew did smile to himself privately over the description of his wife, for Mistress Gilmour, who worked happily most days in her garden, had a pleasant brown shine to her round face and small black twinkling eyes, that made her look exactly like a currant bun. But he loved her none the worse for that.

But the same man, one Ninian MacSkimming, went too far when Matthew overheard him say of Mistress Gilmour that 'if he had married her he would have considered her far beneath him'.

Matthew Gilmour pondered that one. He was a gregarious, cheerful man and, until the perfect answer to Ninian came to him, he had the man quite off his guard by remaining on normal good-natured terms with him. What Matt was after was a more public affront than the likes of a quiet tying of his tail-coat to the back of a chair in the coffee house, which perhaps no one else would witness.

The puzzle came and went in Gilmour's mind, according as the importance of his business affairs fluctuated in it, and it was about a month later that he was walking along the Trongate early one morning, Ninian and his come-uppance quite out of his mind, when he tripped over a workman's ladder left carelessly on the pavement beside the plinth of the great equestrian statue of King William III. Matthew took only a very soft fall on his bottom but as he sat there he had quite a new perspective on the figure and the horse. My, but it was a fine braw statue that . . . the horse looked ready to plunge right down on the Trongate. He had never really looked right at the thing before. He glanced at the ladder and at the statue again, then scrambled to his feet. He lifted the ladder, set it carefully against the statue and climbed up . . . and up. Then he swung a leg over the horse and sat there behind the King's flowing cloak, chuckling mightily and enjoying the view. He could even see into a corner of his own backyard from here with the bonnie bit garden that his little wife made there.

Now, another early bird making for his business premises that morning was Ninian MacSkimming and when Matthew saw him he felt his middle-aged pulse beat a little faster.

'Ninian friend, you're early out the day,' he called down. MacSkimming looked up.

'What in the world are you doin' up there Matt Gilmour?'

'My heaven man, you've never seen sic a view as this. The whole toon's stretched oot afore me. Here, come up and see for yoursel' . . . no, but wait . . . there's maybe no' room for the twa of us ahint the King here . . . I'll come doon and let you up.'

He came nimbly down the ladder and assured Ninian again about the panorama to be viewed from the statue. Up went MacSkimming, leg over, back-saddle to William III. He was about to shout down and agree with Matthew about the view when he saw the merchant calmly lifting off the ladder and walking away with it, calling back as he went, 'If you bide up there for the day Ninian MacSkimming you're sure to see Mistress Gilmour oot at the flowers in her garden . . . way-way beneath you right enough . . . just the way you say about her.'

And there he stayed for the day fuming and fizzing and the butt of all the Glasgow wags who were none too fond of him, and very fond indeed of bun-faced little Mistress Gilmour.

The Hermit of Inchcolme

The night seemed fine, as Alexander, King of Scots, came riding along the coast of Fife . . . a little brooding perhaps but clear enough for his journey across the river. But as he looked towards the cluster of houses on the far side he saw a whip on the waters of the Forth that told of ill weather to come. But not yet, decided the King. There was time a-plenty to set sail and be over there before the storm broke. The crossing was short and he would be in

Edinburgh, safe and sound, while it was still gathering.

The King usually enjoyed the easy sail over the Forth, for the ferry route was the same one his saintly mother, the good Queen Margaret, had taken on her journeys between Dunfermline and her beloved chapel on the Rock at Edinburgh. The plain folk, whom she blessed as she embarked and landed, had ever since called their little shore villages of the north and south, the 'Queen's Ferries'.

He could be careless of his prayers could Alexander, but when he followed in his mother's wake like this, across the Forth, he was always minded of her and would go and stand in the prow of the frail little ship, confess his sins to her God and feel renewed for affairs of kingship in Edinburgh.

He was there now at the front of the ship and, although he prayed sincerely enough, he was not so transported in his religious exercises that he did not see that the whip on the water was uglier now, the waves deeper, and the wind was beginning to blatt warningly against the sail. They were scarcely fifty yards from the north jetty when the storm began to shake itself out in earnest. Winds shrieked across the waters and the boat began to be tossed about, impossible for the helmsman to steer. It swung this way and that, pitched off-course down-river, and began to dip drunkenly from side to side, so that all aboard, a little party of close companions, were thrown about the deck. Alexander's feathered hat disappeared in a black swirl of water and, as he sank to his knees and drew his thick cloak round him, all that the company could see of him, stark in the darkness, was his white face and his moving lips. The King was making desperate bargains with Father, Son and Holy Spirit and with all the Saints. It was Columba's name that came tumbling and stumbling most often in his final vow as the ship shuddered and seemed like to go down.

'In the name of the blessed Columba, bringer of the Holy Gospel to this land; an' it be that we are spared the waters under the earth I mak' sacred vow to raise a Holy Place wheresoever we find safe lodging this night.' Three times he made his vow as the wheel spun loose and the ship plunged yet again into a trough of the sea.

And then the prow was lifted right out of the water, ploughed back down again and, with a grinding roar, lay still on its side on some unlit gravelly shore. Not a soul was lost and presently the whole company was safe on land.

In the midst of the wild black night they saw a torch carried through the darkness towards them, its flames flaring in all directions in the wayward wind. Then it lit up the face of the bearer, a bearded holy man, his cross around his neck.

'The Lord has surely brought you safe hither, friends. Are all of you unhurt?'

'God's mercy aye, good sir,' replied the King.

'Then follow me to shelter and food.'

The hermit's cell was bare and small resting-place for eight or nine men. But it was out of the storm and the hermit lit a fire and gave them of his scant store of oatencake and ale. If he knew his king he did not speak of it for these were but men, all in the same extremity.

'What place is this?' asked Alexander.

'It is the island of Saint Columba. Men call it Inchcolme,' was the reply.

And the King's hand shook with the miracle of his prayer and saving as he raised the cog of ale to his lips.

'For God's deliverance I will raise a priory on your Inchcolme, and for your service and love I will pray by Saint Columba that before you die, old man, men shall know twice more of God's presence here.'

Two nights and days they stayed with the heart-generous hospitality of the hermit until the shouting of the storm died away.

Alexander made good his vow and consecrated an Augustinian Priory on the spot where he had found God's favour.

The hermit was two years older when there sailed past Inchcolme an English raiding ship bearing in its cargo the treasures of a wickedly looted church where its crew had left holy men dead. Now images of the saints, silverware, hangings and fine candles were on their way south. But just off the island a freak storm turned a fine day into a nightmare of terror and the pillagers scuttled back up river, replaced the plunder, buried the holy dead and fled back to their own home waters. And that was the second mark of God's presence.

Alexander was gone and the Inchcolme hermit ancient when another pirate ship, hot from the sacking of a little church in Fife, came merrily towards the island, its sails full of bountiful wind, but its hold full of the modest but precious pieces of plate and carving stolen from the simple worshippers. The crew celebrated and caroused as they gloated over their sacred plunder. Suddenly the warm wind turned capricious, flung itself back on the ship and its now blaspheming crew, and did not blow itself out until ship, treasure and crew lay on the bottom of the Forth.

And that was the third mark of God's presence at Inchcolme. Only then, as Alexander had sought in his prayers, did the hermit die in the fullness of his years.

The Wild Men of Lochaber

In the days of long ago the good people of the hills round Shiel, in the broad stretches of Lochaber country, had two problems. Both of them seemingly insoluble. The first of their difficulties was that they could scratch only the barest living from their soil because it was so stony and the second was they had to live alongside a pack of violent and quarrelsome brothers.

The first problem was one of nature, and they felt they had to resign themselves forever to no more than survival with the greatest effort. But the second problem had a stir of fear about it because the brothers, as well as being violent and quarrelsome, were giant-huge, immensely strong and did not only fight with each other. Their hasty tempers could, and often did, spill out beyond their family into the community and quieter people went in dread of their lives. It seemed there was no prospect of their leaving, for of all the land around Loch Shiel theirs was the least stony and anyway there were six of them, strong men all, to work it and, when they were not trying to get the better of each other in some contest of strength, they coaxed more out of each rig than anyone else in the whole of Lochaber.

The modest folk of the countryside kept as far as possible from the brothers and struggled on with the clearing of their land. But fury against the giants rose to a pitch one morning when they came storming down from the house above the loch, their legs and arms flailing as they argued and fought about which of them was truly the strong man of the tribe. In their battling progress, and hot in the powerful usque they stilled at their cot, they knocked over little Mistress Alison Maclean throwing her aside, senseless, and they strewed her children flying across their stony kailpatch.

Colin Maclean's dander was up fine now. He was one of the smallest and puniest of the Loch Shiel folk but he was Alison's man and he would take steps to avenge her.

He went to the Sage in the next glen who listened gravely to what he had to say.

'Go and walk the glen for an hour and I'll promise you an answer when you come back.'

With a half-smile on his face and the Sage by his side, Colin walked the six miles home that afternoon. And, while Mistress Alison, a bandage still round her head, served the wise man some of her kail-broth, her husband made a round of the other cots except that of the quarrelsome brothers, and warned folk to stay safe in their homes next day. Then the Sage called on the giant-brothers.

Next morning the people, peering from their doorways, were astounded to see the six wild brothers apparently working frantically to clear everyone's ground of stones, so that the air above the whole district was full of rocks and boulders flying out beyond their glen, over hills, beyond burns, into sunless gullies and bleak moorlands where no one lived or tried to cultivate the land.

By nightfall there was not a stone to be seen save on the shore of the loch, and the brothers lay spreadeagled on the ground exhausted. But still arguing which of them was strongest.

Seeing that there would be another tulzie when their strength came back, the Sage walked from Colin Maclean's cottage and stood over them.

'You are mighty men indeed . . . surely the greatest in the whole world!'

'But which of us *is* the strongest?' demanded one of them pettishly.

'Ah that you can find out for yourselves. You must go out from the glen and look to see which stone, of all that you threw, went farthest, for each one bears the mark of him who threw it. It will take you a long time, but you are strong men, one of you the mightiest of the mighty. But *which* one you must go and search out.'

And do you know? They may be looking for it yet, while the land they left, stone-free, blows rich with golden corn, and lies peaceful, with quiet cattle grazing there.

The Landmark of Newhaven

Above the fishing town of Newhaven on the Forth there is a brae, covered now with crescents and rows of neat houses, but once green with grass and bonnie with great surges of gorse.

One day long ago, when fishing-boats were little more than weathered planking, and the skill of the sailor was of more worth than the design of his craft, a young wife sat high on that green brae, waiting for her brown-curled merry fisher-lad to come back to her. Her bairn happed in swaddles lay in her creel beside her. The 'cradle' was new-woven willow wands, springy and kindly, and the child slept while the rosy little mother knitted a new spring jersey for her man. She had been skilled since girlhood with her needles, as were all the gude-wives along the Forth, so that she had no need to watch the purlings of her flying fingers as she looked out over the March waters of the Forth to catch first glimpse of her young husband sailing home to her with the catch for her creel.

She had been an hour there waiting and watching when the watery sun dappled the Forth and now, at last, into one of the far patches of shifting brightness bobbed the little craft she recognised as his. Quite suddenly the sun disappeared. The sky grew gurlie and threatening but her man was in view and with a croon to the child the girl stood up, began to stow her knitting in her pouch bag, ready to take the baby in one arm, the creel in the other.

It grew darker all at once and, as she looked out, the Firth she had watched all afternoon might have been a desert mirage for all she saw of it now. Between her and the north shore there was only the grey shroud of a wet mist hanging over the water.

Then, as if some hand had drawn it aside, it cleared momentarily and she saw the heaving water. The mist dropped again, but, in that moment of seeing, there had been no little fishing boat where it had been before.

Fisher-wives were realists, even at eighteen, and as she gathered the child close she knew beyond hope that her ruddy brown lad was lost. The mother stood still. The child slept. And the freezing mist banked and swirled and turned into snow around them. Even if she had had the will to move and look for the path downhill she could not have found it.

The snow was not the gentle lacey flakes of poetry. It was sweeping, icy, and soon furred everything it met. It lodged on the woman's clothing and her hair and the cold of the air bearing it caught at her throat. She floundered about on the hill-top for a few moments, suddenly remembering the need to save the child. Then she fell, moaning, and willing nothing more.

They found them there . . . mother and child . . . a long time after, when spring came and melted the snow on the brae. The two were laid to rest in the old kirkyard and nothing remained on the hill to mark the tragedy . . . except the willow creel, fallen from the girl's stiff fingers. It had lain unheeded when they gathered up the girl and her bairn. It had stayed there while spring turned to summer and warm suns and soft rains nourished the brae until one of the fresh sauch wands that had been woven into the creel, took root.

Many walking there on summer evenings saw it and wondered, but no one touched it and an old woman of the village, held in awe by those who thought she had the second sight, climbed the hill with the fishermen to see it.

'Let the willow bide there for remembrance, for it comes to me that it will be a sign up here on the brae for boats to come in to safe harbour. Let none tear it oot as a saplin' nor no' cut it doon when it's growed, for it maun stay where the Lord started it, until the time comes when the sma' boats comes in no more wi' fish or when big ships put oot to great oceans fae the harbour here.'

Maybe Betsy Cullen just liked to hear her own voice, for she'd had it close on eighty years and it would soon be silent. But the Newhaven folk had warning that if the brae tree came to harm Newhaven would lose its fishing, and the fish was its life.

Year by year the willow grew, old folk gossiped at it, lovers kissed under it, children played, and fishermen coming out of storm were glad to see it high above the town. When they put up houses on the brae, the law said none must hurt the willow. And life in Newhaven turned on much the same from year to year.

But around the middle of last century there began to come changes in the fishing from Newhaven. The new trawlers were beginning to leave precious few fish for the small-boat men and when a storm carried off a weakly branch of their willow-tree the line-fishers, seeing an omen, came to blows with the trawlermen.

The minister of the time in the parish was sore to see division among his people. He was a godly man, but far-seeing and shrewd for the good of his flock.

'The willow tree is old now,' he reminded them as they gathered at his bidding in the kirk. 'And so are your ways of fishing. Mind that the old woman said as someday big ships would go out from our harbour to the wide seas. Be ready for that. Don't blame the tree and bemoan that it's fate takes away your living.

Don't look back but at the new days that are coming. Every crew as can raise one half the cost of a decked ship I'll someway raise the other.'

Sucking thoughtfully on clay pipes, and with many a glance uphill to the ageing sauch, the fishermen gathered in knots along the harbour wall and talked the strange language of bank loans, interest and investment.

And before the willow-tree that had leapt up from the young widow's creel was finally blown down, a handsome fleet of decked, brown-sailed smacks was to be seen scudding out to sea in fair winds from Newhaven harbour.

Brose and Butter

There was that Laird of Cockpen, of course, who went wooing in his 'pouthered' wig, his blue coat and white waist-coat, his ring, his sword and his fine cock'd hat and was dumb-foun'ert when he was refused. Whether that hapless suitor was the same as the one in this story tradition does not tell, but he was certainly as lively in going after what he wanted.

Our Laird of Cockpen comes first to fame as the merry companion of a merry monarch who, at the time, did not have much to be merry about. His father had been executed at Whitehall the year before in 1649 and now he himself was in the wings in Scotland, heir to a throne in London which he could not reach for the ruling presence of Oliver Cromwell.

But meantime in Scotland, having carelessly promised almost anything, he was King, crowned and eager to please. Charles was young and high-spirited and not entirely weighed down by the politics, battles and sieges going on in England. His bosom companion and fellow reveller during his six months in Scotland was the blithe Laird of Cockpen, whose house was on the South Esk River in Lothian. The Laird was companionable, witty, philosophical, and a skilled minstrel who might have reached considerable musical heights had he not had his duties as laird to keep him busy. But whatever pleasure Charles had in Scotland, that was not with the ladies, was in his company. Whenever gloomy news came of defeat for the King's supporters Cockpen could be relied on to cheer him by fiddling Scottish airs and jigs. And when, over and again, Charles was told it was not ripe time yet for a foray south, the laird filled his glass, brought him good company and sang the jaunty folk-songs of Edinburgh and the Borders. Lilts and reels and strathspeys . . . Charles had taken to them all, but the tune that most tickled his fancy was the romping tirl Cockpen called 'Brose and Butter'. It was quite a royal favourite and he had it played morning, noon and night till it deaved his menservants and his serious counsellors.

Even when the charade of kingship in Scotland was over and the Battle of Worcester had sent Charles into exile in the Hague for many long years to come, the Laird of Cockpen, stripped by the new regime of his lands round Dalhousie, went with him to Holland. And when the King was not too much engaged with his Lucys and Shannons and Eleanors, the wit and wisdom of the laird cheered him, and the playing of 'Brose and Butter' kept his buckled shoes tapping.

The years of the Commonwealth rolled by, Oliver Cromwell died and his son dabbled briefly as second Protector. But Richard Cromwell's heart was not in the role, the country was weary of the Puritans and wanted its King back. Charles came home to great rejoicing and the chance to put into practice some serious plans he had made when he was abroad . . . plans for the Navy, for the advancement of Science, for Art Galleries and the Universities. So many plans he had, in fact, that the likes of the loyal and lightweight Laird of Cockpen were almost forgotten and were certainly not included in the new scheme of things.

The Laird went home to Scotland. His lands had been forfeit for nine years and he wandered sadly round the land that had been in his family for generations. Then, as he trudged, sadness turned to indignation that he had been cast off to fend for himself without any suggestion of *his* Restoration to his inheritance.

He wrote letters to the Court in London seeking reinstatement in East Lothian, reminding the new counsellors to the King of his past services and asking for reasonable favour now. But either all the King's men were too busy on Charles's business to pass on messages that might, after all, be only begging letters from a passing acquaintance, or else Charles had simply forgotten him. That was hard for Cockpen to believe when he looked back on some of their youthful exploits together.

He had the bit between his gritted teeth now and made his determined way to St. James's in London, at first asking, then demanding, audience of the King. But whether by polite shake of the head in the beginning or active throwing out latterly, the Laird was no nearer Charles than if he had stayed in Lothian.

He had presumed almost long enough on the hospitality of friends in London and would have to be off soon to the rooms he had taken in Edinburgh. There must be one more try. Letters had failed him, so had straightforward requests and a more pugnacious chin wagged at palace guards. He would have to try a wee bit of Scottish guile.

The Laird had already met the organist of the King's Chapel in the company of his friends and set out now to cultivate him as a fellow musician. He laid out a little of his dwindling money to dine and wine the organist. He talked church music with him knowledgeably and gave an impromptu audition on various instruments, playing just the dignified voluntaries and hymnals best to delight a serious musician.

'Mind what's my real ambition, Master Organist, is to play yon instrument you have in the Chapel there for they tell me it's a braw player in gude hands. . . . I would give a lot to play that for one of your services. I couldnae ask to play before a King but. . . .'

'But why not? The organ isn't seen from the Chapel. I'll come up with you, show you where to go and you can play the service.'

Cockpen shook his head but without smeddum to his protest.

'Och I couldnae . . . but mind it would be the great thing for me, that.' And so it was arranged.

The service went smoothly, the organ sang soft alongside the choir, and swelled out true and ripe in the hymnals, and there were those there that morning that had never heard it played so mellow. The hour was nearly over, the last Amen drawn out and fervent and the worshippers were ready for the voluntary to take them in dignified file out to the doorway. Suddenly there was such a skirling at that organ as it had never let out before. It sobbed and jiggled as if it was bagpipes and fiddles and whistles. The whole congregation was transfixed as if the Devil himself had been playing. The King stood stock-still on his way out and then turned. The real organist had come down from the organ steps two-at-a-time and was grovelling on his knees before Charles.

'It's not me your Grace. You can see it's not me playing.' He was going into the whole tale of the ungodly Scotsman who had inveigled his way into the chapel, when the King stopped him.

'Of course it's not you. You couldn't play like that if you practised for a hundred years. That's my 'Brose and Butter' he's playing and there's only one man can play it like that.' The music danced on. . . .

'Cockpen!' roared Charles. 'Play it to the end then come and dine with me!'

'You had me nearly dancing in the Chapel,' said Charles later. 'But when your fingers are so merry, why is your face so sad?'

'I used to fiddle for the dancin' on my Lothian estates,' said the Laird, 'but I hae none noo, no' a yard to call my ain.'

'Shame me, Cockpen! You're never still out of your land? I've been so busy with all that wasn't done the last ten years, that I haven't seen good fellows like yourself put back to your rights. What good to you is an open playhouse in London, a Science observatory or paintings in a gallery? You'll have your acres back and your right to them for your heirs as long as they have children, but be sure you teach them your music so they can play me 'Brose and Butter' whenever I come back to Edinburgh.'

Cockpen's bairns had no need of their music lessons to entertain their King, for he never set foot in Scotland in his twenty-five years reign after his Restoration.

But the laird was granted back his lands round Cockpen House. He busied himself with his family and with the running of his estates; and from time to time travelled south to take 'Brose and Butter' with his old companion.

The Darlings of Duich

Once upon a time, almost before all the lands of the West Highlands had come out of the mists to be charted and named, there lived a man in what had recently come to be called Kintail.

He had a home at the head of what folk were calling Loch Duich and, although he had long since lost his wife, he had seven beautiful daughters, each one year younger than the next. They had played happily as little girls along the shores of the loch, gathering pebbles and shells and trailing their pink finger-tips through the water of clear, cold rock pools. There were no other children round the lonely lochside but they had each other and were content.

But one by one, as they grew to be bonnie young women, they began to sigh and wish that they could meet handsome young men as their mother must have done when their father had been a gallant in his twenties. Sigh as they might, there were no taking youths round Duich. Even the ships bearing small cargoes from far places in Loch Alsh passed the end of their loch and the girls would wave forlornly to sails as they blew by in the distance, and feel sure that wooing, love and marriage were going to pass them by.

And then one morning, after a wild black night of storm when the girls had huddled together by the fire, fearful that even their sturdy-built house would be swept away, the wind fell and a soft innocent, new-born kind of morning broke over the loch. The girls took their shawls and went down to the shore to see what the waters had thrown up, that might be of use to them in house or herb-garden.

But they did not search for seaweed or driftwood that morning, for there, limping into Loch Duich was a ship, belaboured by tempest, its mast broken, a jagged hole in its prow, its figure-head battered and its rigging torn and dangling loose. The girls stood quite still on the shingle as a small oaring-boat came down over the side of the ship. They crept to the water's edge, shawled so that the men on the ship thought they were old women. Then two young men clambered into the small boat and began to pull towards the shore.

In twenty minutes they had drawn it up on the pebbles and one of the two looked round at the girls and the house behind them.

'Well now, what have we here? A house . . . and is this not a miracle of the angels . . . a posy of pretty flowers.'

His black eyes sparkled, his teeth were white like the inside of shells and his voice had a lilt that was not of the Scottish glens or shores, but close-kin all the same. And he spoke sweet-tongued and easy as they had never known Kintail men to speak. His companion was busy with the boat but when he too turned round, although he was brown where the other was black, he also had merry eyes and a melting smile.

'Holy Mary, but you're right Michael, unless we were drowned-dead in the storm and these are saints in heaven.'

'Bedad Patrick, I doubt it'll be saints for you when the time comes. No 'tis just girls, Pat, beautiful, lovely girls.'

They were young and they were safe, two brother-lads on their first terrible voyage and it was thankful relief that made them seem bold, for truly they were upstanding lads, well-reared sons of a godly mother. So they introduced themselves properly to the girls, said they had come ashore to find out where they were and if they could get supplies of wood and rope for the ship's repairs.

Would they not come to the house and talk some with the girls' father, seven voices pleaded?

Never were two young men pressed more earnestly to break

their fast in a strange house. The girls fluttered round them with porridge fresh-made by the eldest, bramble-berries in ale, which was a speciality of the youngest, soft cheese-bannock, goat-milk, and the favourite dish of the second youngest, the shiny fish of Duich broiled in oatmeal over the fire.

"'Tis getting back to the ship we must be,' said Michael at last, remembering the other sailors waiting for word of where they were.

"'Dade you're right Pat.' The girls were sad and implored them not to go.

'Faith girls, 'twill be a day or six before the *Lady Shamrock's* fit to put to sea again,' Michael assured them with a smile.

'A full week of more breakfasts,' murmured Patrick dreamily.

It was much more than six days, for the ship was worse-damaged than they had thought at first. The other sailor men had been too busy that first morning to see the girls so far away on the shore. They were older, they had their rum and thought they were making sport of the two young ones sending them away every day on errands ashore. But Mick and Patrick were not so gormless and never a word of the Duich darlings did they let drop. 'Only kind old wives gathering sea-stuffs,' they told the others of the figures on the shore.

The seven sisters and the two boys laughed and sang together, and roamed the fields and the burnsides behind the head of the loch.

'Not the shore, girls, we are too much on water to relish that.' And so they kept out of sight of the ship.

At first it was all light-hearts and laughter, and their father was glad to see his lasses happy. But, as the days wore on, more and more it was the two youngest girls who found themselves hand-in-hand with the Irishmen. Michael was thinking now of a lifetime of brambles-in-ale with a rosy-cheeked companion, and Patrick of bringing his mother a daughter-in-law who could make oatmealed fish into a dish fit for the saints. Then they began to talk, as well as think, of it, and the father glowed to think that two of his girls had found husbands.

But the older girls began to fret and become touchy, for it was ill-fortune for the youngest to marry before the older ones, and they began to nag their father that if any married the sailor-boys it must be the two eldest. The father saw the sense of that.

'They're right, friends, the girls must take their turns,' he said at last, after a long walk to think over the solemn matter.

But Patrick and Michael did not want to marry daughters One and Two, it was daughters Six and Seven they had firmly in mind, and heart. And now the ship was in order and ready to sail. So they conferred long and carefully with each other as they rowed to and from the *Lady Shamrock* next day.

'Sir, you have seven beautiful daughters with never a husband among them. Now we love the two that are nearest us in age . . . but at home we have five grand brothers, handsomer than me and Mick here. Up in the Mourne mountains they are, lonely and sufferin' to find good wives. If we was to take our brides home to show what ravishing creatures the rest are (for sure, sir, they're all ravishing) they would come quickly over the sea to fetch them for their own.'

So *there* was an offer for a loving father anxious to see his daughters set up with likely men! He sent for the priest from over the hill, and the bramble-girl and the fish-girl, attended by their excited sisters, were married and sailed away joyfully to Ireland with their sailor-lads, to send back bridegrooms for the rest.

The other girls stitched at their marriage linen and watched for the ship that would bring them their grand and handsome lovers. But no sail came into Loch Duich that year, or the next. They grew angry and impatient, then wae and sad, so that their sewing fell from their fingers, as they looked out over the waters.

The father went to see the Sage of Kintail, who was the seventh son of a seventh son and had the second sight.

'I can see no brothers to these men. They are their mother's only sons,' he pronounced.

When the dejected father told the girls what the Sage had said, they were indignant and did not believe it. They took to their sewing and watching again with renewed vigour and fury, and became so difficult to live with, that their father in despair went to the seer again to plead with him that he might be mistaken.

'I am not mistaken friend. If your daughters persist in waiting and wailing for these phantom husbands, they will grow old and wrinkled and they will be hags before their time, and then, if some other ship of menfolk should come by, nothing will come of their chance with them.'

'What can I say to my beautiful daughters?' asked the father.

'Tell them that if they are thirled to waiting for these brothers and if they want to remain beautiful (for men who will never come) here is what they should do. They must go to the head of Loch Duich and stand there, warm in summer, cold in winter, looking out all round so that wheresoever their suitors come from they will see them.'

And so the Five Sisters of Kintail took the old man's advice and have stood there ever since, always beautiful, always admired and always waiting.

Baillie Hunkers and the Dancing Bear

The antics of a performing bear and the controversy over the sober religio-political document called the Solemn League and Covenant may seem oddly assorted matters to have become part of the same tale. But strange things happen. And when Mr. Antonio Dollari, an Italian travelling entertainer, with no wish in the world to acquire money-capital and its responsibilities, joined with his dancing bear in certain frolics in the small town of Linlithgow he had no notion that he was laying up any other kind of capital against a future evil day.

Normally Antonio was best content to wander the Lowlands of Scotland, giving shows at fairs and markets and earning himself and his 'friend' a modest living from town and country folk alike. But that day had been a Gala holiday at Linlithgow when the Minister and the Dean of Guild had ordered the public burning of copies of the Covenant. That document, once popular, was now held in some distaste by many plain folk, sickened by certain excesses of Presbyterian zealots. There at the celebrations Antonio had piped on his tin whistle, the bear had danced to its music and all but the dourest Presbyterian Councillors had laughed and clapped . . . the Dean of Guild loudest of all.

Now Antonio and the bear had come to Glasgow.

Baillie Hunkers of that town was not a well-loved man. Many an honest citizen had smarted under the lash of his tongue or nursed bruised shins from the staff he used to clear his way along its streets. He best-fancied himself in the official civic costume with its gold buttons, yellow braid and show-sword and was often to be seen of a noon-time strutting pompously along where the ground was firm or picking his way among the muddy puddles of the Old Vennel after rain. People who had nothing to fear from the swaggering Baillie simply shied away from him or skirted his path, while those who owed him livelihood or preferment touched their forelocks and smiled at him through gritted teeth.

But on the morning of this tale there was one figure in the Baillie's way who did neither of those when the merchant came stalking along, silver-knobbed staff in hand. That figure was the massive performing bear owned, trained and well-beloved by the flash-eyed Italian known affectionately in Glasgow as Anty Dolly and greatly welcomed on his infrequent visits to the city.

At the moment of the Baillie's march along the street, the bear was executing a paw dance to Antonio's whistle-music. The animal was straddled across the Baillie's path taking not a blinker of notice of the approaching figure.

Baillie Hunkers was angry at being obstructed and hit out at the performer with his staff, but the bear merely thought that he was being taught a new sequence to his choreography, caught the stick with his great forepaw and held it to his chest till the ash-wood cracked. Hunkers was now outraged enough to draw the sword which had scarcely left its scabbard since it became part of his official costume. He jabbed the bear viciously in his dancing rump and, whether out of excitement or outrage in *his* turn, the animal lumbered round quickly, snapped the leading rope that held him to Dollari and gathered up the terrified Baillie in his arms. Although Antonio had abandoned his music in consternation, the bear took no notice and waltzed around with his new partner, in the ring made by the growing crowd of half-delighted, half-fearful, spectators. Dollari tried frantically to release the Baillie but could do no more than soothe and humour the bear, to keep his victim from the harm his 'friend' could do in ill-temper. Round and round danced bear and Baillie. The 'stage' was an area of beaten earth surrounded by deep ruts, which formed thickly muddied puddles left by a week of rains, and when a baker, attracted out of his work-place by the babble of excited voices prodded the pair with his barrel-stave, the dancers stumbled over it and toppled into the sticky clay of one of the unsavoury puddles.

The timid fled and even Antonio cravenly disappeared down a lane. The baker's two assistants rushed out bravely with their staves and thrust them between the bear's arms and legs from opposite sides so that they made a cross-spar to imprison him. The Baillie crawled up from all fours smelling, spluttering and beside himself with fury at the state of his muddied clothes and tattered dignity.

The poor bear was held now in a grid of newly-arrived sticks and staves, until a party of soldiers arrived and secured him with ropes. Then they dragged him to face judgement outside the Tolbooth. There Antonio's friend was deemed guilty of the heinous crime of bringing ignominy on the worthy Baillie, said to have been on his way to dinner and claret after a rigorous hour or two's cogitating on the city's affairs and welfare.

Alas, for the welfare of the bear! Amidst cries of 'Shame!' from the boldest citizens, he was taken out to the Butts and shot by a barrage of bullets from the soldiers' muskets. Anty Dolly himself was found, hours later, on the Cathkin Braes above Ru'glen and brought back to face a charge of deliberately causing his bear to torment the fine Baillie. There was a low muttering of protest round the doors of shops and in the town's inns and alley-ways, for the truth had licked round all corners about the Baillie's provoking of the animal, a performer who had given much more pleasure to the community than the overbearing Hunkers. Now it was widely and angrily expected that the popular Antonio would share his old friend's fate.

And indeed official heads *were* wagging and perhaps coming to a concensus that to spare Dollari would be to encourage ribaldry against such estimable men as the good baillies and councillors, when there arrived in the city another traveller. A kinsman of Linlithgow's Dean of Guild and one of the party who had so loudly applauded Antonio earlier in the week at the Covenant-burning, had come to visit his old friend Merchant Brodie of the High Street.

Now in Glasgow, as in Linlithgow, the offended dignity of one of its Baillies took second place to the city fathers' distaste for the Solemn League and Covenant, which looked to them as it had done to those of the other town as if it might bring in an era of bickering and snarling over religious government. The visitor made much of Antonio's contribution to the celebrations in Linlithgow and the Glasgow fathers felt that they could scarcely shoot dead one who had been yesterday's hero in Linlithgow.

But the city had its ounce of flesh and sentenced Dollari to an hour's penance in the jougs* with the skin of his old comrade round his shoulders. When the poor fellow saw all that remained of the faithful companion who had tramped the roads with him in all weathers, he wept so uncontrollably throughout the hour that no one had the heart to throw anything at all at him. And when he was released a number of men of substance, who enjoyed the thought of cocking a snook at the self-important Baillie Hunkers, offered Antonio the choice of a variety of more settled and less dangerous ways of earning a living.

He stayed for a time, working for Merchant Brodie in the city, then he disappeared, and a travelling packman who came to Glasgow told how he had seen Antonio around the Border towns, in Stirling and Linlithgow with a young bear, well-secured this time on a chain, who was fast becoming as accomplished as the old one.

But Anty Dolly never came to Glasgow again and most folk in the city felt themselves the poorer for his loss . . . except of course the Baillie Hunkers, who never again aroused quite the same awe in people who had seen him dancing with a performing bear and spread-eagled in the glaury puddle of the old Vennel.

*jougs — a metal collar chained to a wall into which law-breakers and nuisances were locked.

Note: I do not know whether 'Hunkers' was the birth-name of the villain of this piece or whether he was known by the name *after* the adventure. If the former, then name and mishap form a queer coincidence, if not, perhaps the expression 'down on one's hunkers' is derived from his predicament at the climax of this story.

The Weaver of Strathaven

In the twenty-five years since word of the French rebellion had echoed up from the south, the Wilson's cottage in Castle Street, Strathaven, had been a meeting-place for disgruntled weavers.

Although James 'Purlie' Wilson was a book-learned man, well-versed in the work of Robert Burns and Thomas Paine, with their championship of the worth of the common man, the weavers did not need him to point out that they laboured under injustice, exploitation and cruelly low earnings. But what he could do was to articulate their grievances before they even voiced them, and rally them into coherent anger.

Along with other groups they had prepared and circulated petitions demanding just returns and conditions for their labour. A government in London, still nervous from events in France, had sent instructions to authorities and councils in the centres closest to the fermenting radical groups.

That evening at Strathaven, Purlie Wilson (named in more

contented younger days for the new stitch he had perfected) watched from a hummock of grass as the motley company of craftsmen weavers and knitters in front of him marched, counter-marched and presented pitchforks, hidden from the main road by a ridge behind them.

Suddenly a horseman, riding hard, topped the ridge, reined in for a moment, spoke to one of the men drilling and was pointed, with a spade, in the direction of Wilson. The rider cantered round the edge of the make-shift parade ground and then, flushed and perspiring slid off his horse in front of Purlie Wilson and, without pausing to catch his breath, began to speak.

'My name's Jack Shields, Purlie Wilson,' he reported. 'They tell't me in the town I would find you here. I'm bid to tell you that there's an army of reformers . . . weavers and suchlike . . . gathering thegether the morrow at the Cathkin Braes near Ru'glen. And there's Jacobin generals fae France comin' wi' them, to face up to the army troop. And I'm to say that we're sure to win the day for all of us that thinks we're misused.' He grasped the weaver by the sleeve and spoke urgently. 'Will you come Purlie Wilson wi' your men there?'

This was just what all the drilling and arms practice had been about, was it not?

'All we want's the chance to ask for our due withoot bein' run off at the end of troop-guns. If this is that chance, then we'll be wi' you on the Cathkin Brae the morrow.'

Wilson gave the messenger Shields his hand and the man remounted saying he was making for the other weaver villages of the Loudon valley to rally support there.

When he spurred on his horse towards Darvel the men broke ranks excitedly to hear their rallying instructions for next day, and in the midst of their briefing a second courier arrived with the news that skirmishing between weavers and soldiers in the Glasgow High Street had turned to fierce fighting and that after weeks of mutter and complaint, and hopes of peaceful settlement, the time for action was on them.

At dawn next day two dozen men gathered at Wilson's house in Castle Street. Shotguns and hagbuts, used mainly for rabbiting and hare-hunting and not enough even to arm each man, had been gathered, oiled and stored against the great day of action. Wilson himself carried an ancient blunted sword which had served him as part of his home-built loom. The arms-store, such as it was, was handed out from separate barns and thatches where they had been hidden, and the Strathaven weavers set out across the countryside to gather a few more recruits at Kilbride and other hamlets.

It was at Kilbride that they learned the truth, Jack Shields and the second messenger who had followed him up, had betrayed them. The Strathaven weavers, like other groups from north of Glasgow, had been duped into coming towards the city and were to be rounded up by dragoons sent out on government orders.

'Best we disperse, no more nor two together . . . all try to find cots or barns where you can hide your weapons. For we mustnae be taken wi' them on us . . . then each take our separate paths home to Stra'ven.'

Purlie's brave little army disbanded, seething at Jack Shields. Most of them found sympathetic cotters with wall-beds and haylofts where they covered up the old hagbuts and rusted blades, before taking their despondent ways home.

The sky was gurly and low when Wilson himself set out for Strathaven, having seen his men safely off, ahead of him. He was overtaken by thunderstorm and such a lashing of rain as he had not seen in years, as he plodded across a stretch of empty moorland. Sodden and chilled to the heart with cold and disappointment he stumbled towards a cottage under a curving rim of woodland. A sensible motherly body took in the old knitter-soldier, blanketed him, set him down at the ingle to a jug of ale, and dried out his clothes with scarcely a word spoken on either side before he took the road home to Strathaven.

But all her ministrations served to save him from only his chilling. A party of troops came after him to Castle Street only two days later when he had gone sadly back to his weaving and begun to tidy up some of his abandoned ravels. His daughter could give him only a few minutes warning to scramble out through his back garden to the old village graveyard beyond, where he hid behind one of the ancient headstones. But he was discovered, arrested and carried to Glasgow to await trial before the circuit judge who would hear and pronounce on his case.

The sturdy little weaver, whose crime was no more than that he had been prepared to voice to authority the reasonable aspirations of highly skilled but exploited craftsmen, was found guilty of high treason.

There were doubtless hot heads among the Radicals who might have been dangerous to authority but, for the most part, they were family men who only wanted a small share of the prosperity enjoyed by the merchants and gentrymen who showed a good leg in their stockings.

But the lesson of the French Defarges was too near, across the channel there. Purlie was dragged through the streets on a cart to a scaffold surrounded by a solid block of soldiers at the edge of the Glasgow Green, for public execution. Twenty thousand angry citizens saw him hanged and beheaded, and only their mutinous fury stopped the hangman from quartering his body.

His remains were taken to the Cathedral graveyard where his felon's mort-kist was buried by an outraged sexton who made sure that the shallow grave was not hidden from the eyes of the stricken Wilson family. And by the time darkness fell, the daughter of James Purlie Wilson was sitting beside her father's coffin on a Strathaven farm-cart, trundling defiantly towards home. There he was laid to rest just outside of his own garden in the yard where he had taken refuge after the betrayal at Kilbride.

The false courier Shields, kenspeckle all across the countryside around Strathaven, never knew again what it was to have a kindly word spoken by a neighbour. And some folk say that even his gude-wife bundled him out of their wall-bed to a cold chaff in their spence-room.

The Simple Tale of Tibbie Shiels

An Ettrick lass of the early 1800s, who was not a lady, was either a married woman or a servant-girl. Tibbie Shiels was neither a lady nor wedded wife, so when she met John Richardson from Westmorland who came moudie-catching round the Scottish Border farms, she was, like others of her kind, working in service at one of them. There were Ettrick lads a-plenty who found Tibbie winsome, but none that gave her a moleskin lining to her cloak or kissed her hand as if she was a lady. The unwed menfolk took it ill at first that she gave her heart to the Englishman but as he settled with her, close by the tiny Loch o' the Lowes, and contentedly grafted himself on to Yarrow life, the lads accepted him, and turned their attention to more accessible girls.

Tibbie was no slip of a girl when she married but she was built for childbearing and made up for her spinster years by giving her husband six children in not many more years. By then there were too many bairns tumbling about in that first home and the family moved to breathe more easily in a bigger one on the spar of land which separates the Loch o' the Lowes from the lovely St. Mary's Loch, among the wide hills sweeping up off the Yarrow valley.

But the happy married years were coming to an end for, while the bearing and rearing of her six youngsters had assuredly not exhausted Tibbie, something about them had sapped the moudie-man's strength, for he fell sick and died, a year after the flitting to St. Mary's Loch, leaving Tibbie with her sizeable cottage, her sizeable family, and her far from sizeable income.

After a decent period of genuine grief for her moudie-jo, Tibbie had to shake herself into some sort of plan to support her brood, which was growing up fast, ever hungry and country-sore on its clothing. Her chief talents did not seem promising to turn to much financial account being only common-sense, a happy nature and a way with spirtle and cooking pot. While she was considering what a woman with six bairns could do with these mundane talents to earn their bread, chance brought a visitor to Ettrick and Yarrow.

Robert Chambers had taken a holiday from his publishing affairs in Edinburgh to come south, walking and riding at his leisure in order to gather material and absorb atmosphere for a book he was writing to interest the biener members of the public in taking similar tours in Scotland. He had almost completed what he judged was his stint of travelling for the day and was coming down by the Yarrow Water looking for a small inn when the exquisite sight of late-afternoon sun on the little St. Mary's Loch burst on him as he topped a shallow rise in the riverside path. A lone fisherman passed the time of day with him and Chambers stopped.

'D'you live with this on your doorstep?' he asked enviously.

'Aye, aye,' said the fisher and looked suddenly at 'this' that he had lived with for fifty years, as through the eyes of a stranger. 'Aye, it's bonnie when you come fresh to it, is St. Mary's.'

'Is there an inn nearby the loch I could tak' a bed at?' The man scratched his head, then thought to do a kindness to both the stranger and the Widow.

'Like enough Tibbie Shiels would be pleased to give you a room,' he suggested. And Tibbie Shiels was.

Robert Chambers stayed a day or two and, so successful was the arrangement, that while Tibbie was mulling over the inkling of an idea to answer her income problem, Chambers was writing glowingly of her cookery, housewifery and hospitality in his travel book. So warmly did he praise her that, first, two or three of his own friends came seeking rooms and then a spate of his readers, so that the cottage was a busy little inn in no time at all.

At first it provided shelter for simple intinerants or travelling parties, but increasingly it became a gathering-place for the tribe of writers at that time making Edinburgh the prime literary centre of the day, and for poets over the Border who wanted to meet them. It was to Tibbie Shiel's Inn that the great men escaped for a few days' retreat on their own, or to meet up in cheerful company with others of their kind. In her day Lady Stair might have been the famous formal hostess entertaining the Capital's literati in her gracious apartments overlooking Edinburgh from the Royal Mile, but, in these days of the 1820s there was gustier, couthier laughter under Tibbie's eyes. Walter Scott found his way into her kitchen from Abbotsford, Wordsworth and his sister from Grasmere, Wilson from Edinburgh. To one poet the inn was a haven of peace, to another the heart of the Borderland, to Christopher North it was, in five particulars, exactly like a wren's nest . . . dry, warm, sheltering, quiet and not too easy to find, round and 'theekit wi' moss'.

But among all the famous visitors to St. Mary's Loch, it was Ettrick's own shepherd-poet and his dog who were most often to be found at Mistress Richardson's ingle, and whenever Tibbie Shiels and her inn are spoken of in Scotland, and far beyond, following them in the same breath comes the name of James Hogg.

Both tetchy poet and good-humoured hostler became well-known far furth of Ettrick and Yarrow, yet neither strayed far from home, save on occasional brief visits. They were true peasant children of the Borders and their very fame rose out of these roots. Hogg, his pen and ink-horn at hand in the button-hole of his coat while he sat watching over his yows ready to write of Kilmeny or of his beloved sheep-dog, drew out of his home soil that strange fey poetry of ghosts and goblins and far-off things. Tibbie's practical hand produced something different, but also of the Borders, from its loch-trout and fowl, its grains, its cheeses, its savours from the herb-garden, and combining them in ancient country ways with girdle, swee and kail-pot, turned them into famous fare, fit for poets who had written themselves into a great hunger and beaten a pathway to her door to have it satisfied.

Those were brave days at St. Mary's Loch in the 1820s and '30s, before Scott wrote himself to death to pay his debts, and Tibbie attended Hogg on his death-bed a few years later. She survived poet, sangster, diarist and tale-teller and was widowed of her beloved moudie-man for fifty-two years. So she had long days to remember them and to offer her inn specialities of welcome and cuisine to travellers not even born in the hey-day years. She grew old in the pleasures of her craft, and the humorous peace of her face, in portrait, as an old wife in mutch and plaid nearing her span of ninety-five years, suggests that Robert Chambers and the lone fisher, of half-a-century before, had served her well by thrusting her into the hostelry business.

The Little Gods of Lewis

Once upon a long time ago there lived a good master-farmer whose cattle grazed on the sweet grass behind the foreshore around Loch Resort in the west of Lewis. He had many beasts and needed many herdsmen to tend them and keep them content, for good milking. The herdsmen were cheerful, sociable fellows, almost always within hailing distance of each other as they worked. But there was one of the company who was surly and ill-natured, not much liked or trusted by the others. Black Donald Dhu spoke little and never laughed, but he had a good hand with the animals and the best the farmer could do to keep the rest in their normal good humour was to have the unpleasant cattleman use the most remote grazing behind a wild lonely shore, where he was pleased enough with his own company and that of the cows.

One evening at dusk, as he walked along the dunes, he saw limping into view in the sea-loch, from where it had been hidden by a small promontory, a greater-sailed ship than he had ever seen before in these parts. It must have suffered in some storm away to the north, for the evening air here over Resort was quite calm, and the creak of its broken mast came eerie to the cattleman across the stillness of the Loch. Then Donald saw the figure of a man climbing down over the side of the ship and beginning the long swim towards the shore, perhaps sent to find help. The herd had come on to the dune-land from the grazing and sat watching from among the coarse marram grass. The swimmer made struggling progress and did not seem to cut the calm water as cleanly as he should have done, then, as he rose to his feet to trudge through the shallows for the last few yards to the shore, the cattleman saw that he was cumbered with a dripping bundle that he carried close to his body.

Whatever was in it was surely precious and the herd changed his position from crouching to lying, so that he could peer through the grass unseen. The sailor had sunk exhausted now above the tide line, his grasp of his treasure loosened. The cattleman rose and ran towards him in the dusk, drawing his dirk from his stocking as he went, then, as silently as dusk was wrapping the foreshore, he drove the blade deep into the man's back towards his heart. Then he eased away the treasure. He would go back now, quickly to the master to win his favour by telling him of the ship waiting to be plundered, but this trove, at least, would be his.

Hastily he scooped a deep hole, buried the wrapped bundle, unopened, and lined-up the place mentally with a landmark twenty yards away. Then he dragged the man's body to the lochside and dropped him into a deep pool.

The farmer heard only of the distressed ship which his cattleman had left keeling over before his eyes, and nothing of the sailor's murder. But his fury at the herd's suggestion of looting and killing was great. He paused only long enough to send the man packing from his service, before he and a party hastened to bring the unfortunate sailors for safe shelter in his home and to offer help with the repair of the ship. They recovered their spirits in the kindly welcome, sad only that their messenger had seemingly not survived the swim ashore.

'He surely went down with his bundle,' said one, 'that pack went wherever Bjorn went.'

'It drowned him in the end.'

'Poor Bjorn!'

So they spoke among themselves, but in a Norse tongue that was strange to their hosts.

Meantime, knowing that he must leave the district, the herd hurried back to the shore and scrabbled frantically in the sand to find the planked treasure that would change his life. With shaking hands he lifted it out and opened the several strips of linen wrapped round the gold, or rubies, or whatever had been so greatly cherished by the sailor.

Inside he found neither gold nor silver, coins nor gems, only a collection of strange squat little figures; for cursing the enemies of the owner perhaps, or . . . horrifying thought . . . perhaps his sacred sailor-gods! Like many another cheerless, brooding man Donald Dhu was superstitious and fearful of what he did not understand. The thought that these little sea-gods had witnessed his knifing of the man who had prayed to them, terrified him. Almost sobbing in his panic, he threw them into the cloth, folded it over and buried them again, kicked sand over the bundle, and fled.

The crew stayed long enough with the farmer to have their ship repaired and then, full of gratitude, they sailed away home to Norway, leaving their shipmate in his loch grave, his fair hair waving in the green gulping waters of the pool, his precious gods buried in the sand thirty yards away. A new herd took the killer's place and soon he and his black tempers were all but forgotten around Loch Resort.

But whether the curse of the sailor's little gods was on him, or some ill wish over him from birth, from the day he coveted the sailor's burden . . . cursed he certainly was. In his wanderings to find casual work, he killed a second time and a third in hasty-tempered brawls, before he was finally taken, tried and found guilty, then led to the gallows at Stornoway. The man now faced his Maker, and, lest it went as ill with him as he knew he well deserved, he gabbled a confession to a priest, of that first killing and the burying of the victim's private gods, and of all his malefactions since. He mounted the scaffold steps, if not comforted by the priest's saintly murmurs, at least in less anguish for having told the truth.

Whether or not those who heard the tale of the buried gods and passed the clash round every village and hamlet, feared the gods, as much as Donald Dhu, or whether the priest told them to forget such unrighteous superstition and unlikely story, no one from that day, for many centuries, disturbed the sleeping gods.

During the great new days of Queen Victoria, a young Skye man was visiting Lewis and walking round its summer shores, exulting in the beauty of the place, silent and still, save for the gentle pulse of sea on sand and the cry of sea-birds wheeling above him.

His feet were sinking into the soft sand at every step and he shuffled them happily as he plodded along, his jacket thrown over one shoulder. Then he almost tripped on the ancient bundle and revealed the wrappings. Curiously he opened it up again and found, as Black Donald Dhu had done, so long ago, the collection of squatting figures. Unlike Donald, however, this young man was not superstitious, nor had he any crimes behind him that the gods could have watched; so he had nothing to fear from them. He sat down and handled them one by one, sixty-seven pieces . . . in ivory, he was sure, each one carved differently from the rest. They were quite beautiful and the young man laid them carefully, with the rotting cloth, into his jacket, tied the sleeves round them and carried them back to his lodging.

There he laid them out on a table to admire and consider. They were exquisitely hand-worked and, he suspected, valuable and, though not certain what they were, he never thought of them as gods to curse or bless him.

Edinburgh . . . he would take them to Edinburgh and have them examined.

In the city, a pair of antiquarians gloated with excited pleasure at the sight of them.

'Chess set,' one murmured, 'Part of several maybe.'

'12th century . . . Scandinavian,' added the other.

'Walrus tusk ivory, would you say?' enthused the first.

'Norse, yes, surely,' agreed the second.

'And every one different . . . one king bearded, one shaven . . . each knight a different helmet.'

The little men sighed with pleasure, and so did the young man from Skye.

So the kings, bishops, rooks and pawns of Lewis, whose curse could have brought about nothing more deadly than a lost game of chess, were sent at last to the British Museum where, after lying hidden on that lonely island shore for generations, they were put on view to hundreds of admirers every day.

Jock Howieson and
the Gudeman of Ballengeich

As Jock Howieson tied up the last sacking of the day's millings and stacked the bag plump and floury on top of the others, he sighed and dusted himself down. There was many a man breaking his back on ground around Cramond who envied Jock the miller's half-indoor life, and thought it vastly easier than his own hard graft in all weathers. Besides, millers were reckoned bien men who were fortunate in their traditional share of everyone else's ground barley for their own use, and who were reputed to have well-lined pockets forbye a comfortable life.

But Jock did not see it so.

'Spare me that talk,' he would say when the clash in the ale cot came round to his own good fortune. 'Here's me, that has a pride in my own good milling, that's just to tak' whatever scanty corn an ill-doing farmer harvests. And all the time I'm thinkin' I could be growin' ten times better a crop of my ain.'

That was true enough, for the small bit-rig Jock did cultivate (not more than from mill to cot-house) he farmed well and had fat ears of grain and better kail and herbs than most.

'Besides,' he went on, 'I've just the same darg day and daily . . . Tuesday no different fae Friday, summer no different fae autumn.'

Jock was as much a realist as family men in the 1500s had to be, but he was a secret romantic too and, though he would never have said so to his earthier neighbours, it was his dream to have a real stretch of land of his own . . . to see the seasons turning as he worked, to hear corncrakes among his own grain and yellow-birds singing as they perched on his baulks, to see the violets in the spring and streaming tassels of alder by the river bank, to feel the sun and the wind and the rain on his face as he worked. Aye, Jock

Howieson of Cramond would have given a fair lot to be a man of even quite small property and, though he well knew the hard stint every day would bring to work it, he clung stubbornly to a dream not much like to come true.

Another made in the same romantic mould, had Jock but known it, was his own King. James V of Scotland was a romantic in more senses than one, for, long before he sired the tragedy-Queen of Scots, he had love-children a-plenty and, to mother them, a great variety of ladies had fallen to his charms. But *his* real dream was to know his people, hear what they had to say, see and feel how it was that they lived. Certainly, like other monarchs and great landowners he moved from one residence to another with his retinue, not only so that he could hold court at various centres but, more practically, to ensure that court supplies and local hospitality could be enjoyed in lieu of taxes less easily connected. So a courtly procession was a common enough sight passing through the countryside, but it was like a pageant, a memorable spectacle swiftly past and certainly without any chance of courtier or king meeting peasant.

That was not the 'being among his people' that James wanted and from time to time he slipped out from Falkland or Linlithgow, Stirling or even Edinburgh, and wandered the farmtouns or the street markets to taste what life was like for his subjects. On these excursions his clothing was plain, his staff like that of any merchant or laird and he felt free and satisfied that he would be taken by those he met for any Lowland gudeman.

Perhaps James deceived himself a little for, however douce his breeches and coat, they were not of peasant stuff and although those who saw the Gudeman of Ballengeich, as he called himself, would not have known him as their Royal King, they did not mistake him for a labouring peasant.

Part of the pleasure of these adventures for James was to depart on one of his 'gudeman' outings, unnoticed, so that he was not accompanied at a discreet distance by any of his counsellors who worried about such stravaigings.

So it was, that of the people to the north-west of the dark Edinburgh Nor' Loch who saw the lone stranger passing through their hamlet, it was not only the tailor, measuring and cutting outside his cot, who noticed the close weave of his broadcloth or the fine feather that curled round his hat . . . a man of business perhaps, or a laird going home after a visit to Edinburgh town. Most glanced his way, wondered briefly and turned back to selling their wares or plying their trade that market morning.

But for others who marked the cut and quality of his cladding, their business was with any such unsuspecting man who came their way and who seemed like to have on him a good purse of money. At the tail of the market now a group of tinklers was mending cooking-pot handles, horning spoons and selling trinkets. Trade was not very brisk and a quick look exchanged among them, as the Gudeman spoke in passing to a woman selling hot oaten cakes and a man offering to read or write letters for a small fee. The tinklers worked on half-heartedly until the traveller was out of sight round a bend in the track, then hastily gathered their gear, left it with their womenfolk and set off casually in the same direction.

A stringing-out along the way, a silent hasting-on ahead of two of the gypsies . . . and by the time Jock Howieson's mill was come into Master Ballengeich's sight, they were at his back, on each side of him and in front. If these had been political enemies intent on assassination James would have been a dead man. But it was only his good cloak and his money that these men were after, and beyond a kick on the hand that clutched his purse, a hefty blow across his mouth to keep him from crying out and a pair of battered shins, all the harm the Romanies dealt their king was to hurt his dignity and to make off with his money and the best of his clothes.

It was the miller, dragging an empty delivery-sled back home who found him scrabbling in the dust of the track, dabbing at his bleeding face with his untied neck-cloth and shaking his bruised knuckles to let the air take the sting out of them.

'Sakes man, was it the tinks I saw making to the toon did this?' said the miller helping James to his feet.

'Aye, I suppose.'

'Here, here, come you to the hoose and let me tend your bruisings and get you a cog of ale.' James was up now and the miller oxtered him across the rigs to the mill-house.

Some oil on his scarted face and bindings on hands and legs, a slaking of berry ale, a platter of bread and cheese and James was his own man again. Mistress Howieson was a quiet shadowy creature who filled stoup and trencher and otherwise flitted about the shadows of the small room silently, ever admiring the way her big man could talk easy to strangers.

'There's a bit more colour to your face now, but you've a nasty score there on your jaw'll tak' a wee while to lose . . . what name sir?'

'Och, I'm but the Gudeman of Ballengeich, friend.'

'Jock Howieson, miller, at your service, Ballengeich.'

James looked round the jimp-kept room with its swept lum-stone and scrubbed table. It was as pleasing and comfortable as most that he had seen on the same kind of outing.

'You're thirled to the mill then, are you, Jock Howieson? They say it's a good life and that never a miller starves.'

'Weel, no' thirled by my own will. It was my faither was here afore me, but it's the land itself my heart's in, gin I could ever hae got my name on a stretch or two.'

'Aweel, you've done me a service the day and they've left me no' siller, the tinklers, to mak' my thanks to you. But maybe I can put you in the way of gettin' a bit growin' land.'

The miller laughed.

'I think you'll no' can do that for it's the King's land hereaboots.'

'I have the King's ear when he's a mind to listen to me. Mind and you come to Holy Rood this day sennicht. I'll take you to his person mysel' and you'll can put it to him you'd be a farmer sooner than a miller. Here's my hat for good faith. See and keep it on your heid when you come, for sign that you're the man I'll have spoken about.'

Accordingly Jock Howieson presented himself at the palace under the Salisbury crag and was met and escorted to the long hall where the court was assembled, shortly to dine. The stranger's hat clapped firmly on his head, he looked round the throng, at silk-hosen legs, blue and green slashed doublets, bejewelled ladies . . . even his escort was not the plain man he had seemed at Cramond.

'Which of the lords is Majesty?' whispered the bewildered miller.

'The only one, saving yourself, that hasnae doffed his hat.'

Jock saw bonnets dangling from every hand except his own and Ballengeich's.

'Majesty?' the miller faltered, wary that somehow his own simple doings added up to treason.

'What was it you had in mind to ask the King?' said James, while the rest of the court smiled at yet another of Ballengeich's escapades come home to roost.

And so Jock the miller became master of the land at Braehead, by Cramond. Three hundred years later there were still Howiesons there, and the families of that name that are in Cramond yet, are surely kin to those that farmed its run-rigs long ago.

The Faery Flag of Dunvegan

They say that the nine-feet thick walls of Dunvegan Castle are nearly five hundred years old, its deep dark dungeons and guard-room maybe older. Built by Alasdair the Hunchback, 8th Chief of the Macleods, it has been their stronghold ever since.

Clan fortunes have risen and fallen over the centuries since then, but never has dire calamity come to wipe out the Macleods, nor will it, says tradition, while they keep faith over their ancient talisman. Some say that King Harold of England won it as a sport of war from the defeated Harald Hadrada in 1066 when, having vanquished the Norsemen, the King dashed south to tackle William the Conqueror, less successfully, at Hastings. Somehow, in the strange way of legend, the trophy found its way to Skye. Others again say that one of the Macleods had a love affair with a faery woman and that she gave him the charm as a remembrance.

But those who believe most strongly that they have the real story, see these others as only insubstantial drifts of fancy, and tell it their way.

A child, the tradition goes, had been born to the Chief of the Macleods and there was such joy and pleasure over the infant that he planned great festivities and celebration at the Castle. Sewing-women stitched at velvets and tartans and froths of lace, silversmiths hammered out brooches, bracelets and necklaces to mark the occasion, meat-cooks and pastrymen worked for a week preparing a banquet. Minstrels and sangsters rehearsed in the Great Hall and armies of servants scoured the guest-chambers and prepared fit stabling for visiting horses.

Good folk from islands and mainland came to rejoice with The Macleod and his happy wife. Bad folk, of course, were not invited. And yet the Chief feared that they might come. He feared most of all for the child. It would be a simpler attempt on the clan's future by an enemy, to dispose of a helpless infant-heir, than to face up to a fighting man like The Macleod himself. Carefully accomplished, it could even look like an accident. The Chief sent for the child's nurse.

'You must listen and obey me, girl. Take the baby with his cradle to the highest chamber in the house, the farthest from the hall here. He must not be disturbed by these revels and music, nor even looked upon by any stranger. He must be peaceful through all. And you must sit by his side even when he sleeps. Never for one moment leave him unattended.'

'I understand, sir. I'll watch over him even when he sleeps. I'll not sleep myself, nor will I take my hand from the crib.'

She gathered up the tiny babe against her yellow dress and with a boy following her bearing the cradle, took the winding stone stairway to the small turret-room, high up looking out over Loch Dunvegan to the north west sea, and the great spur of rock below. The boy grimaced when he saw the bare room and thought on the celebrations downstairs.

'Hard on you this is, when there's such brave ongoings and feasting for everybody else.' Then he clattered downstairs to join the fun, and nurse-girl and child were left alone in a silence broken only by the rhythmic lash of sea on rocks, while the eating, drinking, dancing and minstrel-singing went on far below.

The child slept soundly and peacefully and the girl sat, content enough, for a while. Then she began to think on what the boy had said.

'Hard on you . . . brave ongoings . . . everybody else.' She was young and a little sorry for herself. The child was quiet. She could surely just go down far enough to hear the reels and old sad-romantic songs of the islands, without harm coming to him for a few minutes. Down she crept and when she was into hearing of the fiddler she sat on the cold stair to listen. Then she smelled the roasting of the animals on the spits and was tempted further until she was mingling with the other maid-servants at the back of the hall, who were enjoying the fragments of meat too small for guest platters, the sweetmeats the servers brought back to them in their napkins and sips of the French wines the cellarman kept back from the tables.

It was long past midnight when she realised she had been gone from her charge for over an hour and, terrified that the child might have fallen from the cradle or been stolen away, she fled upstairs sobbing with fear. She opened the high chamber door and her heart pounded like the sea against Dunvegan's founds. A woman with a yellow shawl sat beside the crib on the stool she herself had so wickedly left, in just the position, hand on crib, head bent over child, that she herself had taken before she was tempted away.

As the nursemaid crossed the threshold of the room the woman's figure grew less clear, the girl moved forward and now the form became fainter until it was no more than what might have been her own shadow. And then, when she would have put a hand on the figure's shoulder, it was not there at all. Shaking, the nurse looked at the baby. He was sleeping peacefully, but then he opened his great Macleod eyes and she knew that he was unharmed. The only trace of the woman that she had been so sure was there was a flimsy yellow silk plaid, the colour of her own dress, draped over the covers in the crib.

When the night was over the boy came upstairs to bid her bring the baby down to be shown off to the close Macleod kinsfolk, who were all of the merrymakers who were still present. Bravely she carried the child and the yellow banner downstairs into the company and, walking straight to the Chief, confessed her lapse and told of the strange visitation.

The Macleod was grave. He examined his son and found him well. Then he spread out the fine-woven square of silk and bade the family come and look at the strange, ancient symbols embroidered on it.

'These are self-made stitchings on this banner. The favour of the faeries of this island has been over the child in sleep to guard him from harm. Now hear me this . . .', and it was as if another strange voice was speaking through the Chief. . . . 'Let this flag ever be revered as the Macleod's protector from all ill . . . never to be used lightly on pain of punishment or to save us from evils we can fight in our own strength. And to keep us wary of misuse let us say that thrice it will be waved from Dunvegan in dire trouble, and that after that its power will be done.'

The flag has been waved in earnest twice in all these centuries; once when the Macleods were in grave danger of decimation by marauding Macdonalds and the enemy suddenly mistook a mist for the movement-dust of a huge host of Macleods, and fled. A second waving was when their cattle were ravaged by a plague which seemed likely to carry off every beast. But the ailing ones revived, no more took the smit and indeed the herds grew sleeker and stronger after the period of sickness.

Once it was waved in mischief, without authority or ceremony, and, not long after, the clan heir was killed in battle at sea.

The third serious unfurling of Dunvegan's faery flag has still to come, and doubtless the Macleods are saving that against the gravest mischance, for then, unless there should be some other strange visitation at the Castle, the protection of the West Highland faeries will no longer cover them.

Let's call him Enoch Walter, for that's a good Glasgow name with
a whiff of tobacco about it, and it will serve without maligning any
particular one of the great merchant families of the time.

Enoch was a wealthy tobacco lord, pompous, disdainful and
mighty self-important and, much as all the others of his trade and
status also enjoyed strutting the plainstanes of the Trongate in
their scarlet coats and cocked hats, he was the peacock of them
all.

The other tobacco merchants avoided him as much as possible
but he spent so much of his day pontificating there that, if they
were to show themselves off at all at that part of the town which
was peculiarly their own, it was inevitable that they had to bear
with his company some of the time. Apart from his insufferable
vanity there were three matters on which he deaved Glasgow
citizens so, that they could barely stomach him. One was,
naturally, his constant declaration that there wasn't a merchant in
the world, shrewder, cleverer or more knowledgeable than
himself on tobacco matters. On these he discoursed uninvited and
at length and, though he spoke only to those wealthy men he
deigned to walk with at all, he did so at the pitch of his haughty
voice so that he could be heard from end to end of the Trongate.

Another of his favourite subjects was his courage during his
army days and the glory with which he covered himself at every
skirmish and seige, but particularly at the great Battle of
Dettingen in Bavaria at which, apart from some wise direction
from King George II who deployed his troops personally, he,
Enoch Walter, won the victory over the French almost single-
handed. The citizens of Glasgow knew the strategy of the Battle of
Dettingen by heart and especially Enoch's part in it.

The third matter which gave his fellow citizens a real staw at
the merchant was that such a man was said to have it in mind to

wed the fetching, gentle and merry daughter of their much-loved Baillie, James Guthrie. Such a mismatch between the paunchy merchant and the young Lily Guthrie seemed to ordinary folk almost criminal.

It was on yet another of those days that Walter was parading on the plainstanes, one pudgy hand holding his scarlet lapel, the other on his long gold-knobbed walking-staff, and telling the whole of Glasgow how to do its business. He was just at the part of his rigmarole, about it having been the same kind of boldness that had won him King George II's grateful praises at Dettingen, when a small woman walked up towards him along the Trongate. She had come for the day from the country, all fresh got-up in snowy wrapper and best dun-brown dress, and with a very particular purpose in mind.

She gazed round her at the throb of town business and then at the bewigged merchants in their red coats perambulating on the 'stanes' conducting the day's affairs. In her awe she edged towards the forbidden promenade in time to catch the word 'Dettingen'.

She caught shyly at the speaker's sleeve.

'You maun be Merchant Walter?'

He knocked her away with his stick and dusted down his sleeve.

'I am indeed. But how dare you, woman, pluck at my coat. Awa' wi' you . . . you're but litterin' the plainstanes. I dinnae gie charity on the street to the likes of you. Awa' wi' you afore I take my stick across your shouthers.'

He saw the good Baillie James Guthrie approaching with his bonnie lass and was glad to have them see how he dealt with such beggar-wives. But the little country woman was back, holding up her hands beseechingly.

'No, no. You dinnae understaun'. It's to thank you for a noble service you done me and my only son that I make so bold.' Enoch Walter preened himself. This was even better for the Guthries to witness. He raised his voice.

'Indeed. I havenae mind of a' the services I've rendered in my day. Which one would this be?'

'It was a rare service to my laddie.'

He looked benignly at her and paused to let Baillie Guthrie and his daughter closer, to overhear something of this service he had so modestly forgotten.

The woman took both the merchant's hands now.

'D'you no' mind my Willie? He was one of your soldier-company at yon Dettingen and when you ran awa' safe, he ran after you and got his life saved an' all.'

There was a bellow of laughter on the plainstanes and by night every hostelry in the town was rocking with mirth. Tradition does not tell how the sweet Lily Guthrie and her father reacted, for they had witnessed the whole incident from the little woman's first ignorant step on to the tobacco lords' territory. But there is no record of a wedding between her and Enoch Walter in any of the old city Marriage Registers. None at all.

The Pirate of Inchcape Rock

In the days when the town of Arbroath was called by its ancient name of Aberbrothock (for the Brothock Burn on which it stands) there was a good Abbot there. He was concerned, not only for the welfare of the Brothers, but for that of the townsfolk as well and even of the sailors passing by on the wild, cold German Ocean.

The seamen had need of *his* prayers in particular more than those of clerics in other towns for, some ten miles south-east of Aberbrothock, lay the notorious Inchcape Rock, a perilous half-mile of red sandstone on which many a tossing, ploughing sail had smashed to smithereens. Seamen called it the most dread spot along the whole length of the Scottish and English east coast and tried to steer their ships well clear of it.

One day, after the Abbot had seen twenty bodies laid out for burial, silent and long in the town's winding sheets . . . bonnie lads who had been the crew of the latest victim ship, he said the prayers for the dead over them and then walked, meditating, along the white fringe of that cold grey sea.

Then he came back to the town and ordered a bell to be made, with a ring wilder and louder than the sea, and with a sturdy pitched rope attached that would resist the salt-rot of the sea.

Two weeks later the townsfolk of Aberbrothock were startled to see their Abbot, who was most often to be found by those who came seeking help, in the cloisters or quiet garden-places of the Abbey, clambering aboard a small boat and heading south-east towards the Inchcape Rock with a party of fishermen. Their tale later, to the knots of people waiting for word of what the Abbot had been doing, was that he had had them wedge a stake firmly into a crevice between two rocks so that there would be no movement of it in wind or wild weather. On that he had hung his bell, the end of its rope dangling into the water so that it rang without cease with the motion of the sea. The fiercer the sea the fiercer the ringing and the louder the warning to sailors straying too near.

For long years after that, skippers and men blessed the Abbot's bell and came to call Inchcape, the 'Bell Rock'. There were deaths still in the German Ocean but far fewer now from being dashed on the red sandstone of the Rock.

But there are villains in the world as well as saints, and one of the most infamous in later times was the pirate whom sailors knew and feared as Sir Ralph the Rover. There were many ways of being a plunderer of the sea. The cargoes of wrecked ships were sometimes taken aboard the pirate-ship and never delivered or returned to the merchants waiting for them; other ships were boarded as they sailed, and everything in their holds or on the sailors' own bodies carried off as spoil; shoreland villages were often ransacked and maidens carried off for the pleasure of the pirate-king and his band, and then set ashore in strange places to survive as best they could. Sir Ralph the Rover knew them all. And he had one other fiendish practice, adding murder to pillage and rape . . . that of actually luring ships to destruction and their companies to death, then looting all that could be found.

It was therefore a great stumbling-block to Sir Ralph that, however hard he tried to draw small ships off course, to break themselves on the Inchcape Rock where he could close in and strip them of valuables, the bell would clang its warning and the ships would veer away.

In an impatient fury the pirate waited for a calm day, when the Abbot's bell tolled gently, then he took a small swift boat into a creek on the Rock, climbed over the sandstone, cut down the bell and threw it into the depths of the German Ocean. Then, smiling grimly at the thought of the spoils in store, he sped back to his own ship and rubbed greedy hands in anticipation of the next storm.

For a year he rode the Ocean, the scourge of every honest sailor taking spices and silks, wines and gold, and every desirable cargo from land to land across the sea. He grew richer and more merciless and increased his wealth, most of all from the shipwrecks on the Bell Rock.

The next good Abbot of Aberbrothock looked on sadly and buried the simple sailor-dead as the un-belled rock took its toll, and wave after wave shed their bodies on the shore. What use to replace the bell? The pirate had but to cut it down again. Something . . . some warning beacon was needed, that Sir Ralph could not have his way with so easily. And so the Abbot had a great rose-window put in the Abbey with a light always behind it that would be seen far out at sea.

But such a project took time and the builders had not quite completed the wall where the window would be, when the worst storm for a decade shouted and shrieked across the German Ocean and battered the Scottish coast. Sir Ralph's ship was laden heavy with plunder and he had his wheel-man steer in towards land near the Bell Rock, where he would sit out the storm in a sheltered creek, ready to gather in the flotsam from the wrecks. But steering was not so easy. Now and then the pitching, heaving sea tore the wheel out of the men's hands and it spun wickedly, so that the pirate-ship itself was at the mercy of the waves. Then one of the pirates would get a grasp on it again and steady course, wondering where to steer for safety. The Inchcape Rock itself was quite hidden by the spume of breaking waves, and only the clanging of the old Abbot's bell might have kept them off it. But there was no Abbot's bell now, and Sir Ralph had only a moment for bitter regret that he had cut it down, before one more lunge of his ship through a rising wall of sea threw it down across the red sandstone, doomed in one crash, and flinging all of its crew into the sea.

By the next winter of tempest in that fearful sea there was a steady beautiful circle of light sending out a shaft from the Abbey's new rose-window, warning ships to keep their distance, and for a time the high seas out from the east coast there were a little safer. But eventually the Abbey crumbled and, though the window space remained, the light went out and the toll of death on the Bell Rock rose again. It reached a climax in a gale of 1799 when over sixty vessels foundered to total destruction on its half-mile length.

He had been a bold, imaginative man, that first Abbot of Aberbrothock, braving the seas to hang the bell on Inchcape, and it was another bold imaginative man who succeeded in planting another warning there, when Robert Stevenson, sire of an imaginative grandson, built his lighthouse on the Rock. It took four years, in the teeth of wind and tide, to prepare foundations, to build the hundred-foot light-tower and place the lantern there, a beacon to guide wandering ships and, in its way, stand memorial to the first Abbot of the Bell Rock.

The Lordship of Lorn

It was ever a matter of regret to Lady Stewart of Lorn that although she had three handsome daughters she had never given her husband a son and heir. She did sometimes feel however that this misfortune was perhaps retribution on him for having sired his only son, Dugald, out of wedlock and for having kept a mistress over at Loch Earn while she, as his wife, had ever been loving and true to him.

Sir John Stewart did not think of putting away his lawful wife. He was one of those see-saw men who could be as happy with the wife as the mistress, and perhaps spent so much time on his own marital and extra-marital companionships that he did not notice until it was too late that his daughters were keeping courting-company with three sons of a family he held in great contempt and distrust, the Campbells of Argyll. When he found out he blustered and ranted.

'You cannot wed these men, Campbells have been enemies of this house at Dunstaffnage for generations.'

But the self-willed madams assured him that they could and they would, and were indeed already betrothed to their three Campbells. He sulked and pinched over the wedding celebrations but his wife and daughters simply flouted his wishes and went ahead with arrangements for priests, supper and linen-kists for their marriages. Being at heart an affectionate father he had to accept the unwelcome situation and make the best of it.

As time went on, however, it became increasingly apparent that the best of it was in fact the worst of it, for no son but the illegitimate Dugald followed the girls, and by now Lady Stewart was past the bearing of children. Sir John was forced to face the unpalatable fact that at his death the Lordship of Lorn would pass to his Campbell sons-in-law who would share its lands and properties among them. Stewart brooded constantly on this distasteful prospect as he rode over his lands or took the path to Loch Earn to visit his mistress Betsy Margaret and the ruddy-complexioned upstanding Dugald, now rising eighteen, who was everything that a father's heart could desire. If life had been fairer he would have made a brave and worthy Lord of Lorn.

And then, shortly before the boy's eighteenth birthday, although there was sadness when it happened, there seemed to be an amnesty in what his lady-wife had so often called his just deserts over the future of Lorn. For she herself ailed suddenly and died.

Sir John mourned her sincerely enough, but as the days went by he decided that as soon as it was decent he would marry Betsy Margaret and legitimise Dugald into his inheritance. He waited impatiently for weeks to become months and then, amid the winks and nods and nudges of those who guessed what was afoot, he had the tailor make him a fine new suit and the servants scour the castle rooms. He had the Dunstaffnage chapel refurbished and all the plate and brasses polished till they gleamed in the candle light. Then he sent to Loch Earn for his mistress to come with Dugald on the appointed day for the triple celebration of marriage, the legitimising of Dugald and the boy's official recognition as heir to the Lordship of Lorn.

Sir John was a popular laird and those bidden to the wedding were glad to come and cheer on his nuptials. Among the guests naturally had to be his daughters and his Campbell sons-in-law, although it gar'd his teeth grate to send them invitations . . . not so much, however, as it gar'd theirs to hear of Sir John's plans. Their own plans would be sent considerably agley when Dugald stepped ahead of them in line of succession, for they had long since made arrangements to split Sir John's land into three, and even decided which areas would make the fairest packages for each of them.

On his wedding day the Lord of Lorn arrived early at the chapel in the woods of Dunstaffnage and stood with a priest and the early guests at the entrance. From there he would see approaching in her finery the comely woman who had pleasured him for over eighteen years. There was no doubt that, staunch helpmeet as his good wife had been in life, her death had been fortuitous for Betsy Margaret, for Dugald, and indeed for himself.

Not, however, for the three Campbells. They joined the party at the chapel door, barely concealing their ill-temper as the woman and her son stepped lightly over the grass to join bridegroom, priest and guests.

Then, amid the clapping and cheering of tenants pleased for the master, there was a swish of blade leaving scabbard, a flash of steel, and a Macdougall-lackey of the Campbells daggered John Stewart where he stood. He fell back against the priest who knelt with him to comfort his spirit with due rites. But the priest was alert as well as holy and looked sharply about him as he murmured over the dying man. He saw not only the naked satisfaction in three pairs of Campbell eyes, but their deliberately clumsy attempt to grasp at the escaping killer. The priest's own eyes narrowed at what he understood of their plan. John Stewart's pulse was only fluttering now, but the Father leant over him.

'You are mortal hurt Sir John, but if 'tis your will to honour your son and his mother, there is time for me to say you husband and wife.'

Weakly the laird squeezed his arm. The priest took Betsy Margaret's shaking hand, helped Sir John Stewart's greying fingers to slip the marriage ring on her finger and, in a few words bound them wedded partners.

A few minutes later he was dead and Betsy had been mistress, wife, widow and dowager, before the good Father closed her husband's eyes.

Dugald Stewart was the new young Lord of Lorn and the word of him that comes down the centuries since that day in 1463, is that he was a just and well-loved laird and that his brothers-in-law had to settle for the possessions they had had before they tried to add them to the lands of Lorn.

Plaid, Philabeg, nor Little Kilt

It was all of seven years since the Forty-five and the bruised establishment in the south had studded the Scottish Highlands with a network of forts, designed to pin down any further flutters of rebellion . . . Fort George, Fort Augustus, Fort William, all named for the Hanover princelings, all full of redcoat soldiery.

But there were resistance men still in the mountains and it was on an eerily misted day of 1752 that a nervous young English officer, who was travelling to Fort William with two saddle-bags of gold to pay the troops there, thankfully reached the inn at the south end of Loch Lochy, in safety.

There were few others in the inn sitting room. Perhaps some had gone upstairs to bed, but Captain John Shields was glad to warm himself in silence at the fire with his boots off, a tankard of hot-pokered ale at his hand, his coat off and slung over the back of his chair. He fancied no one knew him for an Army man in his plain clads, but tongue and bearing had betrayed him and he might just as well have sat there in scarlet and gold braid.

A lean dark man, all of six and a half feet tall, who had been standing in a corner, lifted a chair as if it had been matchwood, dumped it down beside Shields, then threw one leg over it and sat down, his arms wrapped round the back.

'You're a stranger in these parts sir?' The soft Highland voice issuing from the great frame disarmed the officer.

'Not native certainly and though I know some of the glens, I don't know my way hereabouts. They say it's bleak country.' Then remembering his manners . . . 'but very fine.'

'Indeed, indeed.'

They shared a pipe and half-an-hour's companionable silence, for the few others had retired now and the inn-keeper was snoring beside his keys. John Shields' nervousness had left him now. There wasn't so far to go next day and perhaps this man was bound in the same direction.

'You know the district here well, friend?' he asked at last.

'Aye, fine well, yes, yes.'

'You're not by chance making for Inverlochy . . . Fort William?'

'The very place. I am so,' said the tall man.

'I would take it a favour then sir, if we could go on together for I hear bad things of some of your freebooters coming down from the hills against travellers.'

'I can direct you towards Inverlochy certainly for I'm going very near there myself.'

So it was settled, and if the Highlander had guessed before that his companion was an officer of King George's army, Shields' little bow as they separated for the night would have confirmed it. Nor was it difficult to decide what his business was, that he was not travelling openly in uniform.

At daybreak they saddled up and set off south, alongside the River Lochy. Shields' fears were back, and gratitude that he had this towering guide with him loosened his tongue, and over the next hour or more he confided to the man some of the tales he had heard of mountain robbers . . . told by more seasoned officers, who boasted of the times they had got the better of such ruffians, but had been eager enough to remain at Fort Augustus and allow young Shields to carry the money and cover himself with the same kind of glory.

'There are men like that in the hills since the time of Drumossie Moor,' said the guide, 'Men that did not take kind to having their very hunting knives taken off them, and their very clothes forbid . . . outlaw men.' And they talked of the orders from London nailed to every market-cross in Scotland, that no man or lad might wear 'the plaid, the philabeg or the little kilt', on pain of transportation.

'Proud men do not like that, friend,' said the Highlander softly, 'and take to the hills to *be* and *dress* as they wish, and as their fathers have ever done. It's maybe the Government in London's blame if they plunder a little to live.'

'Yes, they say some do have courage and a kind of honour, but there's one thieving murderer they talk of, that's vicious and cruel and thinks nothing of leaving his victim's throat cut,' insisted Shields.

'And what was it they said was his name?' asked his companion curiously.

'Oh, a Highland name . . . "Mhor" I think . . . Iain Cameron Mhor.'

'A thieving murderer, you say?'

'They tell me so.'

'"Mhor" is but the word that means "big". Your thieving murderer is name of Big Iain Cameron.' Something in his tone and the way he curled the word 'Big' round his tongue, alarmed the Captain.

The Highlander put his hand on the officer's bridle and halted both horses . . .

'. . . thieving aye, for that's but gear, and there's more where it came from, maybe hostaging for a wee bit ransom money and maybe reiving a few beasts for vittles on a winter's night. But murderin' . . . never! Cameron Mhor does not murder. Now sir, I'll thank you for that gold at your saddle. The soldiers can wait awhile yet for their pay. You'll be glad I don't want your life to go with it. I gi'ed you my word to take you safe to the road for the Fort. I'll keep it . . . along with your saddle bags. That there's your way to Inverlochy. I wish you a good journey.'

Trembling, John Shields handed over the satchels and Iain Cameron Mhor stowed them under his own saddle, slapped the rump of the pay-officer's horse, then rode hard himself for the cold mountain cave where he wrapped himself in his Cameron checkered plaid, sat down to his poor supper and contemplated a better one tomorrow.

The Shrinking of the Porridge

So beautiful are the Uists, Benbecula and Eriskay that it seems hard to believe that the Holy Christ and His mother never walked there. So strange legends of their visits to the white Hebridean shores have been passed from mothers to their children and their children's children, mixed with their Bible learning, 'inasmuch as to the least, ye do it unto me.'

Once upon a time Christ and Mother Mary were walking as plain people in South Uist. They wandered down a west shore track, refreshed themselves at a lochan shaped like a little bear and came at dusk-time to a cottage by the shore, looking out over the cream rim of sand to the sea. There they sought shelter for the night and a little of the simple fare they could see the wife was cooking. She had a great pot on the peats, full of fine porridge.

'We seek food and shelter Mistress. Can we rest and eat with you?'

The woman was flustered with her chores and scarcely looked at them as she spoke.

'Not here, I have but meal for my husband and my son when they are home from the field and there is no room for strangers to sleep at our fire.'

And so Christ and His mother left the house, and when husband and son came in presently and she went to ladle out their sup, what she had said was true. There was only just enough for two small coggies of porridge and none at all for herself.

Ever since that day, have you noticed, that when porridge is cooked ready, it has shrunk away from the sides of the pot and become less?

From South Uist Jesus and Mary passed to Eriskay and were wearier than ever when they reached a poor fisher-cot there. A thin woman was at her door throwing fish-bones to a screaming of sea-gulls. She bade the strangers a shy, surprised good evening, for few travellers ever came past her door.

'We seek food and shelter, Mistress. Can we rest and eat with you?'

'You are welcome to my thatch for shelter but I have very little food. These fish-bones are of last evening's supper and today I have but one small bannock. But we can share it and be happy together.' Christ looked at the bannock, small and flat in her bowl, and still unbaked.

'Set it there by the hearth-stone until we are rested, then put it on the fire.'

In an hour the bannock proved to be three times its size and when it was baked to perfection, soft inside and crisp to the bite, there was more than enough for all three . . . and the sea-gulls.

And ever since that day, have you noticed, that dough set by the fire to rest, makes into bread much bigger than it was in the beginning?

Seven miles out of Edinburgh tucked away like a green backwater in bleakish countryside under the Pentland hills sits the village of Roslin, with its old inn, its castle and its ancient chapel. Parts of the stronghold have stood there for seven hundred years, since the Baron St. Clair settled after his soldiering years, in lands given him by his companion-in-arms King Robert the Bruce.

The castle was lived-in modestly by his successors with their wives and families and just the number of retainers such a place required. It was died-in equally modestly for there was no elaborate kisting or laying-out in rich vestments; each one was simply coffined in his own armour and laid so, to a soldier's rest.

It was William St. Clair, the 3rd Earl of Orkney who changed all that and created at Roslin Castle a pretentious style of living, with a court out-kinging the King himself. He had none but noble lords to serve him and not country hobbledehoys from local homes. He lived a life of gold plate and tapestries, rich foods and wines, minstrels and jesters and, apart from his own lordly retinue, his lady wife could scarcely move between Roslin and her rooms in Edinburgh without a bodyguard of two hundred men and a company of ladies in silks, velvets and cloth-of-gold.

It was this same William, the 3rd Earl, who around the year 1450 began the building of a large chapel separate from the castle but nearby, on the River Esk. The whole church was never finished but the choir was completed as a small chapel, a feast of sculpture overlaying the basic style of the building, and it remains his monument to this day.

Two rows of short pillars divide the nave from the side aisles, and the arches joining them to the side walls are extravagant with carvings of Bible stories. There Samson is seen bringing down the pillars in the Philistines' house. Here is the Prodigal Son, the Dance of Death, the Seven Sins, the Great Virtues. The old masons had a joyful celebration of their craft in stone, not pausing to consider taste (whatever that was) or restraint. There was scarcely an inch of bare unsculpted stone in the whole chapel. Ceilings were ribbed and bossed and pillars garlanded with acanthus leaves, with oaks and ivies, and topped with hosts of angel-faces.

This exuberance of carving occupied several masons and their teams of apprentices and, as frenzied as the bursting-out kail-ferns round the arches, was the rivalry between the master-masons. Theirs was a craft known in medieval times for its tetchy jealousies and sharp rivalry for the highest honours and praise.

It was in the preparation of the pillars that the rivalry at Roslin had its sharpest edge. There were fourteen main pillars each with its riot of carving. The stones for them were sculpted individually, meticulously designed to fit together so that the full glory would be seen when the stones were laid one on top of the other. Master masons worked in shadowy corners, sometimes with lanterns so that only they could see the patterns of their own particular pieces. Then apprentices chipped away blithely at the simple leaves and stems or perhaps the trail and fold of a gown.

When the lads were let out by the masters they guddled for fish in the Esk, swung on overhanging trees and released their young energies in horse-play in the water. But there was one apprentice, Tam Nimmo, who did not often join them. He preferred to watch his master's deft hands holding the chisels, seeing when the tap-tap of the hammer was gentle and persistent and when one sharp knock made, cleanly and exactly, just the cut he wanted. The lad lived in a riverside cot close by with his mother and, after work was over for the night, he would come back into the chapel and wander round to admire the work of other masters, then go home to draw up his own ideas and designs. Then his mother would scold him to his bed and bid him mind his place among these great men from all over Scotland and even foreign places, brought to work for Earl William.

There was no doubt in Tam's thinking that it was his own master who was the best sculptor with the most original mind and supplest chisel, and it was the prentices's ambition to grow up equally creative and skilled. If he had known he was more so, he might have been more canny with his talent. But best sculptor or no, it was this master who became worked out and spent, during the making of the pillars, puzzled into fatigue by a particular problem with the composition of various features of one of the pillars, according to his design. Accordingly he decided to travel to Italy to study the patterns of chapels in Rome and the great doorway of Donatello in Florence. Then he would come back and finish his work at Roslin with a flourish and skill outdoing all his rivals. He left his apprentices with the scrollery and chip-work which he had trained them to do quite competently.

The boys worked away, perhaps larking about more than usual in his absence, certainly not looking for extra work. Except Tam. Tam would have worked all God's daylight hours and more. He kept his chisels sharp and bright and anyone who had bothered to look would have seen his lattices, bosses and leaves that were as exquisitely worked as any of the more difficult work of the other masters.

He was carving one day, rapt as ever, when Earl William came by to see how his chapel was progressing and remarked on Tam's work with great favour.

Tam, flushed with his praise, was now fired with ambition to finish his allotted task and also give his master a surprise by completing the pillar and overcoming the problem that had taken him to Italy. He studied the designs, made drawings, took measurements and honed his blades to perfection.

'Tam, mind what you're aboot, master masons are weel kent for their ill-temper when they're crossed. Dinnae you cross yours.'

'It's *oor* pillar, Mother, surely he'll be pleased to find we've made the others jealous.'

'Heed me, Tam. Dae weel what you've been told, but let the rest be. You're that knacky at the stonework you'll maybe show the master up.'

Tam could not believe that, but the very fact that his mother thought it, decided the matter.

In the next weeks the chisel in his quick hands tapped and scored and rang, and chips flew from the pillar as if the figures and dragons, birds and flowers were released from inside the stones and not imposed from without. The shepherd, the lovers and trumpeting angels were so breathtakingly real that even the other masons gathered round and nudged each other as he worked . . . they muttered too, dark predictions of what the boy's master would say, hinting that he would lose his place for disobedience. But Tam thought them only jealous and whistled with joy as he turned back to work, and flicked a whirl into a dragon's tongue.

The master came back from Italy, refreshed and inspired, and certain that the Roslin carving he would now complete would set his name above all names in the narrow-eyed world of masonry.

He stepped out of the sunshine, his hammer and chisel in his hand ready to begin, into the chapel, and the proud Tam met him and led him to the stones now mounted into a pillar of surpassing beauty.

'This is my welcome, Master. Just as you taught me,' he said and stood back waiting for the words of praise and gratitude that would be heaped on his head.

The master walked round the pillar, speechless. There was no doubt that this was the work of a hand more cunning than any other in the building . . . more cunning than his own. It was not to be borne that this skinny lad who had never been beyond Glencorse village, (never heed Florence or Rome) had done this wonderful thing. And what enraged him beyond telling was that he knew that he had not taught the boy more than the very rudiments of what he had done. The rest was his own genius. A great cry of rage and frustration came up from his boots, the masonry mallet came alive in his hand and he struck Tam a blow which felled him for ever.

Apprentices, masters and even the Earl, passing on his afternoon walk, crowded round. The master, stricken at what he had done, broke through them and ran along the riverside.

They buried Tam two or three days later. Perhaps they put a stone at his head — the story does not tell, but his pillar still stands as his memorial and somewhere in a felon's grave the master's bones moulder unheeded where they were laid after his hanging.

There's another memorial to three of the actors in the tragedy.

Among the feast of carving in the chapel are three figures, which tradition has claimed through the ages to be Tam, his mother and his furious master. It's said that the boy's apprentice friends were determined that the incident would not be forgotten . . . that to carve the three in stone would ensure that generations to come would remember what had happened during the building of the chapel. And they do, for the piece he himself carved was known ever after as Roslin's Prentice Pillar.

The First Fair

In the days long before there were pedlars, packmen or market stalls, men met by fords or under trees and bartered their beasts for such necessities of life as they could not make themselves, but that others had skills to fashion.

Girls went without trinkets and ribbons, and made pins and sewing needles from bone, brooms from heather and milked into buckets planked and girded by their brothers. The joy of buying and selling and of choosing and comparing was a delight of the future.

Among the first to beat paths across the countryside as packmen was Will Nimmo, a youngest son with the wanderlust and skilled fingers to work spoons and beads with carved designs. His sisters had country knowledge, greater than most, of the plants and flower-heads to dye their weavings into soft and pretty colours for shawls and kerchiefs, to flatter every colouring. . . . Against pale skins and blonde heads, sky blues and pinks were gentle. With ravens, berry-reds were vivid, and the autumn girls were winsome in russets and greens. Will would pack his basket with his goods and set off on month-long walks in hills and glens. He would take and deliver orders at cot and castle doors and pass on news from one farmtoun to the next.

Will was generally as sure-footed as a goat on rough ground and, as usual, on the day of this old tale, he had safely taken the screes and rushing burns of one steep Perthshire hill, from a high shepherd cot. Then he grew careless as he teetered across a peaty burn on low ground beside a cross-path used by all the folk who lived in that glen. A sudden slip and he was spread-eagled in the water among the mimulus and the crowfoot flowers, spluttering, laughing and watching shoals of minnows darting away from him in dark clouds. He was drenched, his packgoods were sodden and half of them were floating away, down the stream. Hastily he scrambled after them gathering his kerchiefs and gee-gaws.

It was a fine day. The sun was high and strong and he laid his wares out beside the track, to dry. He hung his own outer clothes on a gorse-bush, and dozed off for two hours.

His goods had dried out in the sun, the last drops of water shaken off, and he was ready to pack up and move on, when a group of barefoot women happened along who had been weeding crops on rigs outside the next hamlet and had the few pence of their wages in their hands. The bright colours of the merchandise caught their eyes and in a moment they were round him, clucking and feeling the soft weaving and smooth woodwork between their fingers, ready to exchange their money for their choice of pieces. Then they went off, pleased and delighted, with their purchases from the selection spread out for their consideration. Before they were well out of sight, the laird's lady and a friend came by, taking the air in their grand gowns and buckled shoes and they too pounced on the display. Then a fine fellow, going to visit his bonnie Nansie over the hill, had a notion to take her a knotted string carrying-bag and a twist of sweet-smelling dried herbs. Ten parties gathered round the pedlar before dusk.

Altogether Will did a brisk trade that afternoon and counted out a 'fair' day's takings. Word spread across the countryside of this new, easier and more pleasurable way of selling and buying, for pedlar and customer, and in no time at all there were smaller and greater fairs such as Will Nimmo's in every town and village in the land.

Somewhere along the shallows by the shores of the Pentland Firth, in times long past, there roamed a mermaid, but whether on the Orkney shores or along Caithness, the young fisherman she desired above all men was too glamoured by her wiles and beauty to remember.

She had first noticed him from the wave-lashed rock out a little from the lowest of the day's tide-line, where she sat when she was wae, and wondering which of all the sailor men she knew she might take swimming with her into the deep green depths of her own home seas. When she first saw Hev Sinclair, the lad was baling out his small boat to go a-fishing. His hair was black, his cheek-bones high and proud and his skin had the brown ruddiness that had been left behind long ago when the Spanish went down and cast their sailors on these shores. The beautiful mermaid forgot all the other menfolk she had ever enticed away and lost her heart to this one.

That first time she had slipped into the water behind her rock, admiring the deft hands that handled the baler, fastened the rowlocks and set the oars, angled blade-up, ready for the turn of the tide. Then as the brown boy took to the sea she swam over and shyly offered him gifts of sea treasures, pink shells and the rare little Caithness cowries, a smooth clear pebble, blue-veined and with the sun casting shadows through its depth. And among the gifts was a jewel of purest red that had never grown from the sea. Then, as silently and smoothly as she had come, she slid back under the sea leaving the fisher-lad scratching his head and swaying his boat dangerously.

In most stories of mer-girls and shore men the mortal is stricken with love for the sea-woman and loses all taste for life on land in his desire to go away with her, but this maid's beauty was too unearthly for the boy to appreciate, and he wondered more at the red jewel she had given him, and the sparkling shells.

The next day the mermaid, dearly wanting the lad for her sweetheart, brought more of her gifts, urchin shells of surpassing shape and colour, sea-washed driftwood in fantastic exquisite shapes, and this time a moonstone bracelet. And again she swam away.

That evening, hugging his secret, the fisher-lad held court at the sea-wall with the uncomplicated red-cheeked fisher-girls of the village and bought their salty kisses with the mer-lass's sea trove, the shells, the pebbles, the stones, and the moonstone bracelet one of them clicked on to her wrist as if it had been no more than a cheap bauble.

But one of the girls, with a finer eye to know a chip of glass from a true stone with its depth and mystery, lingered behind with the boy when the others had gone home. Her whispers and kisses asked for more such treasures and the fisher-boy, wild with her promises, waited for the mermaid the next day in the last sun of the late afternoon.

Her pale head rose, as before, from the waves and he pled for more of her beautiful things.

'You must come with me to my cave and choose,' she bargained and the boy slipped into the sea, side-by-side with her, and whithered-away through the green and silent world below. She touched him, to guide him and to pleasure her and they turned and looped and swerved until he had no idea where he was. And then they reached her cave among rocks stroked by the sea's green fingers.

There his eyes were dazzled by the mass of treasure laid out on the sand and the rocky ledges. Necklaces of gold and jade, great opals set in silver rings, anklets, bangles, gold coins, and brooches studded with sapphire, emerald and amethyst. And finest of all the sea's own treasures, pearls of a perfection never seen in any earthly crown or tiara.

'But how does a sea-girl like you come to have these stores of jewels?' he asked in wonder.

'Save for the pearl-stones, I find them on the sea-bed in the wrecks of great ships, the Norse ships bringing the little Queen-maid Margaret, and the Spanish coffers of the drowned Armada,

and from the bodies of lost sailors from ancient voyages to the
waters of the East.'

'Why do you keep them hidden here?'

'They are love tokens for the man of my heart. He shall have
them all,' and she curled twice round him and laughed softly.

A sudden fear took hold of the boy and he thought to have none
of her treasures for fear of the price to be paid. But then she began
to sing and her singing was enticing and soothing, echoing eerily
through the cave. She drew him into the white shell-sand lodged
deep in the rock and fettered him in golden necklaces.

And there he fell asleep and slept through all the years of
normal life so that when he awoke and the chains fell off, he was
part of the sea world for ever, and had forgotten any other.

And the fisher lasses on the sea-wall found other sturdy lads to
marry. They grew old until, as grandmothers, they told their
grand-daughters of the beautiful trinkets the sailor boy had given
them before he disappeared for ever. And they told their
grandsons to beware of gifts from the spirit of the sea.

The Hanging Basket

Alexander III, hero of Largs and King of Scotland's Golden Age of
peace and prosperity, was dead, under the cliffs at Kinghorn. He
had shared a grand-daughter, the little Maid Margaret, with his
old enemy Haco of Norway. Now she too was dead, on her journey
to take her crown, and Scotland was thrown into disarray with a
whole clutch of claimants to her throne. For a time the country had
tholed John Baliol, who had danced like a puppet to English
Edward's string-pulling, before William Wallace took on the task

of rallying Scots to fight for their independence. But now Wallace too was dead, drawn and quartered, and his mantle fallen on Robert the Bruce.

In the opening days of this old story Bruce was flitting about the countryside, creating, everywhere he went, the myths and legends of his prowess that still surround his name. In spite of that, in those early days of his wanderings, peasant folk were hesitant to throw in their lot with him, but a core of Scots nobles declared their intent by cocking a snook at Edward I of England and crowning the fugitive, at Scone, as King of Scots.

It was a brave but not very glittering occasion. What it lacked in pomp it made up for in courage, for every man or woman who attended would be marked out for punishment by an angry Edward who judged himself to have hammered the Scots into accepting him as their king. The only one there who trembled was Robert Bruce's own sister, the quiet Mary, who was happier back in Carrick, watching the grey and yellow water birds swooping along the stream's edge of her home burns of Ayrshire, gathering yellow iris there in fine weather or dreaming over her needlework by a chimney fire in winter. Now she was thrown into this reckless fight for kingship by her brother. At her side, but as different in temperament as eagle from dove, was the proud and fiery Isobel, Countess of Buchan.

'Courage Mary . . . would you no' be a Princess of the Royal house?' she demanded as she felt Mary quiver. Mary would have answered that truly she did not care for jewels and silks and coronets. But Isobel's penetrating whisper came again.

'No' for the show of it, or the power . . . but just that it's right for Scotland to have a King as can hold his head above Edward's of England.' Mary knew that this was so, and that her brother was just such a man. She put her small hand in Isobel's and took heart.

The modest ceremony began. The Stone of Destiny, traditional coronation throne of Scottish Kings, was long gone as part of Edward's spoils of war, along with the royal robes and ancient crown. And so Bruce was settled on the Bishop's seat with not many more than a dozen loyal companion-adventurers round him. The Scottish standard was unfurled and the winds of Perthshire streamed out its rampant lion. Four of Scotland's Earls stood guard around it, while only five out of the great number of her holy men, four good bishops and a single abbot, were there to bend their heads in prayer. The two women, Mary Bruce and Isobel MacDuff, Countess of Buchan attended the new Queen, Elisabeth. Now the thin little assembly gathered close to hear solemn vows from the King, and to offer theirs to him.

It had been a longstanding, hereditary privilege of the MacDuff tribe to place the crown of Scotland on the heads of her Kings, and it grieved the sturdy little Isobel MacDuff sorely that her brother, the present head of that house, was that day in the custody of Edward of England and like to remain so for a long time coming. Isobel was well aware of the risk she was taking by supporting this itinerant King, but boldly she stepped forward, took the makeshift circlet of gold which was to pass for crown and placed it firmly on the head of Robert Bruce.

When Edward heard of the ceremony he was just as enraged as those Scots had expected, who had circumspectly stayed away from Bruce's coronation. Edward stormed northward with an army to put down the insolent new 'King'. A troop of his soldiers came on Bruce and the small following he had gathered since the crowning at Scone, when they were resting in the Woods of Methven. The Scots resisted furiously, Bruce at the eye of the storm, but it was an unequal struggle and he and his men were finally routed. Some lay dead, some were taken prisoner, and one hardy pair drew the King away into the cover of the woods, to survive and fight another day.

It was a warm kindly summer for Robert and his faithful little party of lords, ladies and servant-soldiery to be roaming the hills, keeping always but a step ahead of English parties hunting them. They lived on the rabbit and hare they hunted, and the sweet little river-trout caught for them by their blithe and good companion Sir James Douglas. But autumn cut in sharply, in that year of 1306, with keening winds soughing through bushes heavy with the scarlet berries that foretold a bitter winter. So the Queen, Mary Bruce and the Countess of Buchan went to spend the cold months in Kildrummy Castle, while the menfolk continued their fugitive wanderings all over Scotland, trying to win more support for some decisive battle which would strengthen Bruce's claim to the throne he had already taken. As James Douglas was the beloved mainstay of the King, Isobel MacDuff was the support and strength of his Queen, rousing her when she wearied and chiding her when she grew faint-hearted and spoke her fears.

'I doubt, my Lady Isobel, they made but sport of us at Scone . . . that we were but King and Queen for a summer play.'

'Your lord is King of Scots, Elisabeth, and you maun act his Queen!'

But the men were safer on the moors and in their caves than the womenfolk behind the thick walls of Kildrummy Castle. Edward stormed it that winter and took them all into custody. The Queen was sent to London, Mary Bruce to Roxburgh and Isobel to Berwick Castle.

Chin held high and eyes blazing with the kind of defiance that her nurse had scolded her for as a wilful child, Isobel was paraded triumphantly into the busy, English-held town of Berwick. She was taken past the Tower Green, past the two-centuries-old church, past the Ravens' Dene, the Tolbooth and the Woolmarket and, at last, into the stone stronghold of the Castle itself.

For several days she was held in a small room in one of its towers. The walls were thick, so that all she could see through the slit window was the grey winter sky above the Border countryside, and all she could hear was the echo of hammer on iron. Then she was taken roughly from that chamber into a wide upstairs hallway, where she saw at last what the clanging hammer had produced. A wicker cage, banded closely with iron straps, sat there with its small door lying open. Into this the Countess Isobel was bundled, for the crime of crowning her King.

But that shame was the least of Isobel's ordeals. The cage was taken from the hall, carried by four Southron soldiers to the outside wall of the castle, Isobel clinging to its spars as it lurched along. And there she was thrust out, her basket-prison hooked to an arm from the wall, suspended high above Berwick.

It was not a day's punishment, nor a month's. She hung there for four dreadful years, winter and summer, with only the close weave of the wickering for shelter, and for fare, only the food and drink thrust at her through an aperture in the wall. And it was no comfort to the spirited countess to be taunted with the fact that the gentle, timid Mary Bruce was dangling from Roxburgh's Castle in exactly the same way.

Robert was still a fugitive, but the Scots folk, who had so far not flocked to join him, were watching and taking note of such brutalities as the caging of the women and the horse-dragging and gibbeting at Carlisle of Bruce's captured boy-brother young Thomas Bruce. And whether from awakening national pride, or anger, or from the rumour that Edward the Hammer was dying, the common people and the clergy began to muster behind their King, and the tide turned. When English Edward did die, the new Edward proved to have no stomach for war and conquest and, though Isobel in her swinging eyrie did not know it, as the slow years turned, one after another of Scotland's castles fell into Bruce's hands.

Berwick Castle was one of the very few still holding out against the Scottish King, but its commander began to tremble at the thought of Bruce's merciless fury when he came, as come he surely would, and found the Lady Isobel, frail and ailing from her long exposure, still hanging above the town. So he gave in at last to the repeated entreaties of the Carmelite Friars of Berwick that she should be given into their care, confined if needs must, but at least chambered as befitted a great lady.

Tradition does not tell how ravaged in health the Countess of Buchan was when she was finally freed from her cage, but her spirit could not have been broken or there would have been only her bones lying on the willow-latticed floor, pecked clean by the Berwick ravens. But she survived her ordeal. The friars nursed and nourished her tenderly and she exercised her wasted limbs quietly in the monastery walks and gardens, until body and mind were healed. And perhaps the siege months together in Kildrummy had steeled also the will and spirit of Mary Bruce, for when the man Isobel had crowned was at last hailed undoubted King of Scots and the Countess was finally free from even the friars' custody, she found that Mary too had survived her incredible ordeal-by-elements at Roxburgh.

Note: It is difficult to believe that any human being could have withstood four
       years of Scottish winters in anything but a much more weather-proof
       shelter than the word 'cage' suggests.

A History of Berwick-upon-Tweed of 1799 by John Fuller, states that the Countess of Buchan was caged *in* Berwick Castle, but that was written 500 years afterwards and the whole tone of his description of the incident is so partisan to the English perpetrators that perhaps the admission of the worse atrocity was unthinkable. Certainly the tradition of the Hanging Basket persists, as does that of the one at Roxburgh.

The Business Acumen of the McNairs

No one took much notice of Robert McNair and his wife Jean when they first set up their tiny shop near Glasgow Cross, in the middle of the 1720s. Most would have put him down then as a nondescript young man, without real capital (except his inventive mind and a purposeful intention to succeed). Anyone who was sufficiently interested to assess his prospects would have judged him doomed to make no more than a small living in drysaltery for the rest of his days. Jean appeared to be an unremarkable helpmate, bonnie enough to look at and pleasantly twittering and quick in her manner over the counter. Certainly neither seemed to be the stuff of which great business entrepreneurs were made.

And yet, when Robert, then a single lowly assistant in somebody else's store, had offered his hand to Jean he had assured her that it was only a matter of time before there would be a fortune to go with it. Jean, who had aspirations to become as near as possible a lady, dressed and mannered like Mistress Brodie to whom she was maidservant, caught something of his confidence and perhaps in his slightly bohemian garb, that made her throw in her lot with him.

Robert had saved a little, and so, high-handedly, he left his job and took that first tiny shop where they slept under the counter and ate behind a screen at the back. Jean was tireless, attending to customers, sorting through the small stock Robert went out to buy, and re-arranging it so that different things would catch the public eye on different days. Whether, at that penny-and-twopenny level, the two concluded any of the kind of astute deals they were later to be known for in their shilling-and-sovereign days, no one noticed. But they did prosper. And they moved into bigger premises at the head of King Street facing the Trongate. The shop had two bow-windows and Robert painted the outside with fresh green and white paint.

Above the door was the legend:

ROBERT McNAIR and JEAN HOLMS in COMPANY
GROCERS and GENERAL DEALERS

They opened their new place with confidence and the certainty that real success was now within their grasp.

Robert and Jean did begin to attract biener custom than in the old days. They bought quality merchandise and displayed it attractively . . . but not in quite enough quantity. The years were turning and the real merchant-class trade still eluded them tantalisingly. Robert had made an abortive attempt to raise bank capital to establish a broader line of wares, and was frustrated to be refused as being comparatively unknown to either the bank or the other backers from whom he tried to winkle a little credit. They were modestly comfortable however, and any other couple, risen as they had done, might have settled for the level they had now achieved. Not so Robert McNair and Jean Holms in Company.

One winter evening when the takings had been counted, entered in the book and locked away, they sat over their back-shop ingle in conference.

'We must get oorsels to be noticed better, Rob,' decided Jean.

'Noticed who by, Jean?'

'The big merchants and them as gives credit, and the bank again maybe.'

'How wid we dae that?'

'Weel, just look at us. I'm grey-headed and nothin' but a fat wee body gettin' . . . and you, your hair's that thin your near baldy and your coat and breeches is wore to a shine. And you dinnae wear your gravat-tie noo.'

They were silent a moment, looking at each other as they had not looked for ten years.

'Maybe . . . .' said Robert thoughtfully, 'it wid be a kind of investment-like to put a wee bit siller into new clothes and that. . . .' He stood up and examined himself in the looking glass. Jean patted her straggling hair, warming to the idea.

'D'you think a wig wid answer me, Robert?' and she joined him at the glass.

Accordingly when the McNairs opened their doors after the ne'erday holiday, both proprietors who had been sinking dowdily into middle age, emerged to the astonished clientele in youthful toupees lightly powdered; Robert had a new cut-away coat of ginger suiting with flowing yellow cravat while Jean rustled about between front and back-shop in a striking violet silk gown, fairly fluttering with ribbons.

Good-humoured clash brought a flood of custom to the shop and the investment began to pay off. They hired an errand boy.

Then briefly it seemed as if the fates were against the McNairs after all when a rival general establishment opened just across the street, matching their stock item for item, their prices penny for penny. And to compound the new threat there was a great scarcity of oranges in Glasgow that very season, a staple line at McNair's, always available till now, when he had no more left than a single small barrow load. To their horror they saw that, wherever the new shopkeeper had come from, he had brought a goodly supply of fine oranges with him. So here was trouble.

But Robert and Jean had not put their feet on the first rungs of the ladder to have it knocked out from under them. Robert talked the matter over with Jean's pleasant and amenable nephew who happened to be visiting them that week. Then while Jean filled the barrow with the last of the oranges Robert put a notice outside the front door:

LARGE CARGOE FRESH ORANGERS EXPECTED HOURLEY
Three quarters of an hour later the McNairs' boy was seen to wheel a barrow load of oranges from the direction of the Broomielaw, past his rival's shop and across to the McNairs. In

ten minutes he brought another load, and then another . . . each time he went through the shop with the barrow and then by a side lane out past the new establishment again.

Now it was the turn of the incomer to be worried at the sight of this large consignment of oranges, fresher than his own, arriving across the road. And when an apparently unsuspecting stranger offered to buy the whole of *his* stock he was only too glad to sell them all and have them taken off his hands. He was too busy counting the money he had salvaged to notice the stranger trundle the cart of oranges down the small alley off the other side of King Street. . . .

Jean tossed her ribbons over her shoulder that night to bake a special pie, before her nephew set off for home again.

One or two more such strokes of business quite demoralised the opposition who soon removed his enterprise further west, while the bank was at last ready to finance Robert and Jean.

Although still dealing in their normal wide range of goods the McNairs had now set themselves up as orange specialists, and were soon advertising the finest sweet and bitter oranges from Spain, PULLED, NOT SHAKEN off the trees and therefore excellent of quality for eating or putting to marmalade.

But it was a second, more major, shrewd turning of misfortune to profit that set the seal on the Company's advancement.

Robert's spelling was not any better now than it had been on his FRESH ORANGERS notice of a few years before and, finding himself low in stock of copperas (which he sold for purposes of ink-making and tanning and for use in the gardens behind the large Glasgow mansions) he accordingly sent to London for two hundred-weight of what he spelled as 'capres'. Mystified London agents interpreted this as 'capers' and with great difficulty scoured the city for this enormous quantity of an item used normally in minute particles for spicing sauces. Indeed the stocks in London were all but cleared and despatched to Glasgow, leaving the very small remnant there priced at a premium.

A less wily couple than the McNairs, not needing capers at all, might have simply sent back the unwanted goods to the agent but, sniffing out the situation in London, Robert and Jean *sold* them back instead, not only to one but to various suppliers in London now desperate for capers, for an enormous profit.

Bankers and merchants in Glasgow were by now more than anxious to deal with the enterprising couple and within a few years were scrambling in competition to supply them, finance them and furnish them with credit to expand their business.

And it was only a matter of time before ROBERT McNAIR and JEAN HOLMS in COMPANY had risen to rival all the titled merchants of the city financially, had bought over even the Great Eastern Sugar House and were up there with the likes of the Tobacco Lords of the Plainstanes themselves.

The Shot from the Hill

On the winter-wild, summer-glorious mountain and glen lands of Appin to the east of Loch Linnhe, in the days before the '45, young Colin Campbell (Red Colin, for his auburn hair) and James Stewart of Appin were close friends.

There was a traditional distaste between their clans but the young men in their own companionship disregarded it. They stalked the animals, guddled the burns and roamed the hills together in their leisure time, and their working days they spent learning to be true sons of their respective houses. They helped in the running of their estates and in the wise and kindly dealings their fathers had with their tenants, great and small. And the peaceful years went by.

But when the standard of the Bonnie Prince from over the water was raised at Glenfinnan the Stewarts came out for the Pretender, the Campbells for King George, and Colin and James went off to take arms on opposing sides.

Culloden saw the official end of the civil war, but the Jacobite cause went underground and there was much coming-and-going, cloak-and-dagger, secret agency and passing of messages and money to the seat of the Jacobites, now in France.

The British Government was still trembling from the fright the march on Derby had given it, and from the tidings that came out of Paris; and certain Highland families remained suspect. Among them were the Appin Stewarts, some of them now back and in their own heartlands. But their great estates were forfeit to the Crown and they had to swallow their pride and accept unemployment or only small tenancies.

The newly confiscated lands, now government-owned, needed factors and when Colin Campbell returned to settle to family life again after staunch service to King George, he was appointed to be Factor of the King's lands with the added charge of supporting his Campbell kin to maintain law and order in Appin.

Red Colin had not been one of Cumberland's vicious lieutenants after the Battle of Culloden and no more was he a harsh factor against the crestfallen and displaced Jacobites he had under his eye in Appin. All the same, his appointment did, at first, rouse ill-feeling in the district until they found him a fair and lenient 'landlord'.

James Stewart, also now returned from the wars, was not one who resented Colin Campbell's appointment. Like the rest of the Jacobite lands James's estate was forfeit, but he was philosophical about that price of defeat, and when Colin settled him as tenant of his old property he took up life there with his family and resumed his old friendship with his new factor.

Appin is a long way from London, and Colin's easy ways with the Jacobite tenantry and his friendship with the mild and godly James Stewart passed unnoticed by the nervous Government for over two years. The two men walked the tracks together, talked late into many a night amiably arguing their politics, and dined at each other's table with their lady-wives.

While Colin's work on behalf of King George was only in the administration of his Appin estates, James Stewart's on behalf of his Cause was to quietly gather the 'second rent', the money which went, not as the official rent did, to the Crown, but secretly, to sustain the exiled Jacobites in Paris.

Perhaps someone spied and reported James for this humane service to Bonnie Prince Charlie's remnant. But although he was well aware of it, Colin Campbell was not the man who cliped, for he was thoroughly reprimanded by the authorities for his dilatory and lenient ways, and ordered to throw James Stewart out of his tenancy at Auchindarroch in Glen Duror and to repossess it.

James of the Glen was a popular and respected man and when word of the coming eviction lapped round the district, men came together, whispering darkly and checking their thatches to make sure the blades hidden there were not rusting. But James was a peaceable man, sick of blood-letting, and he had no wish to see the men of Appin at each other's throats. So he forestalled his own eviction by quitting Auchindarroch of his own will and going to a small farm on a privately held estate.

James's gesture might have succeeded in quietening even those who did not believe that he had voluntarily left Auchindarroch, but just at this time of simmering undertow there came swaggering into Appin, James Stewart's foster son, Alan Breac Stewart, the Poxy. An orphan, reared in the well-doing home of James and his wife, he had grown to be a constant source of distress to both of them, for he was hard drinking, would have gamed away his soul and was violent when crossed. He had started the '45 as a Hanoverian, but changed sides, and now, with all the fervour of the late converted, was busily stirring up Highlanders and recruiting them for a Jacobin regiment being formed in France. For this purpose he had come to Appin. He was a good enough secret agent and loyal to his cause but when he had emptied too many tankards at ale-house tables he became loose-tongued and careless. Among the heedless follies he committed in Appin in that spring of 1752 was to let fall that Red Colin Campbell was planning more evictions and that it would gladden his heart, *and* James Stewart's, to see the factor dirked.

It was true that the unhappy Colin was under duress to evict a scattering of other Jacobite sympathising tenants, but the fact that he had promised to re-house them under the new holders of their tenancies, went unheeded. There were few cool heads in Appin now who saw the factor as doing no more than his duty, and Alan

Breac fanned the resentment. Even James who regretted Alan's rabble-rousing was perturbed and angry at Colin Campbell's new move.

The day before the evictions were to take place Red Colin was coming home from a rent-collecting expedition with a party of companions riding in single file through Lettermore woods. From a slope above the track, near Kentallan, a shot rang out and Colin Campbell of Glenure fell forward fatally wounded.

There were other garrulous men in Appin as well as Alan Breac Stewart, men who talked freely of his threats on Campbell and, at once, the authorities were after him for the murder of the Government factor. But the Jacobite agent had slipped out of Appin as suddenly as he had arrived. The authorities, having failed to catch Alan Breac for the killing, immediately turned their attention to James Stewart of Glen Duror and arrested him. Echoes of the good James Stewart's predicament must have reached Alan but he did not answer them and left his foster-father to face his situation alone. Now government officials had James in their custody. It was true that he had been working in his own fields when Campbell had been shot. That much was well witnessed. But he was a man of known Jacobite leanings, he had lost his tenancy . . . what was more likely, ran the official view, than that he was behind the plot to kill the man who had evicted him? Anyway his punishment, as an example, would make those with Jacobite plots in mind, think twice before they hatched them. Perhaps too they hoped to flush out Alan Breac, but he remained safely in hiding while James languished in prison at Fort William.

Taken without warrant, James was not allowed to see his lawyer during the months he was kept at Fort William. Less than three weeks before his trial he had a brief word with his defence, stopping for a few minutes on a journey with his guard from Fort William to Inveraray where he was to await his trial.

The trial itself was equally farcical, with some evidence invented, some suppressed, some manipulated, some even altered between the trial and final records. (One witness stated that the clothes worn by the assassin were brown in colour, yet by the time they appeared as written evidence, they had become blue, striped with black, to fit known garments belonging to

James Stewart.)

The verdict of 'Guilty' and the sentence of 'Hanging' were never in doubt.

There were wild plans to rescue James but, as word of these trickled through to him, he put them aside as likely to throw Appin into confusion and bloodshed and declared that, innocent though he was, his life was not worth such killing and terror as his rescue would bring.

James Stewart of the Glen was hanged near Ballachulish. His body dangled on the gibbet for three years as a warning to would-be rebels, until an old friend took down the weathered bones that were all that remained of him and buried them in an unmarked grave near the shores of Loch Linnhe where he and the young Colin had wandered in happier times.

But who did kill Colin Campbell? Perhaps someone knows even now, for there are those who say that among the Stewarts the name is handed down from one man in a generation to a keeper of the secret in the next. But two and a half centuries after the murder that secret can surely now be no more than a prized tradition.

The Phantoms of the Marsh

The battle was lost and won . . . lost by a queen who had fled, and won by the Regent Moray's force which was still almost intact, at least in life if not in limb. Part of his army, wiping their bloody blades on their horses' manes as they rode, had pursued a remnant of Mary's troop through the Gorbells and up Saltmarket by the Clyde bridge. But behind them lay three hundred of the queen's dead, littering the small hills and hollows around the village of Langside. The victors' work of digging trenches to bury the bodies, down on the moss-hags to the north-west of the battlefield, went on far into the evening and it was touching midnight when the last mort-spade was strapped to one of the working horses, and silence fell over the Moray camp. There was neither celebrating nor carousing for none knew whether the morrow would bring another wave of support for the queen. The army must be up at dawn to fall in line for the day's orders.

But Mary's faction was crippled. Soon Langside lay peaceful again. The meadow and bog-land grew green over the dead and new generations of village folk, tending their fields to the south of the Clyde, were scarcely aware of the bloody battle of that May morning of 1568. . . .

But here and there wisps of legend persisted. And they were still drifting on the Langside air three centuries later.

Before the rest of her fellow-matrons of Crosshill village were set-up themselves in the grand honey-stone apartments of Regent Park Terrace or the rosy-pink ashlar on the Langside hill, Betsy Tannoch, the Queen's Park lodge-keeper's gude-wife, riled them sorely with her airs because of her fine house at the park gate. One of the women, who had once been in company socially beyond her usual circle, even said of Betsy that she carried herself uppity as if it was her own back-yard that Sir Joseph Paxton had laid out, and as if her man was the park's laird instead of its janitor. And the same wife added darkly that Mistress Tannoch had best mind her fancy manners for *she* would not live in that park for a pot of gold.

It was true that the janitor's wife did consider herself more 'Mistress Tannoch' than plain 'Betsy'. And small wonder, she often thought, for she took the air in the elegant acres of the parkland every afternoon when the weather was fine, strolling along its avenues and lanes and enjoying the maturing gardens . . . an occupation, she was sure, much to be preferred to joining in the gossip in the village cottages around the Langside hillock, or in the narrow black houses on the park's north side, or even among her cot acquaintances in Crosshill. For she felt she had surely outgrown the ungenteel women who were content to consort there. Soon, but not too soon, since she had no wish to be thought ungracious, she would drop them gently for the ladies whose carriages were beginning to bring them driving to the park and to whom in passing nowadays she was already tilting her head and flicking her parasol on what she reckoned to be terms of pleasing equality.

Yes, Betsy felt she had good reason to be satisfied, and, every night when her more earthy James had pulled up the bedcovers over his long shanks ready for sleep, she would stand in her window corner drawing her shawl around her shoulders (as she had observed Miss Maxwell of Rose Villa do) and allow herself a smirk at the pleasant upward lines her life had taken since coming to the lodge-house.

She stood there on one such night, when cold moonlight streamed across the park and into the mossy north-west hollow below the slope. That was an area still not drained so that marsh iris and bog myrtle grew there in season. The hall knock was striking midnight. Betsy's man was sound asleep behind her now and there was never a living soul for near half a mile all round. She shivered without knowing why.

'Too much heed,' she thought, 'too much heed I'm paying to what these clashing women say about this being the hour that kirkyards yawn. Anyways the nearest yard's a good half-hour walk fae here.'

She scolded herself for her superstitions and took a last look over her estates as the final chime of midnight was sounding out. And then, as if that chap had been a waited signal, a long sigh came shuddering through the night and a hundred dark shadows rose from the marsh, then another hundred, and another. As they rose they took form and became a groaning army of mutilated men, some armless, some wanting legs or heads, all ghastly white, save for the crimson of blood along the gashes which had killed them. For Betsy knew fine, even in her terror that not one among them was a living creature. Then the groaning died away and an awful silence fell. The figures began to move across the ground, unhindered by tree or tussock, yet skirting nothing. Passing through reeds and sauches, as if these growing things were not there at all, they made their steady way to form a stream of phantoms, heedless of their broken bodies, folding themselves soundlessly into ranks on the main avenue of the park. At first their faces (those who had them), were turned away from the petrified gaze of Betsy Tannoch, but when every last figure was in place, as one man, rank changed to file, three hundred white faces turned towards her in a single sweep from shadow to blanch white, and the ghostly army began to march up Paxton's avenue with never a sound of footfall or command. Transfixed, she watched them march on and on towards nothingness, the column never seeming to end.

Then, of a sudden, Mistress Tannoch crumpled to the floor in a fainted heap of nightgown, cap and shawl.

James found her there when he woke, cold from the lack of his wife in bed, and went with his candle in search of her. When he roused her and heard the gabbled story through her jittering teeth, he thought she was possessed, and fled into Crosshill for the minister.

That good man was a God-fearing shepherd, who knew more about Bible tales of lost sheep than the exact location of Queen Mary's buried army. But he knew Mistress Tannoch too. He read a psalm to the frightened woman, counselling her to seek out in future the tea-cups and chatter of the Langside cottages and the lowly Crosshill village, and to get straight into bed from her prayer-knees of an evening instead of entertaining grisly imaginings at her window.

But he went away, nevertheless, after his hour with her, casting an uneasy glance over his shoulder back to the bogland where a mist was rising now.

Behind him, Betsy, sitting over a hot drink but still shivering, her night-cap all askew, was left only half-comforted. If she had believed the marsh army to be only 'grisly imaginings' or a trick of the moonlight, she might have tossed her head at his advice and gone on aloofly playing the laird's lady. But she knew what she knew, and was only too thankful to find that, while the other women might have fenced her off from their company for her previous haughty temper, her tale of midnight visitation opened every door to her for its dozenfold re-telling . . . a better story far than the ongoings of the doctor's wife with Baillie Murdoch or the tattered state of the candle-maker's Sabbath coat.

Betsy never saw Mary's defeated troop again. She took contentedly to the women's company and, over the years, rose along with them at a more staid pace of social progress, as one by one they too put up fine curtains at the seemly windows of the terraces round the park.

And, so far as she could tell, the dead, buried under the Camphill marshes slept peacefully in all time after.

But then, she never did look out from her window at midnight . . . never again. Never.

The Revenge of Katie Jack

Katie Jack of the Black Isle was, for the most part, a well-tempered woman, but she had two staws at local men who in different ways had got her dander up . . . a big-wig, who was the laird from whom she rented her cottage, and a small-wig, who thought he was a much bigger one. He was the gamekeeper who worked the estate of which Ladyhill was part.

As well as being good-natured Kate was, on the whole, fairly regular in paying her rent. But there were occasional lapses and it was after one of these that she had the affront of receiving a letter from the laird, pointing out that she was currently behindhand with her payments.

She may have been brooding over this shame and the unlikelihood that the laird was in great need for want of her paltry dues, while she was shortly afterwards gathering firesticks one day on Ladyhill. She had collected a goodly bundle and was binding it together with a twining of long grasses when the gamekeeper came splay-footing across the slope, far more angry than his keepering remit warranted and haranguing her for trespass and theft.

'You've nae right here on the laird's land and lifting his wood as well.'

'Tush man, I'm doing no more than tidy up your brae and put it to my fire on a winter's night and getting a kindling for a few other bodies too.'

But the keeper would have none of her common-sense excuses. He grabbed the sticks out of her arms, threw them down to put a match to the lot and let it flare away to ashes while she watched.

'It's a foolish man that heats a hillside rather than an old body's cold room,' she told him fiercely and, flinging her shawl-ends defiantly round her shoulders marched, muttering, down the hill.

So now there were two matters rankling sore in Katie Jack's mind. But she bided her time and waited for sweet revenge over dunning laird and officious keeper.

Now these were the days when even the Black Isle railway was a miracle of the future (never heed the brave road bridge that leaps the Moray Firth now from North Kessock to Inverness). And it was a steamer made the daily journey with passenger and provision between Inverness and the higgledy-piggledy fishing village of Avoch.

Avoch harbour is tidal and the arrival of the steamer *Rosehaugh* did not always coincide with high tide and so Katie Jack made a meagre living with a small rowing-boat, carrying passengers first from steamer to near-shore, and then humping them for the last few yards, one at a time, on her broad back, to keep their feet dry.

It was the laird's turn first for retribution. He had completed some business in Inverness one bitter afternoon, and he took the steamer back north across the firth. On the other side the rowing-boat was waiting, Katie's skirts hoisted for the wade ashore. On clambered the laird, in deference to his position, the first to be carried. Twice she stumbled him, almost into the icy water and twice he cried out in alarm for fear of the cold and for his new soft leather boots.

'What about the rent-letter then, laird? It's trembling about *that* makes me no' so steady,' and Katie lurched again.

'Carry me safe ashore Katie Jack and we'll put you paid-up in the book.'

'I'm steadyin' wonderful a'ready laird, sir,' and a few steps further on the landlord was lowered, dry and safe, on the shingle shore.

A little later, John, the testy game-keeper, had affairs in Inverness and joined the knot of travellers on the beach waiting to be carried to the rowing boat, for the next lap out to the steamer. Katie plodded back and forth with each passenger, leaving the keeper to the tail-end. She looked forward to carrying him for she had fewer qualms for keeper than for laird. Back she trudged for him. The sands and pebble-bars divided the ground under the water so that there were shallower and deeper pools, and it was just a mite unfortunate that there was a mishap over one of the deeper ones. Katie almost fell, but Keeper John was tumbled right into the sea.

'Tt-Tt,' apologised Katie. 'That was a right unchancy thing!' She gave him her hand and led him spluttering back to the shore. 'I'm sorry I canna let you dry yoursel' at my own cot fire for I'm sore short of firewood . . . but hurry you home afore you get a chillin'.'

They don't say whether, after that, Katie Jack had the run of Ladyhill to gather her firewood, free from hounding by the game-keeper. But the laird laughed, and forgave her and thought her such a character that he even had a fine picture of her painted, which Avochidollies still enjoy.

Anyway Katie was satisfied that she had settled her scores with both of them.

James IV was King of Scots from 1488 until his death among the Flowers of the Forest at Flodden in 1513, and it was in his time that the Orkney Islands were at last declared to be part of Scotland. The days of the Alexanders and the Hacos were over and Orkney was put neatly into its little box on the map of Scotland. It was one thing, however, to call it Scottish, quite another to properly absorb it into the life of the rest of the kingdom.

James decided to firm the links by running a ferry from the most suitable point in Caithness. The fourth James was Scotland's darling, young, imaginative and energetic, and would have thought nothing of riding, himself, to the edge of the mainland, to oversee the setting-up of the Orkney run. But he was a busy man. There was a university at Aberdeen to be founded, acts to be passed insisting that laird's sons all learned the Latin and versed themselves properly in Law. There were the acts to be encouraged, the new College of Surgeons to be established in Edinburgh, the dockyards to prepare for the building of the great ship *Michael*. Scotland was swinging into a renaissance and the ferry at Caithness would have to be attended to by a deputy.

But one finger James did want to have in the pie, or three to be more nearly exact. He would choose the ferrymen. Enquiries led to three Dutch brothers who were brave and experienced short-distance seamen, the brothers de Groot. The King had the young men brought to Scotland in 1496. They were ready to settle if the enticement was adequate and, armed with a letter from James to the Earl of Caithness, the three set off, John, the eldest, a blunt-headed peaceable man who was the more taken with the wild silent landscape with every mile they took northward.

William St. Claro, Earl of Caithness, examined their letter from the King and considered his coast-lands. Canisbay seemed the likeliest part for contact with Orkney and a few days later, in obedience to the King, he signed a charter and gave the de Groots the lands round Canisbay in return for an annual rent of three measures of malt.

The industrious brothers did more than grow and dry the sprouting barley for the malt and set the ferry run to Orkney. They tilled difficult soil in a bleak wind-keened landscape, they fished the cold northern sea, they wed local girls and founded thriving families; until by the time they were grandfathers there were eight small tribes of de Groot in that corner of Scotland. The wives bickered a little, the children squabbled and fought over their skills and games, and over ownership of the glimmering cowrie shells they called Groatie buckies, that sparkled on the Canisbay shorelands and nowhere else. But the tiffing in those days was not ill-natured and the eight families would have closed ranks against the world. They all worked hard. Their social life was meagre but its highlight was the annual feast to mark their coming to Caithness and for the fathers to confer together before the celebration.

For some years it was a joyful, laughing assembly, and then the meetings began to grow sour. Perhaps the eldest grandfather, John, did not have the eldest son, or perhaps the eldest son had four daughters while the youngest had the first grandson. And so the generations who were less wholly occupied in establishing crops and ferry had time to chawner and argue about who was now the head and senior member of the family. Scowls became more frequent than smiles or nods among them, and the anniversaries became year by year a greater trial of status, a race to be the earliest arrival at the scene of the party to take the chief seat.

The Johns, the Donals, the Finlays and the Willems were phlegmatic men and their quarrels never came to blows, but Grandfather John was saddened by the sulks among them for he was a quiet-natured old man. When finally, at one of the annual celebrations, it did seem as if there would be fists flying as well as angry quarrelling about who was to be at the head of the table in front of the door, who to make the traditional speech, John stood up and hushed them.

'The de Groots must live at peace in the land and at the sea, for the sea and land are wilder and harder than any of us and it takes a common will among us to keep them tamed. I declare before you all that this day a year from now I will give you an answer to our problem of who heads the family.'

The de Groots had another year of muttering and arguing as to who had the best case to take the door-seat at the head of the table, and about what Grandfather de Groot was up to on his point of land which they occasioned to pass from time to time. Where John was getting the money for his project, no one knew, unless it was from his share of the 'groats' they asked from passengers who used their ferry. Whenever two of the family worked at the same task they chewed these matters over. Seed time and harvest passed, a hundred times the ferry boat ploughed the Firth. Then it was feast day again.

The eight clans took the path to John's land, the eight fathers came forward and looked with puzzlement at the building that had appeared there on the edge of the sea. They walked round scratching their square Dutch-Caithness heads, for there were eight sides to this house, to each side a door and a window. Each man opened a door to find a chair set before each of the eight sides of a large table. They all sat down, their eyes swivelling to try to detect the slightest index of rank. At first there was silence, then Willem chuckled and Donal and two Finlays, until eight roars of laughter echoed out to the families, as eight silly men saw themselves at last as being all Jock Tamson's bairns together, and none abune the rest. Soon the women crowded in, exchanging weaving patterns and secret ways of smoking partans. The children squabbled happily again; and when night came the eight de Groot men walked home smiling sheepishly and warming again to each other.

The de Groots made that land their own, peopling it sturdily, and for two hundred and fifty years they manned the ferries. In time the fine white shell-sand blew in and covered John's curious house so that eventually only a dune-mound lay there. Later a hostelry went up for travellers who came to look out across the sea, to hear the tale of the Dutch brothers, to see the curious table and the original land charter from the Earl of Caithness. And the old peace-house was remembered in the eight-sided tower of the new John o' Groats hotel.

Every monarch needs an heir and James VI of Scotland was no exception. More than most kings, however, he needed also a substantial dowry and that was probably the basic reason why his choice fell on Anne of Denmark. Her tall blonde beauty was no more than hearsay before their marriage and was no doubt a further compensation after it. What she had to gain is more difficult to understand for, while she was not notably learned or highly intelligent, her suitor was an impoverished and eccentric intellectual with no claim whatsoever to beauty or gallantry. But whatever the incentives, James and Anne made a surprising success of their union, providing Scotland for the first time in generations with a lively royal family with both parents surviving their children's early youth. Five previous Jameses and the luckless Mary, Queen of Scots, had fallen like ninepins while their heirs were yet children.

But two things soured married life a little for Anne. One was James' increasing fancy for having handsome young men about him, the other the scarcely-to-be-borne Scottish custom of having one's own high-born children reared in some trusted nobleman's family instead of at home. Anne, who had presumed that the Danish tradition of a mother raising her own brood was universal, was appalled and left with too much time on her empty hands.

It was perhaps then not surprising that the Queen's attention wandered occasionally from the husband who had other company, and the children who appeared at court from time to time but were normally out of sight and keeping at Stirling or Linlithgow.

But if this was unfortunate for Anne it was much more serious for those who passingly attracted her.

I The Bonnie Earl of Moray
The matter of the care of her children had not arisen when the first of these rumoured romances compounded a political tragedy. In

1592 there were as yet no babies of the royal marriage. Anne was still very young and had a normal girl's eye for a handsome man, which the Bonnie Earl of Moray undoubtedly was, and her ungainly husband was not.

It had been King James himself who raised James Stuart to the vacant Earldom of Moray, partly for the man's services to the Crown and partly because he had married the daughter of the heirless first Earl. The couple's home was at Doune Castle and the Earl was much admired by his peers for his bonhomie, and by their ladies for his virile good looks. His beard was brushed and trimmed in the Spanish style and he wore a pair of fine gold earrings. His dark hair peaked on to a high forehead, his nose was well-formed above amusing upturned whiskers and his eyes were warm enough to melt the heart of any lady, as they had captivated that of his loving wife Elizabeth, and . . . it was whispered . . . that of Queen Anne.

However innocent her sighing after the Bonnie Earl, and however careless of his wife's feelings King James was, in his flirtations with the beautiful youths about the court, he did not take at all kindly to Anne's praises of Moray. Devious or careless companions repeated silly tittle-tattle once too often to the King and he took his resentment to George, Earl of Huntly, presently in Edinburgh at James's command.

There were those, of course, who were not fond of Bonnie Earl James, and Huntly was one of them. He had two craws to pick with Moray. In the first place he was popular, which Huntly might have tholed, but secondly Moray was a Protestant which was not to be tolerated. On this matter there had been two generations of feuding between the Moray tribe and the Catholic Huntlys and, not a week ago, the King had ordered both of them to present themselves before him to make an end of their quarrel in his presence. Huntly had arrived and Moray was ready, at a residence he had at Donibristle, just across the Forth, to come to Edinburgh for his audience.

Huntly was not reconciled to making his peace with the Bonnie Earl and listened with interest to James's complaint.

'I'll no' be made look cuckold Huntly, evensoever there's naught in it but a lassie's silliness. Moray sall have my tongue raspin' on him for kissin' the Queen's hand too tender or too often.'

'Bonnie face fronts black heart, Majesty.'

'No, no, scarce black heart Huntly . . . fool maybe . . . but I'll gie him fair hearin' when he comes, on the other matter of your mislikin' for each other. For that's a thing no' to be borne . . . two great families at each other's throats like yon. I bid you go to Donibristle wi' my warrant and fetch me back the Bonnie Earl.'

Huntly's warlike arrival at Donibristle Castle was not quite what the King had had in mind for, aside from the prickly jealousy over Anne's regard for Moray and his annoyance that the two earls were at feud, he had always favoured Moray and found him amusing, affable and no mean companion sportsman. The warrant to speak with Moray took Huntly past guard, gatehouse and house-servants . . . and into the presence of the Earl of Moray, in his bed-chamber preparing for sleep. Huntly began bluntly.

'I command you to surrender to me James Stuart of Moray, in the name of King James himself.'

'Surrender, my Lord Huntly? The King's will wi' me . . . wi' the both of us . . . is surely to see us put hand in hand, no' to be taken to him, one by the other, in shackles.' Moray smiled disarmingly and adjusted his nightcap from its rakish angle.

'Surrender!' repeated Huntly, his narrow eyes cold as the steel of his sword. 'In the King's name. For he would see you on the matter of the Queen's Grace.' Moray trusted the King but he did not trust his messenger.

'That I'll never do to you George Huntly, for I fear you're but rankled that I've the Queen's favour. I'll see the King tomorrow, never fear, but I'll make my own way there.' And he called to the ante-room of his chamber.

'Dunbar!' The Sheriff of Moray, who was attending the Bonnie Earl at Donibristle, opened the door. 'Will you escort my Lord Huntly to the gatehouse, an you please.' Dunbar was a dauntingly immense man and Huntly retreated grim-lipped.

An hour later the gude-folk of Donibristle hamlet saw the castle ablaze and the whisper that licked round as fast as the flames, was that strangers, bearing malice to James Stuart of Moray, had fired it. The Bonnie Earl had wondered if Huntly would go off so tamely and the first flickers of fire had not surprised him. He ran down the stairway and out of the castle towards the foreshore. Various servants and the Sheriff Dunbar spread out, running in various directions as decoys. But as Moray had put his shoulder to one of Donibristle's great studded doors the tassel of his nightcap swung into a tongue of flame, and in the darkness along the shore he carried his own give-away light. The tassel danced and flickered among the black shadows of the rocks and there George, Earl of Huntly, found him and daggered him to death, adding a vicious disfiguring slash to the handsome dying face. A ghost of the old smile that had charmed the ladies' hearts played for the last time on Moray's lips.

'You spoil a handsomer face than your own this night, my lord.'

King James was always an enigma and never more so than following this occasion. When, after they had brought up the Bonnie Earl from the shore and 'laid him on the green' at Donibristle, he did no more than express regret at the killing and extended only formal sympathy to Moray's grieving wife Elizabeth, at Doune.

There are those who say that he felt himself implicated by having given Huntly a credible excuse for his performance of satisfying for the King's married honour. Others, closer, thought they saw in James a grain of satisfaction that the handsome Earl of Moray would not distract Anne any more. But they detected also a distinct cooling toward Huntly and a niggle of disappointment that murder, and not his own diplomacy, had ended the Moray-Huntly feud, at least for that generation.

But the Bonnie Earl was survived by more than a sorrowing widow. He left five children, with a vigorous mother who tried hard to instil in the new little Earl that when he grew to manhood he was in honour set to avenge his father's murder. But King James had his diplomatic way eventually and romance took over in the end, when the young Earl met and married the Lady Anne Gordon, Huntly's daughter, and the old blood feud died away.

II The Young Master of Gowrie

If, in the next eight years, Anne had notions of any other of the nobles surrounding the King, she had learned from the fate of the Bonnie Earl of Moray to keep them to herself, and so neither history nor folklore has recorded them. But, by the year 1600, the second of the rubs in her marriage to James had grown raw. She had two live children now, Prince Henry and the little Princess Elizabeth, neither of whom she was being allowed to rear. Now she was with child again and she knew that however sick and miserable she might be in the waiting months, the babe who could have made it all worthwhile would be whisked away to some other woman almost at once.

In spite of James's suspicions of one of his noble families, the Ruthvens of Gowrie, Anne was fond of them especially of the Earl's younger brother Alexander, Master of Gowrie. As he grew into his late teens Anne, now twenty-six, felt herself stirring towards him when she compared him with her odd, awkward, thirty-four year old husband.

King James VI's accounting books show that for his hunting holiday at Falkland in 1600 he had a new broadcloth suit in hunting green and a pair of velvet-topped boots. He complained frequently that his wardrobe was sparse of clothing fit for a king and looked forward to the time when, if he made himself pleasing enough to Queen Elizabeth in England, he would have the royal coffers there to dip into for his silks and suitings.

And so on this August morning, in spite of any prickling annoyance he may have had over Anne's foolish interest in young Alexander, James in his fine new clothes was in high spirits as he set out from the Palace with a party of companions to go stag-hunting. He had a shauchling uneven gait to his walk but when he was mounted on a brave horse he always felt more like a man among men, and there was bawdy laughter and the sound of rough singing as they swung out of the courtyard. They were scarcely quarter of a mile from the Palace when a rider galloped towards them from the north-west, swerved in among the party and reined up before James. The King frowned to see Alexander Ruthven, Master of Gowrie. But the boy had news for him.

'My brother has detained a man at Gowrie, sir, a man as has too much gold about him for good intent. There's suspicion he plans ill to your Grace's own person, for they say he spoke treason in a Perth ale-house last evening.'

If the treason had come from Ruthven lips themselves, James would not have been surprised: for this man's father had once abducted him as a youth, and his grandfather held a steel at his unborn self in his mother's womb the night Seigneur David Rizzio was murdered. On the other hand his story might be true, and the smell of gold was ever a lure to King James. If the tale was false then there might be, in punishing for it, the chance of some sort of vengeance for that other lure . . . the fancy the Queen had for this young whelp. There had been the matter of a tangle of gold-threaded ribbons given by the King to Anne and later seen on the person of Alexander. The ribbons had been back in Anne's closet when James asked to see them but a sharp servant could have acted and saved her mistress discovery. James had remained suspicious. The revenge for that could be a spell of imprisonment for the young man or, more imaginative, a dalliance with Alexander for himself, which would help Anne mind her marriage vows.

James cantered on to consider a little, then stopped. He would take time to think it over. The Master of Gowrie was at his side again.

'As soon as the stag's taken I'll mak' for Gowrie,' promised the King.

The kill was over by noon and James took a party of attendants and made for Perth. The Master's brother, the Earl of Gowrie, met him outside the town and escorted him to Gowrie House.

'I hadnae thought to see so muckle a company wi' the King. Your Grace maun pardon me that the vittles are no' ready waitin'. But I'll have them mak' such a table as we have, withoot too great delay. Meanwhiles I'll give you word of the prisoner I've put by in the turret room, and my suspicions what he's up to wi' a' that coin.'

The King and the two noble brothers sat over the table and while James heard of the discovery of the man and the circumstances of his detention, his party went out to take their ease in the fruit garden.

Then the Master led James up by the spiral stairway to the turret overlooking the garden, and a chill of apprehension shuddered over the King as he heard more than one gate clang behind him. At the top Alexander threw open the door of the small tower room and stood back to let James enter first.

When the door closed behind them James turned to ask Alexander where the prisoner was, for only an armed man stood, quite still, against the wall. The Master of Gowrie faced him threatening with a naked blade. The King was not a brave man but he was a quick one. He threw himself at the narrow window and yelled to his men in the garden below.

'I am murdered my lords . . . Treason!'

His nobles in the garden moved quickly, for they had already been puzzled at the word of a servant that the King had left by a side gate and was riding alone back to Falkland. Now they knew that for a false diversion and swarmed through the house and up the corner stair. When the first of them forced his way in, he found James struggling with Alexander Ruthven. There was no question now of simply annexing the youth for his own pleasure as a punishment for a suspected liaison with Anne.

'Strike him to kill,' panted James. The room was wild now with shouting and the flail of arms and sword, and finally with the grunting sobs of dying men. When the fracas subsided the two young Gowries, Earl and Master, lay dead, and James, his fine new green hunting-suit stained and torn was on his knees thanking God for his life. He was taken back to Falkland trembling, by a sober company, while the bereaved Ruthven household tended their dead and went into conclave to discuss the account of the affair they would present to the world.

So two versions of the Gowrie Conspiracy have come down in folklore, the Gowrie tradition that it was all the King's plot to wipe out their family, and James's own account as in this tale. But neither has been riddled free enough of accusation, jealousy, political intrigue or the King's taste for engagingly attractive young men, to emerge as clear truth. On balance the King's story seems the more likely.

Perhaps this death of a second favoured man stopped Anne from further indiscretions among the Scottish nobles. And when the court moved to London three years later she found her excitement in theatricals and masques, while James found his in his new wealth, great English hunting forests, more complex political problems, and no longer in jealous suspicions of his Queen.

The Book of Jeremiah

When the 72nd regiment came to serve in Glasgow in the early eighteen-hundreds, one of the soldiers who arrived was Jeremiah Armstrong, wit, eccentric, and barrack-room wag. He was, nevertheless, dutiful in his kirk observances, even sometimes when not actually at a church parade.

He was sitting in the Reverend Dr. William Taylor's church one Sunday, a duty attendance on this occasion with others of the regiment, tucked modestly behind a pillar apparently absorbed piously in the reading of the lesson. His sergeant sat at the far end of the same row, although only a raw recruit or a fool would have mistaken his half-closed eyes for lack of attention to his men's douce behaviour. As the minister closed the pulpit Bible and there was a general raising of heads, Jeremiah, his head still bent over the pew, became aware that an unnatural silence had fallen over the service. He looked up to find all eyes upon him, and in particular two pairs of eyes, the cold blue ones of Sergeant Peter MacAlister and the sad, brown ones of the minister. Almost at the same moment the two men had observed the spread of playing-cards laid out before Jeremiah, a sight already noted uneasily by his nearest neighbours and now sending a frisson of outrage and awe through the rest of the congregation . . . the Devil's playthings in the Kirk! This was a deal worse than some old wife napping under a head-shawl or a bold lad holding hands with a pretty wench in the niche stone seats at the back.

Jeremiah's offence was in fact too serious for either simply army discipline on the one hand, or only Session appearance on the other. The service proceeded in an atmosphere of mingled indignation and excitement and the minister might have been reciting his A, B, C's for all his flock heard. After the Blessing, Jeremiah's arm was firmly grasped by the lean hand of Sgt. MacAlister who had a brief consultation with Doctor Taylor and sent a corporal to line up the rest of the soldiers and march them back to the barracks, while he and the minister escorted the offender through the kirkyard and the street to Provost MacKenzie's house.

MacKenzie, a florid well-set-up merchant citizen, was not as scandalised by the misdemeanour as Doctor Taylor, nor as angered by the breach of discipline as Sergeant MacAlister, but he was conscious of his position in the community and settled the party in his receiving-room to hear the case with suitable solemnity. He heard the complaint and cleared his throat pompously.

'A grave offence Jeremiah Armstrong, a grave offence indeed. You must surely have something to say for yourself.' Jeremiah was not the son of a County Cork father for nothing, though he had never been to Ireland himself. He smiled earnestly and sheepishly.

'Indeed aye, your Grace.' The Provost swelled happily at the style, but without betraying a smile.

'It's like this . . .' went on Jeremiah, 'we've but a bare allowance of sixpence a day for food and drink and a' the other necessities of life, *and* a pittance to send to the likes of my ailing mother. So there's never a halfpenny left for the thing that myself, and any other decent man like yourself, or the Sergeant, or the minister here wants . . . no' just *wants* but *desires* above a' things. That's a copy of the Good Book itself, be it ever so plain-covered.' Jeremiah's voice held a tremor of sincerity now. . . .

'So you see, I make the best use I can of my card-pack that I've carried since I found them in a midden-tip years since . . . I turn the Devil against himsel' you ken.' He took out the cards from his pouch.

'How so?' asked the Provost, while the minister shook his head and the Sergeant snorted.

'Weel, tak' the Ace here. . . .' He moved to a side-table ignoring the quick stiffening of the Sergeant to thwart an escape, and began to snap down the cards one by one. 'The Ace tells me there's just the yin God. And the Two and Three's the Son and the Holy Ghost.' There was flabbergasted silence.

'And the Four?' came the Sergeant's voice at last, heavy with sarcasm.

'Matthew, Mark, Luke and John,' recited Jeremiah. 'And the Five's yon Wise Virgins, the Six . . . the days the Lord needed to make heaven and earth.'

'And seven?' prompted the Minister.

'The day the Lord rested,' supplied the soldier. 'And Eight . . .' he paused, and the Provost spoke, himself now into the drift.

'The righteous preserved from the flood maybe?'

'Aye,' agreed Jeremiah happily. 'Nine . . .' he mused, flummoxed.

'The ungrateful lepers,' murmured Doctor Taylor gently.

'Indeed, you're richt Minister,' cried the soldier, on the home-stretch now.

'And Ten for the good commandments.' He shuffled the Jack to the bottom of his pack. 'And as to the Queen and King,' he said with growing confidence,

'They mind me of the great Sheba come fae the uttermost part of the earth to hearken to the wisdom of Solomon. And the King . . . ' he held up the face-card with a flourish and stood to attention. 'The King is the King of Heaven, and *forbye,* our own great George the Third, by grace of God, King of Britain, France and Ireland, Defender of the Faith.'

They were dumfounded, but the Sergeant was first to recover himself, spurred on by the thought of losing face to the smooth-tongued Jeremiah.

'But *what?*' he asked nastily, 'what, sirrah, about the Knave?' Jeremiah looked at the others and thought he detected a twinkle in the eyes of the Provost and the Minister.

'The Knave . . . ' he said finally . . . 'is the Sergeant who spiers into a man's holy thoughts in the kirk, and brings him to sic a court as this.' The Sergeant tugged wrathfully at his sword.

'Nae, nae Sergeant, bide a minute,' soothed MacKenzie. 'The man's gie'd a good account o' himsel'.'

For all his pomposity the Provost had a rich sense of the ridiculous behind his dignified public mask. And the Minister, for all his solemn kirk virtue, had in him a remnant of humour left over from high-jinking student days. The Sergeant had neither, but when Provost MacKenzie took out his bottle from the press in the corner and set out four glasses, he put up his sword and resigned himself to quenching his rage with a dram of the Provost's whisky.

The Minister was too old a hand at tangling with human frailty and guile to have been taken in by the soldier's rigmarole, but it did occur to him that if Jeremiah knew enough to have such timely recall of Bible teachings from a pack of Satan's cards, the Book itself might even make a Christian of him. Accordingly, on the morning following, Doctor Taylor left a small package for him with Sergeant MacAlister at the barracks, and Jeremiah had the grace to leave his card-pack behind on subsequent Sabbath Kirk parades.

The Rebel Dog

Historians can tell you, of course, all about the parentage, background, blossoming careers and curricula vitae of great figures like Sir John Moore or stout Cortez. But ask your average fifty-percenter in a general knowledge quiz who they were and you hear no more than that the one was buried at Corunna in dead of night, without drumbeat or funeral note, and that the other stood gazing equally soundlessly on a Darien peak.

James Wolfe too has been pinned to the map like that, at Quebec, scaling the Heights of Abraham, winning the battle for the town and dying at the same moment as the enemy general, Montcalm.

But there's another little tale of the young Wolfe, thirteen years earlier, at Culloden Moor. He was then a brevet-major on the staff of General Hawley, shrewd, brave, and a deal more gentlemanly and gallant than either Hawley or the overall commander of the campaign for King George II, his son the Duke of Cumberland.

Culloden was an unequal struggle from first clash of steel on steel. Prince Charlie's army was weary and hungry after the march from Stirling and it was vastly outnumbered by Cumberland's force. The grim persistent beat of Cumberland's kettle-drums was a warning knell as the two armies lined up.

But the Highlanders were devoted to putting their Stuart prince back on his ancient throne. They were spirited and great-hearted and from the first raising of their bonnets to yell a start to the battle they fought like tigers round Charles Edward. But claymores and swords were no match for bayonets, nor the great Culloden blacksmith's whirling cart-shaft for cannon-ball and grape-shot. Wave after wave of clansmen, happed in the smoke of gunfire, fell on to the lines of Royalist bayonets standing firm.

Now the battle was over, Charles had been led away by faithful officers who had taken his bridle and would have him hidden in the hills of the west by nightfall. Cumberland and his officers were riding over the field where hundreds of clansmen lay dead and dying.

There had been glee and rejoicing among the Jacobites in past days, after the battles at Prestonpans and Falkirk, but none of the vicious victor-butchery that Cumberland and Hawley had demanded of their officers after Culloden. No one sang a ballad of celebration and exultant amusement after Drummossie Moor like that about Johnnie Cope. There was nothing to celebrate the memory of victors stepping their horses heedlessly on top of slain and wounded men, or stabbing savagely with steel at any movement of foot or hand until it was stilled.

General Hawley rode with James Wolfe. The young major was increasingly sickened by his commander's orders to foot-soldiers to kick slumped kilted bodies to make sure they were those of dead men, with no word to instruct burial or the giving of quarter to survivors.

As they made their merciless progress in the sleet that had chilled the battlefield, a pair of clouding blue eyes watched them with contempt. Young Charles Fraser of Inverallochie, a Lieutenant-Colonel of the Frasers of Lovat, lay mortally wounded against a moorland dyke, his blood, like that of perhaps eighteen hundred other Highlanders, seeping into the churned ground.

Hawley saw him stir and beckoned Wolfe to his side. Charles Fraser pushed himself forward weakly, his elbows against the dyke, his head raised defying Hawley to put him down or have him booted aside.

'To whom do you belong?' sneered Hawley.

'To the Prince,' said Fraser with as much spirit as he could muster.

Hawley knew that this was no surrender; that the man did not mean the Prince who was the Duke of Cumberland but the Prince who was of a line of Stuart Kings going back nearly four hundred years.

'Major Wolfe sir, shoot that scoundrel who dares speak so to the General of his King. Shoot the rebel dog!' But Wolfe was not bred to butchery.

'My commission is at your disposal, sir. But I shall not kill a wounded man on the field of battle. That, sir, is murder, not war,' and Wolfe dared, with a glance, two other junior officers to do Hawley's despicable bidding. Then the General roared his order to a foot soldier. A musket barked and Charles Fraser of Inverallochie jerked and fell back dead.

The sordid aftermath of the battle of Drummossie is an old and shameful story and left a trail of bitter memories behind it, but no more of it is part of this tale.

Cumberland went back south to a large increase in his royal allowance and to a hero-prince's welcome. But as tales followed him south, of indiscriminate carnage in local hamlets from Culloden back into Inverness, the visions of him as the greatest

British hero ever, died down and the whispered title 'Butcher Cumberland' took its place.

Hawley, having billeted himself with Mistress Gordon among the comforts of her home at Hallhead, had some time yet to spend in the north before he packed and carried off every last piece of his landlady's pretty china, bedding and library, her clock, her silver teaspoons and tongs, her precious japanned tea-tray and every stitch of her late husband's clothing. Over this matter too James Wolfe tried to resist his unchivalrous will, but it was not a question of life or death, he did not risk his commission over it and had to accept that Hawley saw the little lady's furbishings as spoils of war.

So the General left Inverness with his mind on the dainty plunder. James Wolfe left, with the memory of Charles Fraser's dying face in the sleet of Inverness-shire.

In the years that followed the decimation of the Highlands after Culloden, wiser statesmen came to office in London and absorbed the clansmen's frustrated energies by creating the Highland regiments in the British army. And so, many who had fought against Wolfe on Drummossie Moor were under his command in other wars.

Now, thirteen years later at Quebec, he himself was sinking, fatally wounded after the battle for Canada, and perhaps he had some recollection of Charles Fraser slumped against that dyke . . . perhaps it was not only the victory over the French that made him murmur. . . .

'God be praised. I die in peace. . . .'

For the story goes that the arms which held him as he died were those of another Fraser of Lovat.

The Faery of the Findon Gorge

Once upon a time near the Black Isle hamlet of Culbokie, just a step over a mile from the soft grey waters of the Cromarty Firth, there lived a faery-woman. They said her haunt-place was in a shallow wooded gorge by the Findon Burn where clustered bell-flowers grew, white and purple, in summer time, and a cracking of ice edged the winter flow of the water there.

The children would creep down quietly from their play and try to catch her, and the womenfolk would have given much to pin her by the fluttering grey draperies they fancied they saw when there was a low mist drifting under the branches of the rodden trees and among the flag iris blades. But neither children nor mothers caught sight of any more than that trail of the Findon faery.

But they knew she was there all right for she sometimes stole away their menfolk. The men themselves closed ranks in face of their wives and talked knowingly of the fae woman . . . that she took Hugh Sutherland or John Patience or other of the Avoch fishermen into her clutches for sometimes a whole night or more . . . that she had been known to hold two Flowerburn farmers and one of the Mackenzie's men from Rosehaugh estate, for a whole week. And none of them could ever tell a word of what had happened to them there. They were, however, never stricken or unhappy, never wild-eyed or terrified when they reached home again, only tagled a bit from doing a good stint of work for the faery.

Of all those who were carried off to the gorge, the man who was the faery's victim most often was Tammas Ross, who was a farm-worker near Killen. Sometimes Tammas was gone from home a month or more. There were some women who thought privately that a month away, with even an other-worldly woman, from his scold of a wife could only be a treat for Tammas, for she was known to chase him whiles with her washing-stick and take it hard across his skinny back. But they would never have spoken such thoughts for they had to stick by each other, even by Mistress Ross, against the siren faery of Culbokie. Whatever else she did to Tammas during his captivity the faery left a silly smile on his pinched face that infuriated his wife when he finally appeared again, bearded, crumpled and quite unable to say what had happened to him over the weeks of his absence.

Tammas was the favourite of the faery until his targe of a wife was laid to rest after falling down dead from one of her rages. He married a buxom good-natured milkmaid and was never snatched away again.

But the faery held other Black Isle men in thrall from the last decade of the sixteen-hundreds, curiously enough almost exactly the time that the Laird of nearby Ferintosh was granted freedom from duty on all whisky made from his grain. These happy days of cheap liquor lasted until the freedom lapsed a century later. It was a great blow to local men when the flow of liquor so freely distilled for four generations dribbled to a drought. And only the most sourly suspicious of the loving wives remarked that the Faery of the Findon Gorge seemed to lose her taste for their menfolk at precisely that same sad time.

Maggie Hardie's Bargain

Martinmas rent-Friday that year of 1643 was not a happy day for young Tam Hardie and his wife Maggie. They sat early that morning in their sheep-farm-cot twelve hundred feet up on Tollis Hill eating their oatmeal porridge. They were looking glumly at the few coins Tam had thrown on to the table from the bag where they had always carefully kept enough to make up their rent to the Earl of Lauderdale at Thirlestane Castle.

Tam had certainly worked his days of rent-labour on the Castle ground, and his due carriage of peats to the estate. The Earl was good about the other dues of his near-subsistence tenants and did not insist on taking the share of their small harvest that a harder landlord might have exacted. Two hens was all he asked of the Hardies, no sheep at all and none of the wee bit barley they grew lower down the hill.

Nevertheless the money for adding to labour and kain to make up the full rent was just not there, and there would be plenty of other hardworking men without either rigs or grazing, to try and make something of land that became vacant because of unpaid rent. Most lairds would certainly turn out a rentless tenant and give another man his chance, and there was no grudge in Tammas Hardie against either the laird or the lucky man who would be next tenant on Tollis Hill.

'Gin it just wasnae so bleak Tam, up here on Tollis. But there's the frost and then the snaw as lies that late, it mak's the spring-time too short.'

'Aye it's the snaw lyin' that's the sign how cauld we are up here. That's three-four winters now in a row and scarce a decent lamb at the end of the day to sell at the market. They're that skinny!'

That was true, a bad spell of winter storms howling and juddering the cot walls and near cutting the fleece off the sheep had all but ruined them.

'And yet I wouldnae like to leave here Tam, for it's that bonnie come spring and summer with the burns sparklin' and a' the flowers.'

And indeed there were some advantages in being up here on Tollis, out of some harm's way, for although the great days of the Border reiving were done, there was still a fair bit of quiet plunder went on where sheep were accessible to rustlers from either side of the Border.

But, for all that and all that, they were short of their rent and Tam's heart was heavy as he clapped his sodden bonnet on his red curls and set off for further up the hill to see the puny animals into which these wicked winters had turned his well-covered sheep of a few years back.

Maggie fell to thinking as she redded up hearth and bedding, teased out floor straw, washed the porridge coggies in the burn and fed the few scrawny hens still scratching at the door-space.

'We've aye worked hard, Laird, me and Tam. He's no' lazy. He's out a' weathers wi' the sheep and there's none skeelier at the lambin'.' Thus she acted out how she would call on Earl Lauderdale, and the words she would use to put their case to him for time to find the rent.

'It's the cauld up yonder, you see, Laird, and the way the snaw lies till near mid-summer, it's fair cruel.'

And so she day-dreamed her way through her water-carrying and washing, her humphing-in of the day's peats. Day-dreaming . . . but why just day-dreaming? Why not go and tell him all that to his face . . . never mind the factor . . . go straight to the laird himself . . . him snug down yonder at Thirlestane wi' three-foot walls between him and the sough of a cold wind? Tam would be gone all day. Why not face up to the laird? He couldnae throw her into his dungeon for asking a week or two's grace before they were put out.

She whipped her plaid off the nail, swung it round her mane of black hair and, holding it firm under her chin with two small raw and determined clenched fists, trudged down the hill and marched to the Castle gate. The keeper was an old friend of her father's and no more match for the self-willed girl than he been in her dandling days.

She had more difficulty with a hall-servant, but she held her ground. Now she stood before the Earl of Lauderdale himself, surprised to find herself chittering with nerves, but giving her spiel just as she rehearsed it.

'It's the cauld wind up Tollis, Laird-sir, and the snaw that lies there yet, when it's near summer everywhere else . . . ,' and the bit about Tam not being lazy, but hard-pressed . . . and yet them both loving the hill for all their hardships there.

The Earl of Lauderdale did not often have such visitors. He was easier-going than most who have no real experience of cold, hunger and fear of eviction. It was more amusement he felt, than either anger or real understanding of the Hardies' plight. Besides she was a bonnie wee lass was Mistress Hardie. He laughed.

'I cannae think the snaw lies all that time. But if that's true I'll make a fair bargain wi' you. If you can bring me a snowball come next June to pay your rent, we'll forget about what you're owin' and for another year. That would gie you a fair start on a better winter. I cannae curb the weather for you, so you'll just have to hope the Lord'll see you right.'

All he thought he was offering was a month or two's grace but Maggie's dark eyes flashed.

'A snowball in June. Aye laird I'll bring you a snowball in June as'll show you how it's no' easy up there.'

Maggie toiled up the hill again, the Earl's promise hammering on her heart. No rent yet, but a snowball in June for a whole year's let off rent . . . a snowball in June. . . .

'A snowball in June!' repeated Tam. 'Och me Maggie, I think you overtold him a bit about the snaw. Gin you'd said May maybe, but June . . . !' he shook his head.

The snow came in December, a great plaid of it happing the hill. Tam and Maggie worked hard with their sheep and, as well, Maggie made several dozen snowballs, pressing them firm and hard and stowing them away in different crannies all over the slope where the sun never shone, nooks among outcrops of rock where the coldest of wind whistled and there was no shelter from its keening bitterness.

In June she presented herself again at Thirlestane Castle . . . without the snowballs.

'Oh aye, it's there a' richt Laird . . . seven of them, but gin I was to bring them doon here to you where it's grand and warm, and easy living, there'd be but my wet hands to show you. No, you maun come and I'll gie you your snowballs up there, where they're waitin' for you.'

Curiosity and good humour took the Earl up the hill next day. In good faith he accepted one of the snowballs in lieu of a year's rent.

Forbye that, he came home with a deal more respect for his Tollis shepherds than he'd had before, *and* a glow on his face from high sharp air and the pleasure of an energetic day's climb. But the amiable Earl was not done with Maggie yet and on another encounter the boot was on the other foot for favour, so to speak.

There is no record that the Hardies paid their rent in snowballs in after-years but Lauderdale did not forget the shepherd-wife, nor did she forget the honourable keeping of his bargain. And maybe that wee glimpse of hardship and discomfort he saw on Tollis Hill challenged him when his own rough days came on him in the Civil War. He was a King's man and, after trailing the country in Charles I's army, he was taken prisoner by the Roundheads at the Battle of Worcester and sent captive to London, as a possible candidate for the death penalty.

London keeps and dungeons were not built to be breached, but in civil war, more than any other, it is not always easy to know friend from foe, and word trickled back to Thirlestane that a little gold for his imprisoners could bribe Lauderdale into freedom in Holland until Cromwell was defeated.

Perhaps his concerned friends and servants in Lauderdale felt that the best carrier of the gold secretly to the prison in London, would be some innocent country girl making a once-in-a-lifetime visit to the great city. But where to find one with spirit as well as innocence? Perhaps on Tollis Hill.

The journey itself might have been adventure enough for Maggie Hardie, after spending all her years in the Lammermuirs. But there was London itself ahead and then the real mission. Someone else had played his part and, when the Earl in his prison-room heard, above the bustle of the streets and the cries of 'Sweet Lavender!' or 'Pretty Violets', a clear voice carolling songs of her Leader-Haughs and Yarrow countryside, he seemed to his gaoler to be much affected, as indeed he was.

'You wid gie a great favour to a condemned man, gaoler, if you would let yon singer bring a home song or two in here to me, for it's no' easy to hear right wi' the wheels and the street-cries. It's been a weary time since I heard a voice from home.'

The gaoler looked through the window grid. It would while away a dull half hour for him too to have a bonnie lass like that in to entertain them, and no harm would come of that.

Maggie made a slight protest when the big man put a hand on her arm and spoke to her.

'A Scottish prisoner you say, but he would be agin good Master Cromwell (her teeth grated as she said that). But if he's maybe to die . . . weel I can bide but a few minutes for I'm to take this bannock to auld Mistress Lovey afore noon.'

She sang three songs, the last one quickly as if anxious to get away from such a place, then in a final gesture of kindness to a poor soul, she broke off half of the mythical Mistress Lovey's bannock, thrust it at Lauderdale and ran out, the gaoler at her heels to open and re-lock the street door.

Having quickly removed six gold coins from its innards while the man was gone, Lauderdale gratefully shared the broken pieces with him when he came back, remarked on the stranger-lass's sweet voice and settled down to await the right opportunity and the right man for the 'buying' of his escape.

Maggie went back to Tollis Hill. Lauderdale sailed one dark night to Holland to live comfortably enough but in exile until the years of the Commonwealth were past and Oliver Cromwell dead. Then he came thankfully back to Thirlestane.

Whatever is true of the story of exchanged favours between Maggie Hardie and the Lord of Thirlestane, he certainly, after his return, made her a thanksgiving of a silver-chain girdle which is now in the keeping of the Museum of Antiquities in Edinburgh.

The Ivory Casket

It would be strange if a match that united two of the greatest houses in the land had started with the romantic meeting of man and maid out walking by a riverside or at a dancing celebration in some Border castle, meeting and chancing to fall in love. And so good sense dictates, that the marriage between the mighty and wealthy young baron John Balliol, lord of half of Galloway and broad lands in England, and the lovely Devorgilla, heiress also to wide estates in East Galloway and great castles in England, was an arranged one.

When John Balliol of Barnard Castle in Durham sought the hand of the daughter of Allan, King of Galloway and Constable of Scotland, the prize gladly given to strengthen their houses was Devorgilla.

Within a year of marriage the bride's father and other benefactors had died and she had come into her great inheritance. The extent of the joint possessions stretched for long distances from the North of Galloway to the middle of France, outposts five hundred miles apart. This no doubt pleased the Balliol family and the royal kin of Devorgilla, but much more important to the couple was that by then they truly loved each other. And it is as faithful lovers that they come down the centuries in story, although they lived in a time of wild turbulence, warfare and massacre when knightly chivalry went hand-in-hand with barbarity; and Christian and Mohammedan struggled against each other to pin down their God in earthly places they considered sacred.

When he was not enjoying the charms of his young wife at either his main stronghold of Barnard Castle or in the lovely Galloway hills where she was most at home, he was out striding the bigger world. He was a man of politics and war, playing his part in altering old boundaries to his country's advantage and juggling finances in huge trade enterprises to line the war coffers of his king. He may perhaps have grown a little arrogant in his power, and yet it is not for state and warcraft that he is best remembered.

Wild nobles had wild followers and there were men retained at Barnard Castle who rode rough-shod over the countryside, especially lawless in the absence of the lord. It was during Balliol's travels in the mid-years of the century that a band of his men went on a plundering rampage across the land of the pompous little Bishop of Durham, one Walter Chirkham. The Bishop was outraged and pronounced excommunication on the hard-riders of Barnard Castle.

In due season John Balliol returned from his continental journeyings and was incensed to find his own men cast out of the very kind of holy places he had risked his life, limb, inheritance and reputation to preserve against the Saracens. He thundered into the Bishop's presence demanding the restoration of his men to Communion. But no half-princeling of this world was going to change the peppery little Bishop's decision as to who was to populate the next, and he would have none of Balliol's demands.

A few days after their bitter exchange the Bishop and his retinue were making a visit to a nearby monastery on invitation to sample the season's brewing of berry ale. Their short journey took them through a thick planting of woodland and, while they sang to entertain themselves as they walked, a shadowy band of Balliol's men unfolded, each from behind a tree, threw ropes round half the Bishop's men and the other half into disarray. When the remaining brothers recovered themselves, their struggling, kicking friends were being carried off to Barnard Castle.

It was now the Bishop's turn to be outraged and he made his complaint direct to King. The King knew better than to uphold temporal power against the Church and commanded that John Balliol should make instant reparation at Durham Cathedral. And so the proud John duly appeared, in the cladding of humble penitent, at the entrance to the cathedral, to be met by the smug little Bishop wielding a whip that he could not have cracked hard enough to frighten the smallest altar boy. But the weight of the King himself was behind the Bishop and Walter Chirkham demanded an act of considerable charity from the offender.

John was not averse to acts of charity and after the first burning resentment at having it *required* of him, and for the sake of Devorgilla, he made this one with right goodwill.

The couple had lands near Oxford, and John took a small house close to the town, set it up as a hospice for sixteen impoverished young scholars and paid them eight pence a day to allow them to pursue their studies there at Balliol House. This kind of activity was much more to the taste of the gentle Devorgilla than rape and pillage in the name of her Lord Jesu. She took to the venture as to other godly occupations, whole-heartedly, and became more than ever enamoured of her husband.

But John's days were numbered. It is said by some that he died at Barnard Castle. But others have it that he died while away on great affairs of state in France and that the manner of his going, alone and unattended, grieved Devorgilla so much that she had his heart embalmed and placed in a casket of ivory and enamel, banded with fine silver. Certain it is that wherever he died it was in the year 1268, and that she did indeed have his heart so cased, that she cherished it for the rest of her life. It never left her side and even when she sat down to dine she had food placed before it on the table for blessing, and then given to the poor of whatever was the nearby village. When she travelled from one home to the other by palfrey or litter, the casket was carried with her . . . and so too on her journeys to oversee the increasing numbers of her good works. His heart was close to hers and almost as close was the welfare of her Oxford students.

As the years went on Devorgilla was concerned for the fate of her lord's heart when she too would be gone, and to honour him she had built on Solwayside a beautiful rose-stoned resting place and called it 'The Abbey of the Sweet Heart'.

For fourteen years after it was ready, whenever she was in her beloved Galloway Devorgilla made pilgrimages of remembrance to the tomb which would some day hold the casket. Then in the year 1289 on a visit to England she herself died. The monks of Sweetheart Abbey to whom she had given books and scrolls for study, and sacred presents to beautify their sanctuary, made a grave for her before their High Altar, and she was brought home and laid to rest there with her casket of memories next her heart.

For centuries confusion and battle still raged across the country but the tale of love and faithfulness was never lost. So John Balliol and Devorgilla are remembered neither for their son, the vassal King of Scots men called Toom Tabard, nor for their wealth and great possessions, but for their true, close-heartedness and for the college bearing their name which rose from the little scholar hospice at Oxford.

The Magic Quern

Off the north-west corner of the Orkney island of Stroma there spins a dangerous whirlpool called the Swelkie. It was not always there, anymore than the sea was always salt; and thereby hangs an ancient tale.

In the oldest of the old days, in the land that came to be called Denmark there once ruled the good King Frodi. He was wise and handsome and strong and kind, and possessed of a dozen other virtues, but it was for none of them that he was legendary far beyond his own borders. It was rather for his strange gift of being able to supply any real need faced by his people. If there was famine he could produce enough for them to eat, if there was plague there were medicines to cure it, if there was poverty he found them gold, if they wanted for trade he gave them spices and sugars to barter with their neighbour countries. Strangest of all if there was war he brought them victory and peace. King Frodi's wisdom lay in never giving enough of anything to make either himself or his people lazy . . . only enough to fill their need.

It was a great mystery to every other King, Sultan and Pharoah in the world, how Frodi performed this miracle and every year there came messengers and spies to seek out his secret. Even honoured guests at his turreted castle high on the sea-cliffs, tried to bribe his counsellors to break the vows of silence they had made to the King.

And then one day, to the waters below the cliff at Frodi's castle, the sea-king rover, Mysing, steered his ship . . . Mysing who sailed every sea and fjord, pillaging and plundering other ships and the small villages beading the coasts. But it was not as a notorious pirate that he came to King Frodi's castle, just as a simple minstrel whose only pleasure, it seemed, was to delight the King with his music. Mysing did not take long to charm a little servant-girl into showing him every corner of the castle in his search for Frodi's secret. There was one locked door in the high tower above the sea and Mysing knew for sure that the answer lay in that chamber. He was patient, entertaining the court every evening with his music, but always waiting for a dearth of something in the land because he knew that then the King would use his magic to answer it. At last he was rewarded with the total failure of crops for harvest . . . not an ear in the field, and no more than a handful of meal in any girnel.

And then Mysing saw Frodi making his way to the turret where the sea-robber was sure he would find corn for his people. As King Frodi took every turn of the spiral stair, Mysing was behind him in the shadows. At the top the King turned a silver key in the lock and a door swung open on what was not, after all, a chamber but a great deep niche in the outside of the castle wall so that the fourth side was open to the sea. The place was quite empty, save for the King, and a great quern sitting in the middle of the floor. Frodi lifted his arms wide above the milling stones.

> 'O Grotti quern, supply our need.
> For lack, we crave it, not for greed.
> So grind *meal*, quern, till sundown, grind!
> Then may we modest ample find.'

And three times Frodi passed his hands in wide circles over the stones, the handle of the quern began to whirr and a scattering of meal appeared around the stones.

Then bowing three times as he walked backwards Frodi came out of the chamber, passing the sea-king in the shadows and, leaving the key in the lock, descended to wait quietly until sundown, when he would stop the mill he had called 'Grotti', with another magic chant, and prepare to distribute the first day's grinding to the people.

Mysing rubbed his hands. Now the great secret was his. He slipped through the door. His sturdy ship *Blackvoe* was immediately below the wall-niche and, summoning all his strength, he edged the Grotti quern to the open side and pushed it over. Down it plunged, still whirring, and landed on the deck of *Blackvoe*. Then he himself, silent as a shadow, slipped downstairs and out from Frodi's castle to join his pirate crew and order his wheel-man to sail toward the nor'west; and his unearthly laughter echoed back to the good King he had tricked.

Still the quern sitting on the deck was hurling out meal. But it was not *meal* that Mysing wanted. The most precious commodity he had ever laid his thieving hands on was salt. It was his custom to carry off the prized stuff from one community on the wide coasts he plundered and sell it for great gain to another. And now Mysing faced the spinning quern, his arms outstretched; then his hands passed over the stones in just the movements he had seen from Frodi.

> 'O Grotti quern supply my need
> For wealth I crave it, wealth and greed
> So grind *salt*, quern, grind, grind and grind
> So may I untold riches find.'

And, instead of meal, fine white salt began to spew out from Grotti. Mysing fairly danced with delight and his crew stood round in open-mouthed awe. By late afternoon there was a thick circle of salt at their feet. Then dusk came and the salt was at their knees. Mysing gloated over the wealth that would soon be his. Sundown came and went, and the salt grew into a great mound, and still the Grotti whirred. Then the salt began to lodge against everything on deck and he decided that now he had enough for one cargo. He wished he had heard from Frodi the spell to stop the grinding. But no matter, he would stop the thing himself. He grasped the handle but it threw him on the deck. Three pirate sailors fell on it and were tossed aside, and all the time the salt was pouring on to the deck. By the second day, when they were halfway to the Northern Islands, the salt was spilling through to the deck below. By the third, it had filled every space in the ship and *Blackvoe* began to sit lower and lower in the water.

Now they were off the island of Stroma. The pirate crew bent every sinew to brush the piling salt into the sea until at last they understood that it was coming faster than they could sweep, and that they were lost. In a fury of mutiny they threw Mysing over the side with his salt.

Presently there was a creaking and cracking, and ship, crew, salt, and still-grinding stones, sank slowly into the sea.

From that moment to this, the ancient quern has spun on, and if you would see the place where it lies under the water, still churning out the salt which savours every pool from Cathay to the Atlantic, then you must venture out to the Orkney whirlpool called the Swelkie. If you dare.

Herman Boaz and the Travelling Shilling

Sandy Park was a man of modest means. He did not drink, and neither smoked nor took tobacco, and so he did not consider himself extravagant for making the most of what he had, by enjoying whatever was available in town in the way of entertainment. His outlay on theatricals and suchlike was not great, but it bought him much pleasure.

Sandy was a portly, jovial little man with a distinctive quiff of greying red hair which made him a kenspeckle figure at plays, pavement side-shows and band concerts. He rarely booked tickets in advance, partly because such seats were too expensive and partly because he found the queueing up outside almost as enjoyable as the shows themselves. The interest of studying the faces and conduct of his fellows in the shuffling line (as everywhere else in his life) was an unending source of interest to him.

It had been almost three weeks since there had been a performance to take his fancy and so he was delighted to see bills posted about the town one Monday morning advertising the coming appearance of one, Herman Boaz, Celebrated Conjuror and Hocus-Pocus Merchant. Sandy duly took his place in the queue at the Palace Hall entrance, breaking off his cheerful low whistling from time to time to smile and nod to passing acquaintances, or to exchange a pleasant word with strangers around him in the queue.

He was not a suspicious man but when he felt himself jostled, even before there was any movement in the line, the word 'pickpocket' leapt to mind and his hand flashed to his coat pocket. There had in fact been nothing in his pocket except his latch-key and he was relieved to find it still there . . . but he fumbled deeper and brought out also a bright shilling which had certainly not been there before (for he had brushed out his pockets that very morning).

Sandy may not have been a suspicious man by nature, but he was quite shrewd. He smiled to himself. When the queue did begin to move he deftly slipped the shilling into the pocket of a spindly man with silver hair who was in front of him. Then Sandy bought his ticket and took his place in the front row. He noticed that the spindly gentleman went to the back of the hall.

There were two rousing turns, a singer of great stoutness and bellowing voice, and an astonishing dancing prodigy, then Herman Boaz came on in a blue coat glittering with paste stones and to a great run of notes on the piano. His ringed hands flashed in and out of his coat-tails and sleeves, losing and finding white mice and coloured handkerchiefs. He drew ribbons from the ears of his 'Bella Assistante', and juggled plates until the audience was gasping. Then the conjuror called for the help of a man from the audience and a sheepish young fellow pushed by an admiring ladyfriend clambered up on to the platform. He was the instrument of several mystifying tricks and then was asked to place a shilling under a cup on the fringed magic-table. Boaz stood ten feet away.

'You are quite sure, sir, the shilling is under the cup!'

'Quite sure,' said the young man firmly. Herman muttered his Abras and Cadabras and tapped his forehead . . . as if trying to catch some transference of thought.

'The stout gent with the plume of red hair in front has it in his pocket,' he said triumphantly at last.

Sandy stood up apparently finding the shilling in his pocket and, showing great surprise, seemed to look at the coin in the hollow of his hand.

'Wonderful, miraculous!' he beamed all round at his fellows in the audience. Then slowly and deliberately he held his cupped hand in front of his mouth and gently puffed across it towards the back of the hall.

'There now, favours must go roon. I've blawed the shillin' to the pocket of yon fine silver-haired gentleman at the back.'

Sandy showed his empty palm and the tall thin man put a disbelieving hand into his coat . . . and sure enough, produced the shilling.

The audience cheered at this bonus of seeing the mystifier mystified. And while Herman Boaz was a mite put out at first and almost bungled his next two tricks, he recovered and was seen after the performance having a quiet word with Sandy Park. That satisfied gentleman had two free tickets for the other two nights of Herman's short Glasgow season, in return for undisclosed services.

And Herman Boaz too was satisfied.

The Hogloon and the Glunchy Farmer

Once upon a time there lived on Sanday a very well-contented Hogloon, one of Orkney's Little People who did more good than harm but could turn coat and do mischief if they had a grudge at some unsuspecting mortal.

This particular Hogloon was happy because he lived inside a comfortable hummock, never disturbed by the easy-going farmer or his merry sonsy wife who sang at her work and so delighted the music-loving Hogloon. In cold weather the farmer would leave a forking of hay at the lea side of the brownie's mound to keep him warm, and every evening his wife would put out a licking of milk or a thimble of ale, neat squares of girdle scone and a fine crumbling of cheese. In return the Hogloon would blow on the fire if it seemed in danger of going out, or stir the porridge to keep it free of lumps while the merry wife heeshed her baby if it cried, and did a hundred other little services.

Then, sad to tell, the kindly couple took another croft and moved away. The Hogloon expected another friendly couple to take their place. But the new farmer strode out into the yard, stomped over the hummock so that the Hogloon's little home shook and trembled; and the new wife swept about her in such a fury of cleaning and scrubbing that even the very house-mice fled. She was much too perjink to suffer saucers of milk or dribbles of ale on her back step and too mean to share her bannocks (which were thin and stodgy anyway) or her cheese. There was never a nestling of hay from the farmer either, even when the nights drew in, black and cold.

But Hogloon trolls are not to be trifled with, and this one screwed up his rubbery face and made a list of mischiefs. To exasperate the wife he stickied the butter-pats, cracked the eggs, mislaid the milk-stools and bored a hole in the meal girnel. And to infuriate the farmer he tied the tails of his cows together and bent his ploughshare off the straight.

The grouchy couple were angry, and they began to have a close suspicion that they had a Hogloon making these disorders for them. They tholed them for a twelvemonth or more but when the troll ruined their crops by creeping underground and pulling down, by the roots, every green blade of the year's crop, they were certain that they were entertaining a destructive and malevolent Hogloon.

So they yoked their horse Maggie, piled table, bed and chairs on their cart, strung along behind them their two pack ponies laden with pots, kettle and rugs and trundled off to find another croft where they would be free of their tormentor. Then, they thought they could go on with their skinflint and house-proud ways unmolested.

As the milestones slipped by, their misery changed to gloomy glee that they had escaped and outwitted the Hogloon. They rubbed their greedy hands together that they could keep their milk and cheese, their ale and scone, for themselves, without being pestered by the brownie. Halfway to their new place they stopped, sighing with relief, and opened their lunch basket. The farmer sat on the cart, leaning against a milk can, to eat his bannock and cheese.

Suddenly, there was a clanging of the churn lid, the Hogloon poked out his head and smiled a wicked smile.

'Fine day for a flit, gude-folk,' said the reedy voice cheerfully, and the troll gee'd up the horse and snipped the string holding up the pots so that they all clattered on the track, as Maggie the mare set off down the path.

The farmer and his wife learned their lesson fairly well that they could not shake off a determined Hogloon. At their next place they measured out a little careful cheer for their 'guest' and sprinkled a crumb or two of mouldy cheese and hard scone. But they did it with such poor spirit that the Hogloon invited back the mice to enjoy the fare, and deserted the place for himself. He went wandering until he found the easy-going farmer and his merry sonsy wife, and set up home with them again.

The Barring-Out of Baillie MacMorin

Edinburgh is a long way from Caithness to come for schooling and in the year 1595 it must have felt like the end of the world. So it was not surprising that young William Sinclair of the Castle Mey, heir to the Earl of Caithness, longed for his school vacation. Edinburgh was a stirring, throbbing town with its castle and luckenbooths, and frequent sightings, in the High Street or Canongate, of James VI and his retinue from Holyrood. They were a colourful sight in their bright doublets and breeches, suits that mortified His not-very-wealthy Majesty as poor cladding for a crowned King of Scotland and grossly unfitting one who aspired to be King of England too. But William Sinclair and such country lads marvelled at them. Yes, Edinburgh was interesting enough in its way but the boys of the Royal High School at Blackfriars were kept thirled to their Latin and Law and did not have time to enjoy all its advantages.

The Castle of Mey, on the other hand, was in wild open countryside, where a lad could swim in the cold, cold sea of the Pentland Firth, fish in its rugged inlets or gallop freely for miles over moorland countryside. No one held his nose in a book there or took the tawse across his breeks for fidgeting in class. Or worse.

For much of what Will Sinclair did in school was much worse. He was spirited, rebellious, difficult and infuriating to his masters. He was too much a son of the wild north to be contained in a schoolroom . . . and he was one of the scholars shocked to the marrow when it was announced, without warning, that the longed-for vacation was to be shortened.

For all the misty picture of Lowland Scotland's willingly accepted curbs of discipline and the toe-ing of lines drawn up by Master J. Knox, from time to time in the High School, as in other schools across the land, pupils dissented, took objectionable matters into their own hands and barred the schoolroom door to dominies until their wishes were met. The frequency or likelihood of such a strike depended largely on whether there was in the school at the time a bold-enough boy to lead it.

On that September day of 1595 they had their general in Will Sinclair. Two boys were first despatched to bring in enough food to keep them in energy for the campaign and those others whose kists of school gear included pistols or dirks brought them into the schoolroom. Then the door was locked and the lads, all under fourteen years old, settled gleefully to await the dominie. Their own master was a thin scholar in a threadbare coat, much less happy facing restless boys who did not care a bawbee about Cicero or Virgil, than in his eyrie atop one of the High Street tenements where he could study and philosophise with other teachers and ministers who inhabited the intellectual attics of the Royal Mile.

When he arrived that morning he was met by jeers and, before the boys even began to chant their request for the full holiday, he had fled for the school Rector. Master Hercules Rollock stalked angrily along to the classroom door.

'To your places, gentlemen. Let us have no more of sic folly.'

'Rector Rollock sir, it's but our fair and just holiday we're asking, that's been cut down.'

'You're ahint in your studies and until you mak' up, there'll be nae long holiday.'

One voice came clear above the rest of the grumbling and, though its Caithness lilt was soft, there was determined menace in it.

'Our due holiday if you please, Rector.'

'You ken weel-enough Master Sinclair and the rest of you, that I'm obliged to your faithers to see you learned in your Latin, and the Laws you'll hae to live to, by and by.'

The ding-dong battle of words came to nothing except for Hercules Rollock's threat to go for backing to the City Magistrates.

'You may bring His Majesty himself, Master Rollock, and we will tell him of this injustice.'

By the time the city officers arrived the boys were refreshed for the fray with their first round of spice-cake and ale, the rest of the food garnered away against a long seige. Baillie MacMorin, who led the officers, would have been better to laugh at the boys, give them their holiday and go home to his dinner, but he was a pompous man who took his position unco seriously and was determined that a spineless academic like Hercules Rollock would see how to treat thrawn schoolboys.

'Unbar this door at once, sirs, or it'll be the waur for you, every last one.'

'Do we get our just holiday?'

'Indeed you do not. That is my last word and this door will come down gin it's no' opened.' The door did not budge.

The Baillie signalled to the officers and they lifted the battering-ram they had brought and ran it against the door. It splintered. William Sinclair's voice rose.

'The first man through that door will get a bullet in him for his trouble.' The ram came again at the door, Will Sinclair lifted his pistol, ran to a window, leaned out and discharged it into MacMorin's head.

There was shocked silence for a moment, the boys inside were terrified speechless. Then the officers, seeing there was nothing to be done for the Baillie, broke down the rest of the door, rounded up seven of the boys and within half-an-hour had them cowering in the Tolbooth.

Even William Sinclair was chastened when he heard that his earlier taunt to 'bring His Majesty himself' to see justice done, was to be taken up and that King James was even now considering the justice to be meted out to Will himself.

The son of a less powerful father than the Earl of Caithness would no doubt have had scanter justice than William and his friends, sons too of noble families on whom the King depended. They were tried, to be sure, and perhaps that was enough to frighten them into better sense, but at James's bidding they were acquitted and sent home. What the family of the determined Baillie thought of the proceedings, or what the next Earl of Caithness thought privately when he looked back on that disgraceful afternoon's work and how best to educate his own sons in their turn, are not recorded.

The Safe-Keeping of Mhairi

On the north shore of Loch Leven there stands a large house with many a memory of fire and calamity, love, sorrow and romance surrounding it. There is one story with all of these things woven into it, and that is the tale of Mhairi, a beloved only daughter of the house.

It was a fine place for anyone to live, with the ever-changing face of the loch waters . . . now still and shimmering in the sun . . . now surly and grey, with windswept trees to make it starkly beautiful. Beyond that there were the sweeping hills of Glencoe. Mhairi had been happy there as a child but she was now a young woman and, although she was happier than ever in one way, in another she was in despair.

The trouble was that the girl's father loved her so dearly that he thought her much too good to marry any of the ordinary young men of the district, or even of the villages over the hills. And yet Mhairi had given her heart to Diarmid from a small house in a hamlet near Loch Awe. When her father was busy on his estate she had long days to herself and she would walk miles to meet with her golden-haired lad and wander with him in the moors of Benderloch. That was not often, for Diarmid had to work hard on his father's small holding of land and only when he had to make a delivery of one of the special goats they bred could he leave home.

But their love prospered and each glowed with love for the other. So bright was Mhairi's face that her father suspecting its cause, followed her one day and found the sweethearts walking together at the head of Loch Etive.

'You will not throw yourself away on that young man or any other like him. Someday there will surely come by a laird or a chief's son for you to wed, and only then will you have my blessing.'

So Mhairi was forbidden to meet with Diarmid and, if she had been the spiritless lass her father wished, she would not have stolen off still to see him from time to time. And if her father had been as stupid as Mhairi wished, he would not have had any idea of it. But she did and he had.

And so it was, that when a trading ship came sailing into Loch Leven and dropped anchor, to sell leathers and silks from Italy and France and spices from the East, Mhairi was locked into her bedchamber. From there her father was sure she could neither run off to meet Diarmid under cover of the stir in the village, nor could she join the other happy spenders, rowing out in chattering groups, to buy from the merchant sailors, and perhaps meet a handsome seaman and run off with him. Because Mhairi's foolish father thought for sure, that his daughter only sought to torment him by marrying beneath her . . . whoever the man.

Mhairi, though, had no thoughts of love for any but Diarmid over the hills, but she was young and pretty and would have dearly loved some shining coloured ribbons, a length of silk for a waist sash or, best of all, a little jar of perfumed oil to sweeten her white skin for Diarmid. Dolefully she watched as the row boats plied between ship and shore, and her little foot tapped impatiently while giggling girls and their lads came laughing and chaffing by, on the path beneath her window. Even the maids from her own house had brought back their trinkets and treasures and . . . cruellest blow . . . her father had been there too to buy soft leather pouches to keep her tocher money in.

Then the last of the purchases was made and word whipped round that the ship would be off in the morning.

But in the morning there was no laughing and the ship was not 'off'. No maid came, and no father, to unlock Mhairi's chamber door . . . all was silence. She rattled the latch but no one responded. She opened her shutters, and there, out on the loch and at the cots and biggins round the shore she saw the reason for the silence. A black flag flew from the ship and makeshift copies of it from half a dozen houses in the hamlet. Plague had come to Loch Leven, brought from the East by the merchant ship.

Horrified she watched all day as more flags went up until almost every house flew one. Still not a sound came upstairs from her own home. Out there, men who had not taken ill began to burn down the homes of the dead to nail the smit. When they began to come towards her own house here, with torches flaring, she knew that everyone in it but herself, was dead.

Frantically she shouted and waved her arms at the window and they thought at first that she was in the last throes and would fall back dead in a few minutes. Then they would fire the house. But then young Donald Cameron, the stable boy, remembered that Mhairi had not been with the others at the ship and that the maids had told him she was captive in her own room.

'You cannae roast Mistress Mhairi alive,' he protested. And they agreed that they would leave her house until next day and whether she was dead or no, would burn it down then. They turned away but young Cameron remained behind.

'Can I serve you someway, lady, for you surely have no food?'

'Och no, my father did not starve me, Donald boy. I have all I need here. But you can do this for me . . . if you have not come near the sickness and can safely travel.'

In ten minutes Donald Cameron was riding for dear life through glen passes and over hill tracks, to bring Diarmid to save his lady.

By dusk Diarmid was at Loch Leven, creeping quietly among the long grass under her window. He threw up a rope and helped her down and with heavy hearts they set fire to the house themselves.

For the sake of others whom they might meet they and young Donald went swimming in the clear, cold, cleansing waters of the loch. Then they left the boy and galloped through the night, by Glencoe and past Loch Etive, towards Loch Awe.

Perhaps Donald Cameron had passed on word of the Loch Leven plague at Loch Awe when he came for Diarmid, for it was common clash when the fleeing couple reached there, and Old Diarmid, the young man's father, would not receive them.

'You will be welcome here in forty days with your bride,' he called to his son across a rushing burn which marked the boundary of his small patch of land. 'But you must spend them in the high fresh air of Ben Cruachan. You will find cave or other shelter there.'

'Father we are not wed. Have we your blessing all the same?' There was a hint of laughter in Diarmid's voice. Old Diarmid growled affectionately.

'I have Father Angus here, he will wed you. Your vows will be all the more binding across the running burn.' A trembling, faltering little priest stepped forward from the group around Old Diarmid, and in brave terror hastily pronounced them man and wife.

Never was stranger honeymoon. In forty days Mhairi's Loch Leven sorrows were drowned in love for her young husband and Old Diarmid was thankful to have his son's strong arms digging his land again, a bonnie gude-daughter to run his house, and Donald Cameron, fetched from Loch Leven, to help look after his goats.

The Bogroy Incident

Songs, legends, claymores rusting in thatch, the trousered leg and the falling apart of the ancient clan system, these were all sorry legacies of the Forty-Five and its savage ending at Culloden. They echo forlornly across the years since defiance almost died. Almost, but not quite.

For there was one rebellious activity that survived in the glen, long after Jacobite hopes were dead, and had the remnant Highlanders laughing up their sleeves at the pro-English establishment. . . . It was a widespread sin, taken up with such zeal by lairds and crofters alike, that many a respected minister was heard to mumble blessings over its working gear and even conceal it in his pulpit.

The word 'smuggling' in the glens did not mean the running-in of foreign goods from the coast without paying duty, it meant the illicit distilling of whisky in cooling 'worms' set up in half-thatched cots, croft sheds or even inside hollow-built peat-stacks, and its safe-keeping until it was delivered to barns and troughs up and down the valleys. It was rough bree and the likes of Rory MacKenzie, of one of the glens that open on Beauly, did not feel they had done a good job unless it caught the throat and slackened the limbs at first sip.

But there was more to the 'stilling than that. There was the joyous outwitting and exasperating of the excisemen, the finding of safe-places to produce their usqueba and safer-still places to hide it.

It had taken the Lowland-born excisemen who were based at Inverness too long to recognise, in the quiet-spoken Rory MacKenzie and his friends, shameless, exulting enemies of the King. But now they were after them or, failing the felons themselves, at least their illicit makings. Twice the gaugers had followed the peat-reek in the hills to pounce on the smugglers, only to find that they were being trailed false. Another time they paid Rab Macphie good siller when he showed them the making equipment in a still beside a gully, only to discover that Rory MacKenzie had abandoned it and that he and Rab had used the money to help set up a new one somewhere else.

Then one fair summer afternoon, the gaugers struck lucky. They found a cask planked by a stacking of peats a mile up Strathglass from Beauly, obviously set there ready for lifting by the smugglers. But it was the triumphant gaugers who heaved it up on to their cart and set out with their prize on the long journey to the customs office in Inverness. Rory MacKenzie and the others arrived with their cart, fresh from emptying another barrel into grateful vessels in Beauly cottages, in time to see their full keg disappearing down towards the village.

A cask of whisky was a sore loss and, keeping their hand-cart and its empty keg out of sight and hearing, they followed it sorrowfully like men behind a funeral kist . . . but not too stricken to think.

For their part the gaugers were certainly not mournful and they would never have heard the sound of wheel on road and the mutter of men behind them, for their lusty singing as they admired their beautiful find. The carts trundled on towards Inverness, the second always out of sight, always a bend or corner behind the first.

They were thirsty, tiring miles and the excisemen very properly thought that they would do the second lap faster for having a rest on the way. Bogroy Inn would serve very nicely. Just as properly for its safe-keeping, they lifted off the precious cask, carried it into the inn, and upstairs to a room where the inn-keeper made obsequious turnings of his hands to indicate that that was where he attended to important clients like soldiers and gaugers. The cask was rolled across the floor then set on end with the burliest exciseman, who had found the day gruelling, if exhilarating, sitting on the lid. There the happy hunters relaxed and called for legitimate drams all round, the keg secure under his bottom.

Downstairs the landlord was setting up the drams and assuring his growling regulars that 'they' were up-by and would not trouble them. He was also making curious measuring gesticulations to the five newcomers who had come wearily into the ale-house, just this minute.

Rory MacKenzie went through the back with the inn-keeper while interested topers watched Rab Macphie and the others bring in an empty keg, which they calmly placed on top of a table they had quietly lifted out an arm's length from a corner of the room. Then Rory was back with a long sharp stave and, following low-voiced instructions from the host, he selected a spot on the ceiling and began to bore. The others jumped on to the table, held up the cask and quietly transferred into it the contents of their lost barrel from the room above.

The gaugers 'rest' at Bogroy was long and convivial and only when the hapless party was ready to move off again towards Inverness did they discover their keg empty. By then some thirty gudemen of Beauly, coal-merchants, kirk elders, fishermen, dominie and doctor, were already warming to the first sampling from the bottles new-hidden in their thatch. And Rory MacKenzie was sitting at home, the Book on his knee, solemnly conducting his wife and bairns through Saturday evening family prayers, with no thought that his day had been spent in anything other than a legitimate altercation with a wholly unjust law.

There used to be a thread of lore that the nearer to the heart of Scotland a family of Little People lived the sweeter was their music and the more nimble their dancing feet.

How that could be, the story-teller does not know, but can only tell the tale of the man called Aeneas Gow who built a house somewhere in the countryside near Schiehallion and close by a burn that rushed and babbled cheerfully. But . . . quite unwittingly he placed it on top of a faery mound.

The Little People heard the thumping as Aeneas set the stones carefully row upon row, grunting with effort and satisfaction every so often, as he laid a heavy one into its place. They were a cheerful tribe inside the mound. 'Live and let live' was their byword and they went on busily with their own life and their work . . . housekeeping likely-enough, spinning yarns and whatever other bogle work was on hand.

Then every evening they entertained themselves. It was only when Aeneas finished his thumping and thatching that he began to hear the faeries at their music-making. At first he thought he was hearing simply the rushing and babbling of the burn, but then he was sure it was Little People at play. Early of an evening he heard them sing lullabies to their bairns and then, when the babies were soundly asleep, there came fiddle reels and shrill mountain piping, weaving lilts and waltzes . . . sometimes plaintive dirges and laments when they were wae.

Aeneas would lie listening, enjoying the music but not able to sleep for it. After a while, so little rest did he have, that he could not properly work the next day, so that his small crops were poor and he fell asleep milking his cow.

One day he went walking in the loneliness of the moors where there was only the sound of a curlew breaking the silence. He must try and decide what to do. It would be a great task to find another place and build yet another house, and even then perhaps he would plant it on some other faery mound. But work he could not, following night after night of the fast and slow music and the tap of tiny dancing feet. How was he to live?

After an hour's walking he was no nearer an answer to his question, but the sun shone on the mountain, the warmth soaked into him through his sark. Somewhere now he heard the soft crying of birds. It was a brave day and he began to sing and whistle some of the faery tunes and make occasional little skips into the air. Then he was walking along a burnside and came unexpectedly on a group of cot women thrashing and splashing and washing their clothes at a scattering of small boulders in the water, while their babies lay nearby in rush cribs. He stopped whistling to give the women good-day and would have passed on.

'Nay, nay,' they protested. 'Pick up your tunes again and stop our bairns their crying. And for us too; were we not rubbing the harder for your whistles?'

Aeneas was an obliging fellow and sat on a hummock of grass, realising now that it had been the babies' whimpering he had heard and not the calling of birds. He sang and whistled for an hour the music he had had of the Little People. The croons heeshied the bairns to sleep, the reels had the scrubbing done in no time, the strathspeys were grand for the swishing and rinsing, and the women were near waltzing as they gathered up babies and bundles ready for home.

Aeneas was thoughtful as he wandered back to his house. He listened carefully to the mound music that night. Next day he made the long walk into the town market and had a simple fiddle made. Then for a month he slept by day and taught himself the fiddling by night as he heard the Little People. After that he gave his cow to a neighbour body and set out from home, going first to the north, then south, east and west . . . for was *his* home not in the very best of places for a travelling minstrel . . . the very heart of Scotland. Wherever he went he was the welcomest of fellows, fiddler-man and sangster, for he made light of work and wailing infants, he played for parties and penny weddings, wakes and ceilidhs and earned a fine living there and at market fairs. When he had had a week or two of good nights' sleeping and good days' taking, he would come home to his well-built house on the faery knoll, not for a rest, but to add to his repertory of jigs and songs for his minstrel rounds. And the Little People in their own way, but kindly, knew what he was up to and always had new cradle-songs and ballads ready for him when they heard him home.

Kinmont Willie and the Bold Buccleuch

William Armstrong of Kinmont, and reiver of renown, was riding with a small party along the north bank of Liddel Water, and to a stranger to the Borderlands it might have seemed curious that across the river and abreast of the Scots, rode their traditional enemies from south of the Border. But the reivers themselves would have understood it for in the strange chivalry of the Border ruffianry, that had held both sides in turbulent uproar for centuries, there was periodically a day of truce. The wardens who policed the Marches of each side met with small groups of deputies to settle fines, hear complaints and generally indicate that their presence was not to be provoked beyond endurance. And one of the inviolable conditions of the Truce Day was that those attending must be given safe passage, coming and going, on the day of the conference and until sunrise on the following morning.

Kinmont Willie Armstrong had been, that March day of 1595, to Kersehopefoot to represent one of King James' great Keepers of the Scottish Marches, Walter Scott of Buccleuch. Willie, although fifty years old to Wat's thirty, was a fair copy of the young Buccleuch to be standing in for him at the Truce Day, both being wild and daring reivers (for even the official Keepers were not above an occasional plundering foray to plump up their head numbers of cattle). Scott of Buccleuch knew that Armstrong would not be brow-beat by the English Warden's party. Nor was he.

The conferring was done, the rough justice of the Borders had been agreed for the present and now, riding in the same direction along the Liddel Water, were Armstrong on the northbank, the English party on the south. The code was strong and should have held firm but these were not parfait gentil knights, they were parties who would tulzie with each other another day, and across the river there echoed threat and counter-threat, boast and better boast.

Kinmont Willie had a notorious history of reiving behind him. Even on his apprentice raid of many years earlier, he had pillaged eight villages, left six men for dead and made off with eight hundred cattle. Three years before this Truce Day he had plunged into Tynedale with a thousand men, taken double that number in beasts and over three hundred pounds in spoil.

Such a man riding bold and free across the river there, was a sore temptation to the much bigger party of English Marchmen, who were under the jurisdiction of Lord Scrope, Warden of Carlisle Castle. And so when a curdling promise from Willie Armstrong of fell reivings to come, rang out across Liddel Water, followed by baiting and insolent gestures of defiance, the party making for Carlisle rose to the provocation and, at the next ford, swept across the river. Willie, in full flight, his head thrust forward, rode for dear life, his mare's flanks steaming in the chill of the late winter afternoon. His party, unmolested and unheeded by the enemy, had fallen far behind him and for four miles Kinmont held his pursuers off. But the English Border riders were some of the fleetest horsemen in the whole of Europe, they were many chasing one, and after leading them a worthy dance Kinmont Willie Armstrong was taken. In triumph the English Marchmen led him towards Carlisle.

Next morning found Willie breakfasting sparsely and ruefully in the castle there, preparing for a confrontation with the Warden, Lord Scrope.

If the captors were in high glee over their prize there was fury across the Border. Had Armstrong been taken red-handed on a cattle-thieving foray, caught with one of his great freebooting troops driving home a plundered herd or two, that would have been seen as capture in fair hazard. But this was a mean round-up and, among fierce men whose whole life was spent in pillage and harrying, there was prim resentment that truce had been flouted.

Angriest of all was Walter Scott of Buccleuch. Kinmont Willie had been his envoy at Kershopefoot and he felt his authority as Keeper of Liddisdale insulted. He first demanded an explanation and satisfaction by letter. Lord Scrope was evasive, hinting, but without really asserting, that Armstrong had assaulted an Englishman at the meet, before setting off for home. Buccleuch seethed. He and Scrope were long-time enemies. Walter Scott was young and proud and felt he was being patronised and he burned to show that he was a true son of the Scott tribe, who would brook no soothing answers while Armstrong was unjustly held. When another wily reply came to a second letter Buccleuch's patience was exhausted.

He was not a rash man and calculated that a carefully planned and spectacular raid that made Scrope look foolish, would be more devastating an affront than blundering in with a great punishing force and causing mayhem which would show no clear victor.

Accordingly he consulted with two groups of adventurers who would glory in such a raid. There was the Graham family, formerly of the Scottish Borderlands but who, for their wild and lawless felonies had been banished across the Border (those Grahams who missed their moors and burns of Liddisdale had slipped back home disguising their origins by reversing their names to Maharg). The Grahams then had the spirit for this adventure. So too had the Carleton brothers, Thomas and Launcelot. They were Englishmen but had a considerable dislike of Lord Scrope. It was not long since the Carletons had raided an Armstrong party on its way back across the Border, but that was all in the day's work, and the pure pleasure of springing a prisoner, even if that prisoner be a Scotsman and an Armstrong to boot, was hard to resist. They were a swashbuckling pair were the Carletons, who gloried in thundering over the Borderlands, striking terror into those they fancied enemies.

'There's no' to be spoilin' or burnin' or killin' on this night's work. It's the liftin' of but one man fae under Scrope's very nose that'll caw the feet off him. Now mind that.' And for four hours some three weeks after Willie's capture Scott of Buccleuch, three of the Grahams and the Carletons planned every last move and contingency for the rescue of Kinmont Willie.

Buccleuch had no difficulty finding spies and informers around Carlisle. The similar lives led by the Borderers on both sides, and the constant coming and going between them, had led to intermarriage, and families who scarcely knew where their loyalties lay, if not simply to their own families and an increase in its head of cattle.

Information flowed to Buccleuch from inside and outside the castle, and from the very town itself, for there were more than a few in the castle surroundings who were piqued by the succession of Wardens from the south of England Carlisle had housed over the years, when there was many a local man they thought better fitted for the task.

Now Buccleuch knew the castle lay-out, where in it Kinmont Willie was held, that he was not in chains, and who exactly inside would turn a blind eye to their secret invasion, even signal or lead them to the right direction.

Final details were fixed at Langholm Races, early in April. Ropes and ladders and jemmy-spikes lay ready at Kinmont's own place and all that was wanted now was a murky Border night and word sent to their allies inside the castle.

A hundred silent shadows of Scotts, Carletons and Grahams moved forward the six miles to Carlisle, flitting in short laps to confound any who might chance to detect a continuous thrust. Mist shrouded them as they crossed the Esk at nightfall, edged forward to reach the castle at dawn and overpowered the gate-keepers. The only miscalculation was the too-short length of their ladders and these they abandoned in favour of spikes to prise, loosen and pull out some of the soft-bonded wall-stone at the side of the gate. The stones were dragged out, a man-hole was made and the rescuers crept inside. Every man padded quickly to his appointed place following his detailed instructions and carrying them out to the letter. There was no attempt to take the castle, not another chamber-door than the prisoner's was chapped. It was simply a swift boring into the strongest hold in the north to bundle out a man they were certain should not have been there in the first place.

There was the slam of a door, grunts of winded men and a brief scuffle in a central courtyard, then Kinmont Willie Armstrong was out and pounding northwards towards Scotland on one of his own horses.

The secret mirth of some and the public fury of others which greeted news of Armstrong's escape did not come from a clear divide of factions into English and Scottish. Carlisle folk, who had seen this snook cocked at Lord Scrope, hugged themselves with amusement, and, up in Edinburgh, so did King James . . . but discreetly. The Scottish Border keeps and cots echoed with celebration and laughter. The fury came from a few sour Scots who had harboured a mean joy that Armstrong, the wild horseman, had had his spurs blunted. Fury came too from Lord Scrope, incensed that not a sniff of the planned break-in, clearly known to many others, had reached him. His reputation was in tatters . . . he who had the safest fortress of the north in his charge, had lost from it his prize captive. Queen Elizabeth too was angry, much put-out over such a dazzling snub . . . and King James in Scotland, waiting fawningly in the wings for her throne, had to hold his wheesht a little and urge Buccleuch to put up with a few months of easy custody to placate her, then go to London and make his peace.

Historians . . . or maybe just story-tellers, say that she was uppity with them at first.

'You have sound explanation Walter Scott, that you broke so into my fortress of Carlisle and outraged my Lord Scrope's authority, for the sake of some Border ruffian better safe-held than burning the countryside? How dared you sir?' she demanded.

'What thing is there in this world Madam, but that *some* man will dare?'

Elizabeth seemed torn between the Tower for this impudent man and the wish that he might have been subject to her, instead of to her cousin of Scotland.

'With ten thousand such men as you, Buccleuch,' she said

enviously, 'King James might shake every throne in Europe.'

In a reign that had had men like Raleigh and Drake doing her bidding and scouring the world to find her colonies, that was no light accolade. And there are those who believe that the Kinmont Willie incident may have strengthened Elizabeth's belief that a king who had this man and others like him, at his command, would sit quite well on her throne when she had done with it.

The Last Request of Jenny Cordiner

John Cordiner was a godly Presbyterian, ageing, but as much respected for the sturdy shoes his skills produced as for his blameless life. He revelled soberly in the minister's Sabbath sermons and was much exercised about the state of his soul. Even on weekdays, as he cut and stitched at his leathers, his mind ranged among texts and psalms to find the answer to the teasing question as to which of the seven sins was deadliest. The short leet varied in order from time to time, but mostly he was certain that the Great Sin was Pride. And for his soul's sake he must fight it.

But John was not entirely selfish in his concern. He was just as anxious for his wife's soul and when the day came, in the ripeness of time, that he was sitting at her death-bed, he was disturbed to find her lacking in humility about her worth to him over the fifty years since they had come, newly-wed, to Glasgow, as lad and lass from the country. Now she lay, neat as ever, cap straight, night-gown snowy, hands clasped, dwindling to death.

'Weel John,' she said, ready to tidy up her life, 'We're goin' to part. I've kep' your table and your linen right and minded your purse. I've reared your bairns and I've been a good wife to you, John.'

Guid-sakes, but here was Pride indeed!

'Oh, just middlin' Jenny, middlin',' he said, brows drawn slightly.

She was too far through to notice the reproach. Or maybe it was so much part of his normal tone that it passed her by.

'You must promise me . . .' she whispered, 'You must promise to bury me in the old kirkyard at Stra'ven alongside of my mother, John. I couldnae rest easy among strange folk in Glasgow.'

John considered long. He was fond of his wife, in spite of her high opinion of herself as wife and mother, but a journey of over a dozen miles to Stra'ven would mean closing the shop for an extra day and the costly hiring of a cart, even idleness at his bench. Thriftlessness. Near as bad as Pride.

'Aye me Jenny! That's a lot to ask.' He paused again. 'Suppose we just put you in the Gorbals yard first, and if you dinnae lie quiet we'll think to try Stra'ven.'

And, with that kind promise, Jenny had to die content.

The Weavers of South Uist

There are people who will tell you slyly that if there had been no God, men would have found it necessary to invent him. Perhaps God sighs a little at his ever-so-clever children thinking they can get rid of Him like that, or maybe He just chuckles quietly that He made them so creative.

Perhaps it was more nearly true to say that kind of thing about the Waulking Faery of South Uist, that the tweed-making women could do their work properly only if they imagined her there to oversee their work.

Whether she was real faery, or simply a necessary figment of imagination, she was certainly present at the making of the best Hebridean tweed. The women knew they must not start the long process of producing a fine length of cloth without her; for they recall the time when one group, not knowing they must wait her coming, tried to do without her.

It was a long, long time ago when a king of the islands was going to foreign parts to bring back a bride and ordered the women of South Uist to weave him a length of the finest cloth to make a suit for his first meeting with the betrothed. The loom must be well set-up, the warp laid true, the weaving close and firm but not too tight, and the waulking or shrinking perfect so that the cloth would wear well.

The women of the chosen village near Ben More were so overwhelmed by the honour of doing such a task that they nearly fell over each other to set up the warp, each one wheedling her way in among the others to be first to touch a thread in the great king's cloth. When it was set-up, they were so anxious to get on to the next stage that they did not notice the threads which went off the straight. Each of half-dozen women jostled to throw the shuttle straighter and more firmly than the rest so that tension was uneven. When the cloth was ready for shrinking by a third of its size, they were so tired with trying to outdo each other, that they found the rolling and turning and twisting of the length tedious and laboursome, and were so anxious to let the king have their own handmade masterpiece that they skimped the waulking, quarrelled while they were doing it, then dried and rolled up the cloth and rushed it to the king.

The winds were fair for his voyage and, although his tailor muttered dark Gaelic mutterings as he cut and stitched, the king urged him on, and just as the tide was right the majesty proudly donned his new braws and sailed for his Princess.

How she laughed when she saw him; her laughter tinkled and echoed up and down the fjords, for the weave of his clothes was squint, there were puckers and dimples and bosses where the shuttle had varied the tension and already, after such a short time, because the waulking had been skimped, the cloth was wearing thin.

She laughed, it was true, but the princess was a kind girl at heart. She fell in love with the island king himself, not with his clothes, and was happy to travel back with him to be his queen.

The king was angry with the women when he came home but the queen laughed him into better humour and went herself to ask them if there was not a waulking faery living on Ben More who could help them with their work.

And there was.

She was with them from the very next time they set up a piece. She took them in hand, looked carefully at their wool, stood over them to check the warping, then the evenness of their weave, and she was especially strict when they began the waulking. She taught them how to sing songs that would make their hands move rhythmically. Each woman had to make up and sing her own verse and so that they would not have to relax their pace to gossip about the village ongoings, the faery had them weave those into the words of their songs, the latest romances, expected babies, what flotsam had gathered on the shore or how Mhairi Macleod's hens had stopped laying. (Some say that it was descendant kin of the Waulking Faery of Ben More who taught sailors to shanty as they worked, and took calypsos to the West Indies.)

When she was not managing the beat and tempo of the weaving work, the faery was something of a mischief with their butter and cream and cheese, for she could take the virtue out of them and leave them thin and wersh. They retaliated sometimes, putting tales of her doings into their songs, and tried to protect their churns and pats and basins from her cantrips by wiping them over with the fluffy heads of bog-cotton, which she did not like.

But they had no real grudge against her, because in their important work of making the finest cloth in the world, under her strict eye their tweed was well-knit, sturdy and primely handsome.

Geordie Dick of Greystones Mansion

Some people say that the man in this story lived in the far north; others put him in the Borderlands. The place does not matter, the foolishness does. So let us put him somewhere about the middle and give him a house in the valley of the River Tay.

Geordie Dick had been a packman in his early days, trudging about the countryside selling his gew-gaws. Then by doing a little bit of sleight business here and another there, he had been able to take, first of all, a stall at each of the local weekly markets on different days, and later a small business-house in town. From rough cobbled biggin he had moved to a two-roomed house and married a gentle, if slightly silly wife. He hired a well-intentioned but rough fellow to see his horse, dig his kail-patch and do his other odd jobs.

When he was approaching his prime, Geordie's business really thrived and he moved with his wife, small son and his honest, obedient, all-purpose manservant, whose pay was suddenly trebled, into a fine, square stone house with ten rooms.

Now, many a new-rich man remains modest and sensible in his new circumstances. The manservant, John was just such a man. He did not change his ways nor flaunt his trebled income in the ale-house and he bought his wife no more than a new trim for her Sunday bonnet.

If only Geordie and Mistress Dick had done the same! But she bought a press-ful of new clothes, a ring for every finger and two dozen silver teaspoons, and she began to talk even fancier than the Laird's wife herself. Geordie bought a new carriage, a gold watch-chain, ordered a box of best cigars to be delivered weekly from town, sent for a dictionary of highfalutin' words, and decided that something would have to be done about rough John. Poor John, and his wife in the kitchen, did not seem to be sufficiently aware of the new station in life to which they had all been called. There was, it must be said to Geordie's credit, no question of getting rid of them. The new gardener and coachman knew what was what, and now he must have John in and give him a lesson in gracious living . . . first his language about household matters. . . .

'Now then, John, I must have a word or two wi' you about a few changes in what we call things now we're to be entertaining merchants and lairds and such. For a start noo' there's this place; what is't you've aye called a place like this?' John was puzzled. After all, what was it but a house?

'It's a hoose,' he said bluntly.

'From now on you're to mind and call it "the edifice of Greystones Mansion of Perthshire",' instructed Geordie. John nodded.

'Och aye, sir. I'll mind and dae that, sir.'

'Not "sir" any more John. You're to say "my lord and master of Greystones Mansion of Perthshire".'

John repeated that carefully, '"My lord-and-master-of-Greystones-Mansion-of-Perthshire", yes. And the mistress, what about the mistress?'

'She's "the lady of Greystones Mansion of Perthshire".'

'Is she no' "the-lady-of-*the-edifice-of*-Greystones-Mansion-of-Perthshire"?'

'Oh aye, that. I forgot that.'

'What aboot the laddie?'

'No, no, John . . . no' the "laddie". He's "the young master of the edifice of Greystones Mansion of Perthshire".'

'It's a lot to mind, sir. What aboot other things? Am I to call your "clothes" maybe something else?'

'Oh aye, John. You dinnae move up wi' oot you use the right words. No' just "clothes" now.' He consulted the new dictionary. 'I think "vestments of richest apparel" would be about right, for they couldnae just be Sunday braws in this place.' John glanced round the room.

'What aboot the lum? There surely cannae be another word than "lum".'

'"The great apple-wood burning fire-place" it's to be.'

'Och aye . . . and Pussy there?' The cat blinked green eyes and stalked away like a duke.

'The "small tiger of Greystones Mansion of Perthshire".'

John was nearly flummoxed trying to get it all into his simple, steady head.

'And your dog Scamp?'

'Scamp'll no' do now, John. He's to be "the hound of Greystones Mansion of Perthshire".' The small dog frisked about the corner of the room chasing his tail.

'He's no' very big to be a "hound", my-lord-and-master-of-Greystones-Mansion-of-Perthshire, sir.'

'He'll grow to it.' Scamp was already ten years old so John doubted that.

'That'll do you for now, John, but there'll be other changes to what you call things. Mind these ones for now.'

And John went off muttering the eight new names he was to learn and practised them while he brought in the wood, rubbed down the horses and took the dog for a walk. Soon he was word-perfect.

Geordie and his wife preened themselves as they walked around their mansion and estate that afternoon. Peacocks, they would have next . . and a lady's maid for the lady of Greystones Mansion of Perthshire. Then after that, Geordie thought, he would have a little more instruction for John as to some of the new niceties expected of him.

But that very night when John was going round with his lantern to make sure all was well with house and estate, he saw a lick of flame round the top of one of the chimneys. Then he heard the roar of fire as it swirled up the stack. He ran inside and up to the main bedroom, going over and over his new vocabulary as he took the stairs. He drew in a deep breath and began. . . .

'My-lord-and-master-of-Greystones-Mansion-of-Perthshire, grab your vestments of richest apparel and rouse the lady-of-Greystones-Mansion-of-Perthshire. I'll waken the young master, son-of-the-lord-and-lady-of-Greystones-Mansion-of-Perthshire, and I'll find the small-tiger-of Greystones-Mansion-of-Perthshire and the hound-of-Greystones-Mansion-of-Perthshire. Because if you don't make haste, it'll no' be just the lum . . . your pardon . . . the great apple-wood burning fireplace . . . but the edifice-itself-of-Greystones-Mansion-of-Perthshire WILL BE

ON FIRE!'
  But of course, by that time it was burned to the ground.

Now if Geordie and his wife had been cruelly proud folk and not just foolish; if they had dismissed the simple John and his wife when they became rich, the tale-teller would no doubt have had them burned to death. But stories without villains should have happy endings. It seems that they were only singed in the fire and when they had a new house built they were just plain Mister and Mistress Dick, with clothes and a lum, a laddie, a pussy and Scamp. And a lot happier they were too.

The Dream of Fergus

Long, long ago, barely five hundred years after the life of his Lord, the hermit Fergus had a cell on the bank of the little river they called Clyde. It was built of rush-and-daub and the hard mud floor had a hollowed place where the holy man knelt constantly in prayer. He lived on river trout, berries in season, and by the small offerings left for him by passers-by.

  Fergus had few possessions, a change of tunic, a bowl and a precious page or two of Holy Writ. This scrap of the good news of Luke told the story of the old man Simeon at Jerusalem and, so often did the hermit read that scripture, that he began to dream the same kind of dreams as Simeon. The one he dreamed most often was of a shining young Messenger-of-God who told him.

  'You will not die, good Fergus, until you have seen the "dear friend" of St. Serf, the holy man of Culross. The young man will come here to this cell on his pilgrimage-way to set the church of

God in Glasgow village. Then, and only then, will you be gathered to your fathers.'

Day by day, month by month, year by year, Fergus waited, growing old in patience as he looked along the river-path for the coming of one he would know as the 'dear friend' of St. Serf. . . .

While Fergus waited, there was a tale unfolding far away to the east, a tale of love and hate, of rage and gentleness, at the court of Loth, King of Northumbria and Lothian.

Princess Thenew, his daughter, of the russet cheeks and tow-gold hair, was the prettiest picture the travel-weary Prince Eugene, outlander from the south, had ever seen. He happened on her as she walked along the stream-path on her father's land. Although he intended travelling further, he sought hospitality at her father's court and passed the days of his stay walking with Thenew, singing love songs of fair ladies and swineherds, and telling her the tales of his own country. King Loth had grander marriage plans for his daughter than the impoverished Eugene and was thankful when at last the Prince had to continue his journey. But before he and Thenew parted, he looked long into her eyes and told her that he would be back to seek her hand, and that their love would surely satisfy her father into giving his consent.

Perhaps they had bewitched each other or perhaps they were simply young and foolish but, when he had been gone a month, Thenew found herself to be with child.

King Loth, her father, was a stern unforgiving man and, moreover, his plans for some enriching alliance with a neighbouring king were now in tatters. Thenew cropped her yellow hair and fled her father's house in the rough tunic of a swineherd. She wandered in this disguise for weeks, exchanging a day's work here and there for a corner of straw at night. Eugene heard from a maidservant of her flight and her disguise. He came looking for her and found her at last, thirty miles from home, wae and forlorn, nettle-stung, and scratched by bramble and thorn. Bravely he took her back to King Loth, to *demand* now, not simply *ask* that she should wed him.

Whether Eugene was slain for his presumption, or just put to flight, the records do not tell, but the King had no mercy for his wayward daughter. First he decreeed that she should be thrown over a precipice above the river and that when lying there close to death, should have the last breath of life stoned out of her shameful body. Such was his order, but when Thenew was tossed over the cliffs by Loth's sorrowful servants, a great wind seemed to catch her up and bear her quite gently away from the rocks below to a stretch of soft sand and sea-weeds. Seeing her unharmed, Loth's frightened counsellors and holy men told the King he must not seek to kill her violently again.

And so Thenew was taken up, set in a coracle boat and pushed out into the River Forth towards the Island of May. She would drift downstream from there until she died of cold and hunger. But a shoal of fish carried the coracle with it, until the little craft was beached at the riverside fishertown of Culross.

There the good fisherfolk tended the beautiful stranger until her boy-child was delivered, then, according to the practice with foundling people, they took her to the tiny Christian monastery of St. Serf nearby.

And that very night was the first on which, far away to the west, the hermit Fergus first dreamed of the young man who was someday to visit him.

Thenew's boy was named Kentigern. He was a well-favoured child, curious, bright eyed, quick to respond to all the sights and sounds of countryside and riverbank, to recognise thrift-pinks, razor shells, turnstone and whaup, and poor soil from rich. He absorbed the routine of work and prayer, the gentle, learned ways of the little monastery, with the calling of the bell, the quiet strength which came from meditation and the study of scripture. But, boy-like, he was nevertheless wayward enough to be endearing so that Serf grew very fond of him. The name Kentigern fell out of intimate use and 'Mungo' the dear one, took its place as his love-name.

As Mungo matured, the holy men around St. Serf began to be aware that there was more than ordinary spiritual strength in the boy. He seemed to have the gift of channelling happy miracles. Most of the brothers rejoiced at this blessing, but there was one man who grudged him his gift.

There was the matter of Serf's red-breast. The old man was devoted to his offices but he also tended a garden in the heart of the monastery where he said his real prayers. There he grew yellow daisies, evening-star bells and sweet-scented herbs, and there he threw crumbs to the tame robin who hopped about all the time he worked the soil or talked with God. Serf loved the little bird and when he came into his garden one morning and found him dead his heart was sad. And it was made sadder by the grudging brother who told him that Mungo had killed the robin. Sorrowfully Serf began to scoop aside the earth to bury his tiny friend, when Mungo came looking for him.

'Did you truly kill the robin?' asked Serf, hoping to hear that at worst it had been a careless accident.

For answer Mungo gently took the bird in one hand and made the sign of the Holy Cross over it with the other. A throb came into the ball of feathers, the robin hopped down to the soil overturned for his grave and began to poke for worms.

And there was the refectory fire. One day in winter, icy winds were blowing across the land and finding every chink in the monastery wall so that the flames of the holy fire in the refectory were guttering dangerously low. It was a discipline of their order that this need-fire, a gift of Heaven, should be kept alight, and on that day Serf had entrusted to Mungo the task of keeping the flame. To the lad's shame he fell asleep in a draught-free corner of the chamber, and his enemy slipped in and doused the fire so that it would shortly go out. Then he went off to clipe to Serf. The old man hurried to the refectory in time to find Mungo at the outside door penitent over his lapse but breaking off a frost-furred wintered branch of a hazel tree. In the name of the Holy Trinity he breathed on the frozen twig until flames began to lick along its length. It was thrown on to the barely smouldering embers, and the holy flame burned brightly again.

The years turned on and Mungo grew into manhood, having absorbed all that Serf could teach him, at least of book-learning. Although the old man would have begged him to stay and be his successor at Culross, the young one felt that he was being called through a dream vision of an ageing hermit, to take his learning and the wisdom he had had of Serf, to the countryside further west. He took leave of his friends at Culross and taking only habit, staff and small bundle, he set off with his mother before dawn of an autumn morning on the path which led towards the River Clyde.

And so it was that after twenty-one years of waiting since his first dream, Fergus the hermit, now ancient and weary for death, saw Mungo take the lane to his hut and knew that this was the stranger who was to bring him peace. The three ate and prayed together and lay down to sleep. Mungo dreamed of a dead man whose remains he had to take on his journey until he found a burial place ordained of God. When he awoke to ask Fergus if there had been a death nearby, he found that it was the old hermit whose spirit was flown.

Mungo eased out the wood planks that had formed the cell and made a sled of them. He wrapped the body of his host in his clean tunic and laid him on the cart. Shy people who had brought their little gifts to Fergus in the past came out of nearby riverbank touns in twos and threes to help. One man brought bulls and yoked them to the car. Then, by grassy bank, alder grove, rowans, and bushes bright with berries, Mungo led forward the sled and followers, until he reached an old forsaken burial place, a green place near a cluster of small houses further along the Clyde river to the west. There his heart told him was the resting place for Fergus and, when a herd-lad out with his goats told him that long ago the holy Ninian had blessed the spot, Mungo knew that his heart was right. And he knew too, that he himself had come home.

Flora and the Prince

Folk sometimes say that there was some spark of love, a brief romance, between Charles Edward Stuart and Flora Macdonald of Benbecula, during the early summer of 1746. But the romance was in the nervous, brave adventure, and not in long tender looks between the two chief players.

For two months Charles had been flitting from hiding-place to hiding-place in the Outer Isles before the two met and, but for some small rivalry between Flora and a kinswoman, they might never have met at all.

There were three ways of regarding the Prince in Scotland; there were the heart-loyal people who believed implicitly in his father's Divine Right to be King and were prepared to spill their last drop of blood for him; there were those who found the whole escapade frightening and unsettling after thirty years of the Hanovers and either fought firmly against the Jacobites or subscribed to letters of gratitude and hero-worship sent in their name to the man others called 'Butcher Cumberland'; the third group were honest people, content enough with the stodgy Georges who had given them a kind of peace, people who had kin serving in their armies or in the King's government, but who would *not* have sent to death a bonnie Stuart beauty like the Pretender Prince. Not for all the ransom money offered by their government.

Flora Macdonald was one of these last . . . not sighing after Charles, not even favouring his claim, and already deeply in love with her future husband Allan Macdonald, a redcoat officer throughout the campaign. Flora's much-loved foster-father, Clanranald, was in command, too, of King George's troopers on Benbecula. So, although Flora would not have seen the Prince betrayed, her sympathies were not Jacobite.

But then she was asked to do something much more positive than just 'not betray' him. She was young, healthy, spirited and practical, and must have seemed to those in the ploy to be one of the most likely young women on the island to guide Charles on the next chancy stage of his journey to refuge on the continent. At first she prudently refused the Captain who approached her.

'I wish the Prince no ill, and would see him safe. But I cannot join in a plot like that, for my kinfolk are King's men.'

'It is your own foster-father who has thought how best to have him taken safely to Skye.'

Clanranald was a kindly man and Flora could believe this of him, for that reason alone, but also when she considered the unease the Prince's presence had brought to Benbecula and the quietness that would drop over them again when he was gone unharmed, she could see that there might be wisdom in helping him.

'What will people say of me that discover I have been alone all these hours that you speak of, with the Prince?' Flora was in truth not much disturbed by that, but people would certainly talk.

'Neil Macdonald will attend you, but if you fear for your repute Ma'am, *I* will wed you before the escape. I would do so for my Prince; though indeed Ma'am it would not be so great a punishment,' said the Captain gallantly. She laughed.

'That sacrifice will not be necessary, sir, but. . . .' She hesitated still, for Allan's sake. But the Captain tried again.

'Your kinswoman Miss Ailie Macdonald would not dare to serve the Prince when she was asked, but I thought you had more spirit Ma'am.' And that was enough for Flora.

She and the Lady Clanranald prepared the clothes for her big raw-boned Irish maid Betty Burke . . . the flowered gown of country-stuff, the coarse petticoats, the snood, cloak and white cap, and the large shoes which nearly gave her away.

After she had agreed to be the Prince's guide, Flora Macdonald first met Charles Edward Stuart on the 20th June, at her brother's home. A week later, when they were ready to start their journey word came that the redcoat General Campbell had landed with orders to search Benbecula for the fugitive. The scene was set now for such a drama as was almost too theatrical to be true . . . an island at the misty edge of the world, disguises, scarlet coats, a fleeing Prince, brave friends, a hunting general with orders to catch him. And *one* traitor.

In all of Prince Charles's wanderings among simple folk who lived an existence of near bare survival, who were offered thirty-thousand pounds to give him up and who, to a man or woman, could have told where to find him, only the Reverend Mr. Macauley of Benbecula sent word to General Campbell of the Prince's latest hiding-place. Maybe the General did not like traitors or maybe he did not care for this hunting assignment. Whatever the reason the minister's advice was not followed up, the searching of the island was oddly delayed, and was unthorough when it did take place.

Wherever Campbell was when Miss Flora Macdonald, her maid Betty and her manservant Neil Macdonald slipped out from the island in their small boat into the choppy waters of the Minch, he was nowhere to be seen.

That was the closing, not just of a chapter, but of an age in the Highlands. And although it might seem charming and more romantic to believe that Flora and the Prince were even a little in love, or that Flora was a loyal Jacobite, perhaps there's truer romance in knowing that her service was the more generous for not being offered to a Cause, or a sweetheart, but simply to a man in need.

The Weeping Willow of Carmyle

Long, long ago, not too many centuries after the good Bishop Mungo set his holy church in Glasgow, there grew up a number of little settlements along the Clyde river, to the west and to the east.

Upstream of Rutherglen and Balloch Mill the river made a loop and its low banks were watered into fertile grain-land when even the gentlest of rains swelled the river. The place became known as Car-myle.

One winter time two men came there from more barren country in the north, their precious seed-corn slung in satchels across their backs. And there they set their homes, daubing together their stone walls and turving their roofs tight against the weather.

They claimed, for their own, adjoining strips of land, the common boundary of which was marked at the end nearest the river, by a sapling willow. And there they dibbled-in the seed for their first crops.

In the weeks of waiting for the flush of green to appear, they took time off to woo and win two sturdy young women from a cottage on the green at Glasgow, and with them they settled to put down family roots.

By the time of the next sowing, each of the farmers was father to a little son, the one Ninian, with a head fair as bog cotton; the other Dafyd, with hair black as a raven's wing. Within hailing distance of one another the fathers furrowed the soil, the young mothers cast the seed, weeded the rows and sang work-songs, then sat in the shelter of the willow nursing their babes and talking over them, making a soft contented sound like the cushing of doves.

The land rigs were narrow and when the seed from the two satchels was thrown it rose on the wind and fell mingling across the meeting of the strips, so that when the two crops grew they merged and blurred the division between one toft and the other.

When Ninian and Dafyd grew too heavy to be swaddled on their mothers' backs and cradled to the rhythms of each season's work they kicked and crowed happily lying alongside one another among the stooks. In their third year they tumbled together at the women's feet and were as much at home in one cottage as the other.

At nine years old they chased each other in the drills, and swam, swift and clean, in the sunlit waters of the river, or guddled the flashing trout in a pool under the graceful willow. By eleven they could give names to the dipping birds on the river stones and the shy grey wagtails under the overhang of its banks. They had names for flower and tree, known only to themselves and when their laughter over the same things shouted at the sky, their mothers smiled.

Then, at twelve years old, they were suddenly man-strength to their fathers. But even if they were working at opposite ends of their rigs, when the day closed they made for each other at the willow tree like arrows bowed to the same target. Then they folded into a double shadow to walk home together in the dusk.

As the willow matured so too did Ninian and Dafyd, the fair one and the dark; and the holy man who lived in the cell-hut at the next river bend called them the Sons of Saul. What was beautiful to one was beautiful to the other. They shared gloom in things forlorn and joy in all that pleased. And they shared puzzlement in the mysteries of growing into manhood.

During the summer of the year when they were eighteen the families watched a stranger-man bigging a turf cot a quarter of a mile beyond the wester rig. By the first mist of autumn he had pegged out a croft of land and was their neighbour. As soon as they had finished the next week's darge Ninian and Dafyd walked out towards his hut by the river path, meaning to make him welcome and offer him a day's stint to turn over his soil. As they went they picked and ate hazel-nuts and berries, throwing husks and pips light-heartedly at each other and puffing out experimental breath clouds on the frosty air. Then they were at the new hut.

At the self-same moment they both saw the cot-daughter planting wild flowers at her doorway. She was a robin of a girl with cheeks the colour of its red breast, gold-brown skin soft as feathers, and her tunic, stained with leaf-dye, olive as its back. To the earthy lads her slender body bending over her slips of plants was a sweet arc of purest beauty. Each youth stared, mumbled greeting and was stirred to his very core.

Ninian and Dafyd having shared this new joy, never shared another.

Not a word passed between them on the way back, not a nut was split nor a berry spilled of its juice. Next morning at sunrise Ninian, meeting the girl at the river, washing clothes, carried back her basket for her, and at dusk Dafyd left flowers at her door.

Over that winter there was a silence on the two long-established rigs. During the working day each young man brooded on what was in the other's heart, and in the twilight each was wooing the lass the other loved. One night Ninian would walk her along the path to the east of the willow tree; the next, Dafyd the one to the west. And the robin girl, entwining her arm with first the fair one, then the black, could never make up her mind which was the lad to marry, for aside from their looks there was scarcely a blade of difference between them. She would kiss Ninian under the willow sauch one night, sure she must be wife to him and then, on the self-same spot where their lands met, tremble to the touch of Dafyd's lips . . . and the youths grew wild with jealousy.

The ground at the willow tree became a place of torment and delight, each watching the other there from behind a hummock, with set and bitter face, when it was the turn of the rival for the girl's favour. . . .

The crop lay burnished gold the noon-day that Ninian and Dafyd fought for the final claim. They fought with blades they had swept across their grain-stalks together throughout their green years. One, mortally hurt himself and distracted at having slain his friend, then turned the blade on his own heart. Their stricken fathers found them lying by the willow on the trampled corn stained red with their blood, and that afternoon the rival lovers were buried side by side where they had fallen.

But the land had to be worked and, bowed with grief, the two fathers prepared their strips and sowed their seed. The sun shone and the rain came and the crop blew bravely along the drills, green and lush . . . except at the willow tree where Ninian and Dafyd lay. There the ground was bare of corn, a strange colour for these parts, different from all other, potter's red and arid like a desert.

The girl fled from the evil-minding the corner brought back to her, into a safe marriage with a dull and solid Cathedral sexton, twice her age. The boys' parents left their riglands and took to herding Gleschu goats and cattle up the Cow Loan grazing-place. By and by each couple had another child but, although they worked about the same common grassland, the two families never again raised their eyes to each other. Many a one afterwards farmed their old strips, but never an ear of barley grew over that patch. In time the name of Blood Neuk was given to the place and few dared set foot for fear of unknown curse.

And so it might have remained to this day. But one stormy winter's day, long long after the local people had forgotten why the Blood Neuk was so called and long after the descendants of Ninian and Dafyd's kin had forgotten the cause of their old feud, even its existence, one of them, a blond youth rising eighteen, had an errand at the Clyde mill upstream from the Neuk. He was hunching his way homeward against gusting winds and rain squalls, when he stumbled and fell into the swirl of the river under the hang of a grove of willow trees. He caught and held to a branch, crying out for help, but his blue fingers began to slip, and all feeling drained from his legs. Then he felt himself being caught and drawn surely from the clutch of the waters, laid on the bank and wrapped in the rough coat of his rescuer, a black-thatched youth of ages with himself, who was also making his way to Glasgow from business at Boghead.

Together they took their way, supporting each other through the fury of the storm to the town. It was a city rather, by now, and the two parted in the crowds hurrying home to dry firelight. In spite of fine promises to be in contact, they never met again . . . never found a common bond beyond the hand-touch in the storm.

But it was a passing wonder round Carmyle next spring when seed, blown in the sowing from a near-by farm, was seen to have taken root and sent up green shoots at the Blood Neuk; and gool marigolds and poppies waved there when the barley turned to summer gold.

The Tailor and the Ferryman

The rain lay bright on the alder trees and beaded the primroses nestling in the grass beneath, but there was sun now on this bright spring day of 1535. Robert Spittal, the tailor and maker of dresses, came jaunting up the path from the south towards the river-crossing which would take him into Doune village. There was no bridge over the Teith at that time, only a ford inconveniently lower down the river, and the small ferry-boat which Robert was making for that day.

He was pleased with life for the present, for as well as being stitcher to the better-happed people of Doune and the Castle precincts, he was tailor to Margaret Tudor, widowed Queen of his late Majesty King James IV. He was on his way to see her now, by appointment, to measure her for a new court dress in which to receive her son, the young King James V, on a visit of some importance. Robert had also in his satchel several samples, lately sailed in from France, of rich silks that glowed in jewel greens and cramasies and gold, and he knew that they would delight the royal eyes and bring great credit on his taste.

What he did not have in that satchel was, however, something more immediately necessary to him . . . his money-purse. Some fifty yards from the crossing he made the discovery that he had forgotten to bring it, but considered that his credit would satisfy the ferryman, and strode lightly on.

But if, as a breed, millers were dubbed proud men and gravediggers glum ones, ferrymen were reckoned close-fisted and avaricious, the more so for having travellers at their mercy. The ferryman of Doune was just such a man. He plied to and fro across the river and sometimes helped the drovers from the trysts to guide their animals across the ford . . . for a fat fee.

Laughing at his own absentmindedness Robert airily explained that he had left his pouch behind in his workroom, that he would pay his way on the morrow, and he prepared to step into the small boat.

'Bide there on the bank, Robert Spittal, for you'll no' cross Teith the day, wi'out you've siller for your fare,' growled the ferryman.

'It's no' the river o' death John Row-boat, I'll be back the morrow.'

'Nae fare, nae ferry,' insisted the ferryman.

'Come man, fine you ken my word on my money's good. The King's mother hersel' waits for me at the Castle.'

'More fool you to come wi'oot your pooch. Were you the Queen hersel' I wouldna carry you,' sneered the man. Robert was angry now.

'Would you have me tell her so?' he threatened.

'An you please, tailor,' said surly John, and pushed away from the bank, empty of passenger, to fetch a laundry-woman from the other side who had the gleam of pennies in her hand.

Robert Spittal would have thrown the ferryman into the water had the man not been well out into the river, and he had to content himself with a shaken fist, before he turned to make his way downstream to the ford. His pleasure in the day was spoiled. He had on his best braws for his meeting with the Queen, his good doublet and breeches, a new pair of cream silk stockings and buckle shoes: a fine state they would be in with the jawps of mud that would spatter them at the ford, for it had rained for weeks until this bright morning and he would not get over the river-bed dry-shod.

He would not get over the river-bed in time for his appointment either, and there was a deal of muttering to himself as he walked to the crossing and uphill to the castle.

Up there in her private apartments overlooking the courtyard the Queen waited. She was a lonely woman now, fearing herself half-forgotten, but she would not have been Margaret Tudor, the great Henry VIII's sister and late wife to the martyr of Flodden if she had not been in a right royal tizz that her tailor was so long in coming. (Indeed there were those who had wondered of James IV and his lady which of them was truly the Thistle, which the Rose.) Now certainly her hackles were up. If Spittal failed her today she might not have the gown she had set her heart on to have audience of her son. It would be an important meeting for she would be urging on him again the necessity of finding a Queen of his own and siring legitimate children. At twenty-two he already had three sons out of wedlock. Better far that he should have a quiverful of heirs than love-children in every keep between here and Edinburgh. The dress must be right . . . regal, stately and cut as only Master Spittal could scissor it with long lines to flatter the dowager figure.

Then there was the sound of challenge from the gate-house and she glanced down to see Robert swinging swiftly across the green . . . at last, at last!

Tradition does not tell what kind of confrontation Spittal had with the Queen Mother. But he was neither hung nor thrown into any of Doune's considerable dungeoning, for he lived to make John Ferryman regret his truculent denial of the tailor that spring morning, and to appease the Queen with more than the magnificent gown in which she ordered her son into matrimony.

Robert Spittal was a bien man for a sartor. He was a superb craftsman, much in demand among the well-coffered of the royal town and he was wealthy beyond the dreams of other plodding tailors whose work was rough-cut and ill put-together by comparison. He brooded for a while on the ferryman's punishment and that autumn had a fine two-arched bridge set across the Teith. Within a week or two the man and his boat were quite put out of business and even the drovers forsook the ford and took to using the brig, for unlike others of the time this one was of stone and the beasts did not panic as they did to hear the drumming of their hooves on wood.

And the inscription carved on the bridge above a pair of tailor's shears pleased the Lady of Doune Castle who feared to be forgotten, for she was there described in stone, for all to see and remember as long as the arches stood, as the Most Noble Princess, Queen of James IV.

Note: Robert Spittal, the tailor of Doune, is recorded as having made so many provisions for travellers, for the poor and for the sick, that it is unlikely that he had the 'brig fundit' out of pique. But the tradition persists and perhaps shame for the reason of his first benefaction motivated the rest.

Three Little Tales of Zachary Boyd

1. The Scolding

In the middle years of the 17th century Zachary Boyd was minister of the Barony Parish Kirk in Glasgow. The Barony was one of several congregations which, at that time, met for worship in the Cathedral building (another being the Outer High parish flock). Zachary Boyd's Barony people were housed in the Cathedral crypt.

No doubt other of its ministers, before and after, shepherded his people as gently through their perplexing paths as Zachary, and preached as earnestly, with as much scholarship and directness. But from these old days in Glasgow it is his name that comes most endearingly to mind as one of the pawkiest, most eccentric, yet sternest, characters ever to occupy a city pulpit, or walk its streets leaving a trail of savoury anecdotes behind.

But on the Sunday morning when this incident began (and it is no more than that) no such thoughts of himself as being worth the time of a chronicler, filled Zachary's mind. He was expounding from eight headings and texts on the double doctrines of justification and the priesthood-of-all-believers, to the great weariness of his hearers on their stools and benches round the walls and in the body of the kirk. The douce days of pew and formal order-of-service were not yet part of church life, and Zachary's expression grew grimmer by the text as he watched, insulted for God and for himself, while a sizeable part of his congregation began to slip away. They turned their heads away from his gimlet recognising eyes, and crept along the shadows of the side-walls then up into the sunlight of the Sabbath morning.

Discretion, of course, brought them back in the afternoon, if only to record their attendance, and while the minister had them as captive worshippers at least for the early part of the service he made the most of the first intercessions to have the backsliders squirming.

'Now Lord,' he prayed, 'Thou seest that many of Thy people do, whiles, go away ower soon from the hearing of the Word, but, O Lord, had I tell't them stories of Robin Hood, or else the bawdy tales of David Lyndsay, then they'd hae stayed . . . and yet none of these is near as grippin' as the good Word that I, Thy unworthy servant, preach.'

Every manjack in the kirk had doubts that Zachary considered himself an unworthy servant, but they sat cowering and rebuked, resolving never to sin so again, but to sit out the sermon in the future, howsomever long. At least until *the next* fine sunny Sabbath.

2. Deuce

There was no way in which an ordinary citizen could have cocked a snook at the great Master Boyd for his long sermons and stern ways, even if it had been thinkable to try. But some rubbed sheepish hands and relished the tale that they heard in the October of 1650 when Oliver Cromwell himself marched on the city.

Cromwell had come to purge Scotland of any remnant of loyalty to the Stuarts and to tidy up the church life of the northern half of the country. He had mastered Edinburgh and now, in Glasgow, magistrates and ministers had fled before his army, except for the two ministers of the Cathedral congregations who, he had heard, were ready to oppose him. Cromwell with his train of attendant Puritans processed to the Cathedral and down into the Barony crypt to hear the wayward preaching of this Reverend Zachary Boyd.

Zachary excelled himself that morning and at first Cromwell glowed with sober satisfaction that his presence was inspiring the minister of this rough outpost of Christendom, to wisdom and acquiescence in sound doctrine. But Boyd did go on at great length and Cromwell found his mind wandering as his gaze took in the ancient stone walls and pillars, satisfactorily naked of Popish ornament. But through his dwam he was taken aback to hear his own name thundering out from the pulpit, in a tone and context which were certainly not respectful. The Protector was alert again now to the minister.

This Zachary Boyd, he soon realised, was admonishing him in no uncertain terms and calling down all manner of punishments and hell-fire, on him and his invading army. Eloquently he recounted and criticised every step of the history of Cromwell's rebellion against the Stuarts with devastating knowledge of its course. The Lord Protector himself was torn between a desire to hear this passionate man out and having him by the ears for his insolence. Indeed Master Thurlow, his secretary, sitting now by his side in church, jumped up, his pistol cocked in his hand.

"Tis treason, my Lord, let me take the scoundrel where he stands,' he cried. But the warted face was thoughtful.

'Don't be a greater fool, sir, than you take him for. Sit down and hold your peace. There are juster ways to better such a man.'

A note was delivered to Zachary Boyd's house the following day and the minister felt that his Sabbath message had hit home and that, under God, he had chastened the Protector, because he was now invited to dine with Cromwell. . . .

The meal was frugal, with Puritan fare that any Glasgow gude-wife would have scorned to put on her table. Little was said about the Sabbath's preaching. Cromwell seemed more interested in the welfare of Glasgow's citizens, the number and state of the town's schools and the condition and stock of books in the University library.

Then, when the bell for 'eleven o'clock night-time' rang through the streets, Cromwell called his household together and invited Zachary to join them at family worship. After the reading from the Book came time for prayer. Oliver knelt down motioning Boyd and the others to their knees also. Then for all of four hours he prayed in sepulchral tones . . . on behalf of himself and those present, in repentance for a litany of sins, for cleansing of hearts; in petition, and in atonement for every conceivable sin, in thanks-giving for a score of blessings, and in endlesss intercessions for all kinds and conditions of men in every thrall, predicament, mis-fortune, overfortune, sin and anxiety, in every social station, profession and country of the world.

Zachary was stoical. He did not sigh nor budge and if his 'Amen' was unusually fervent as he rose to his feet at three o'clock in the morning, it was the only acknowledgement that Cromwell had matched him will for will. Cromwell did not scold Boyd over his preaching for it had given him much to ponder; and the minister did not reproach the Protector about his praying, for it had been manifestly sincere, though easily worth spreading over a week or two if only not to deave the Lord God.

Some time later there arrived in Glasgow, from Cromwell, then safely back in England, a munificent gift of seven hundred pounds, to buy new books for the University library.

3. Zachary's Legacy

Zachary Boyd's career as cleric, scholar and maker of psalms metrical, had been one of conscientious integrity without thought of wealth or plaudit for himself. But his congregation, the citizens and tradesmen he met with in the course of his days, even the other Cathedral ministers, held him in considerable awe. But it was general clash, among those who knew him best, that one who was not in the least intimidated by the Barony 'man' was Mistress Zachary Boyd, Margaret Mure that-was.

During the latter days of Boyd's ministry one of the other pastors using the Cathedral building was James Durham of the High Kirk Parish, a personable and charming man whose notion for Margaret Boyd, and hers for him, was, they fondly thought, a secret between the two of them. Zachary and James Durham, working side by side in the Cathedral precincts, were nevertheless close friends and sat under a late tallow many a night chawing over points where their theology differed.

But Zachary was failing, and during his convalescence after long illness one winter, he sat by the fireside one day, dictating to Margaret the terms of his last will and testament. There were legacies to various of his kinfolk, to this good cause and that project, to the University and to several hospices.

'D'you no' think to leave a wee something to your good friend Master Durham?' asked Margaret, her quill poised ready.

'Mm,' considered Zachary . . . 'maybe . . . but I'll no' make it money or goods . . . I think . . . aye I'll leave him what I ken fine he has already . . . thy bonnie self.'

Tradition does not tell whether the ink spluttered from Margaret's pen or whether perhaps she swooned in outrage. But whatever the end of that quiet fireside scene, it is certainly true that, within a very short time of Zachary Boyd's death, his bonnie relict became Mistress James Durham and manse-wife to the High Kirk congregation.

The Brood Sow and the Border Gipsy

It was a wicked winter night not long after the death of Queen Anne. The woman stirring the broth-pot over a fire in a broken-down Border barn thought about the late Queen from time to time for, like her, Jean Gordon had borne over a dozen bairns but, unlike her, had seen nine sons grow up lusty and as wild as the hills they roamed. She threw in another chopping of kail and turnip for it was near midnight and all nine would be in presently looking for a hot sup.

But the traveller who was frantically looking for landmarks a mile away was not one of Jean Gordon's wights. There was a freezing mist out there, creeping, banking and swirling, changing familiar outlines and hiding well-kent boulders in the valley-passes through the Cheviots. As the drifts came and went, the exhausted man wished with all his heart that he was home at Yetholm where he was gude-man at the farmhouse of Lochside. But he had had to make this journey to collect rents for his laird, from properties he owned a mile or two across the Border. Now he was bound for home, his takings in a leather pouch at his waist.

There were two dangers from his dreich surroundings. One was that he might be set on by thieves who knew where they were and would suspect a lone man out in such weather, to be on important business and probably carrying money. But to meet them might be preferable to the second danger, of growing weary and completely lost in such cold, of being forced to rest and never rise again.

The sight of a faint but steady glow of light, spread and diffused by the mist, cheered him to the core, for only a near light could pierce such thickness and only a building, rather than moving men, hold the light so steady.

The bulk of the derelict barn loomed up almost immediately. There was no home-cot nearby so the building was certainly not in use for its original purpose.

The farmer stumbled to the door space, confused in the light, and the woman inside lifted her lamp, came forward and peered out. She was the fitter of the two that night, and alert enough to know him at once for the gude-man of Lochside. He was too far-spent at first to place her and she had time to gather herself and consider, while she drew him in and set him to thaw at the fire, blazing cheerfully under the roof-hole.

Jean Gordon was in her middle forties, married on to Patrick, of the Faa gipsy tribe around Kirk Yetholm. It was a mark of the farmer's exhaustion that he had not immediately known her for she had once been a kenspeckle-enough figure to him. She was all of six feet tall, with a beaky nose between penetrating eyes, and a bush of wiry hair standing out stiff to her shoulders, under a gipsy-style straw bonnet which she wore even indoors. The odd, short-cloak and the long walking staff which she would have had when Lochside last saw her at his door, or roving the sheep-tracks, were now thrown into a corner of the barn.

But for the moment she had the advantage of him. Many a time in the past she had known hospitality at the farmer's hands; a coggie of brose, a night with one or other of her brood of bairns in his hay, or a few pence in return for a small task. For that reason she had never lifted so much as an egg, never mind the chicken she would happily have filched from any other less kindly household.

That had been a matter of pride to her for years while her boys were young, but she had been black-shamed when, in their teens, the lads had stolen a brood sow from Lochside and in her affront she had never gone near the place again.

With a helping of Jean's thick broth inside him and a measure of rough ale at his elbow, Lochside was better able to take stock. He knew Jean Gordon now and, grateful as he was for harbour, he feared for the laird's rent money and his own ruin if he lost it, and he held his arms close to his sides. He had no reason to think she herself had not been behind that old lifting of the sow, which had meant much to a small cot-farmer.

'Best you bide here the nicht for it's ill out there,' and she jerked a horny thumb at a bed length in a sheltered corner of the crumbling barn.

He hesitated when he saw the size of the broth cauldron on the fire, for the woman was clearly expecting some big gathering of men to be fed. And yet a glance at the fog clouding past the doorspace told him he must accept her offer. She saw his doubt, guessed at his money, and stirred slowly like some gaunt witch.

'I ken you've mind of yon sow, Lochside, and I tak' blame it was my lads took it,' she admitted. 'And you're richt that this is their sup, for when they come by presently. But if, as I trow, you've money somewheres on you and if you would tak' it hame safe, you'll hae to trust me, for my bairns grow no better. . . . Gie me your money to keep for you, not just *all* of it, keep a wee pickle to put them aff.'

Lochside knew that he was like to lose it all anyway, so grudgingly he counted out all but a jingle of coins and watched with fearful fascination as Jean lifted her sark and thrust the money into her own pouch.

Presently there were sounds of men's guffawing voices carried in on the wisps of mist trailing through the wall chinks, and in jostled the nine men-bairns of Jean Gordon. They were a rough, evil looking pack who obeyed no rites of hospitality. For they had not been inside above five minutes when Lochside was on his back half-stripped, in the search for whatever of value he carried. They took the new belt he had bought at Kelso last fair-day and the few coins left in his pouch then, disgusted that it was not any more worth their effort, threw him aside and fell to a long deep carousal round the fire after their broth. One by one they keeled over into a stupor of ale-sleep, and only then did Lochside relax into fitful dozing for an hour or two, while outside the mist rolled away and into the next valley.

At daybreak he woke to the snores of the Faa men and the sight of Jean Gordon leaning over him, the towering height, the shock of stiff white hair, the ancient hat and now the cutty shawl-cape round her shoulders all making a grotesque shadow on the wall. She gave him a kerchief to tie up his breeches, beckoned him to follow and led him out to his path home. Then she thrust a grey-looking bannock into his hand and, but for the stolen pennies, all his money. He held out a thank-offering but she waved it aside as far less than the cost of the brood sow. She saw him go and turned back into the old barn, gave him time to be well on his way, then wakened her lads to plan with them what villany they could do that day to some luckless and less-deserving victim than the farmer of Lochside.

All nine sons of Jean Gordon Faa were eventually gibbeted together on the same grey day at Jedburgh and Jean herself, for all her peculiar code, was caught in petty theft and ducked to death in the river Eden at Carlisle. But Lochside did not forget the night of the mist. While she lived Jean Gordon had ever a bite at his door, and when she was dead he would not have her cursed for a thief in his hearing.

Jinty White and the Sinful Prayer

It was quite an adventure that Mistress Janet White, of the village of Woodside, had that October day of 1773 . . . quite an adventure. Jinty was a wash-wife and she had made her usual Saturday delivery of clean bleached linen to two-three lady-wives she laundered for in town. Now she was tramping through the fields towards home.

She was a comely widow-woman was Jinty, not young enough to be flighty or silly, and not old enough to be past a warm chaffing from a likely man. And she was as blithe as the bright day, singing snatches of songs as she took the path through a bonnie bit of woodland beside a small open coal-pit a mile or so from home.

Small wonder she sang, for she carried her money-payment for the washing and, forbye, she had a whang of kebbock and a round of oatmeal bannock from one of her ladies. The cash was in the leather pouch at her side and the makings of her supper in her big white apron that she had tucked up like a bag and pinned with a great brass pin at her back.

October, so it was nutting and bramble time and Jinty thought to gather a nibbling of hazel-nuts and these plump black berries she could see beading the bushes. The nuts were already opening, shiny and brown, and easily gathered. So was the first handful of brambles. But the very best and fattest were, as they ever are, almost out of reach at the back of the bushes, by the edge of the pit. She leaned forward and oops-a-daisy . . . over she toppled . . . down into the pit.

It could have been two minutes or an hour later that she came out of her dwam, scratched and sore about the knees, but otherwise unharmed. Her purse was still tied firmly, and her food was safe, so she cupped her hands and shouted.

'Help! I'm in the coal-pi-i-it!' Three times she shouted in the first five minutes and then at longer intervals for an hour . . . then another hour. But no one heard.

She had not thought it worthwhile at first to check out her surroundings for a long stay but when nobody had answered her cries in three hours, she began to consider her predicament. She had milk-cheese and mealie-cake, a handful of nuts and she could see bramble wands laden with fruit at one side of the pit. She also glimpsed a trickle of clear spring water and was comforted that she would not die of thirst.

She could eke out her food for quite some time too, so unless an untimely frost came down she felt she could survive awhile yet. She shouted once or twice in vain, then as dusk began to fall, sighed, swept up her flannel petticoat over her head, tried not to heed the croaking of frogs, and went to sleep rolled up like a hedge-hog.

Next day was the Sabbath. She breakfasted on brambles and bannock, then thought 'I to the hills . . . ' would be a sensible psalm to sing in such a plight. But that thought of the Lord put her in a swither as to whether she could properly pray to Him to be saved that day, when she full well knew that it would be only a Sabbath-breaking sinner that would happen along to rescue her, for there was no kirk near, to bring good folk past the coal-pit on their way to worship.

Then it came to her quite comfortably that, since she was a sinner herself, it wouldn't be out-of-the-way to ask for a sinner to come by and pull her out. And so Mistress Jinty White ordered her day in a tidy programme of eating, drinking, shouting, napping, and praying for both rescue and forgiveness.

But the good Lord had a wee lesson in patience for Jinty and it was Tuesday afternoon before she was heard by anyone other than Himself when a man in working clothes peered down from the edge of the pit and saw her there, dishevelled but still cheerful and bonnie. He went off to bring back a rope and two lads to help him pull her up.

Of course he saw her home to her trig little cottage and her bleaching green at Woodside, and of course by the springtime they were man and wife.

It would be nice to record that they lived happy ever after; but indeed no, they did not. He was an idle, graceless scamp who spent too much of her laundry money in the ale-house and Jinty wondered often as she scrubbed and blanched her ladies' linens, if her lot was just what she deserved for her ungodly prayers yon time in the coal-pit.

But no again! It was only that the good Lord was still teaching her that patience, for they say that in years to come, when her man was gone, their son rejoiced his mother's heart by turning out for a minister. She was awed to be the mother of a man-of-the-cloth and, ever after, took a deal more care in her prayers.

The Honours of Scotland

The conflicting details of the great tale of the Scottish Crown Jewels are an irritation to the story-teller who wants to have it plain and true, but the confusion is maybe a measure of the wiles of the conspirators and the various ruses and red-herrings to bamboozle Cromwell's soldiers over the whole enterprise.

The main facts are quite clear, that one day the Crown, Sceptre and Sword of State were in danger, outside the only remaining stronghold in Scottish hands, and the next day they were safely inside; and that shortly afterwards, when the castle itself was threatened, they were carried to safer safety outside again, without the besieging troops having any idea how or by whom either adventure was conducted.

The different versions of 'how' perhaps arise because, not only the Regalia was flitted, but at different times various documents as well; and of 'who' because a dozen or more rescuers were involved.

But all good tales begin with 'once upon a time' and the starting time for this one was the execution of Charles I in 1649 and the dour days when Oliver Cromwell gave himself the Divine Right to rule, which before had always been of Kings. There was a fine healthy royal heir, of course, to be disposed of first, and although the new Charles II made staunch efforts to get at his English crown, the only one he got was the ancient Scottish one that was laid on his head at Scone as it had been laid on Robert the Bruce's three hundred and fifty years before. So Charles was, at least, King of Scotland. He spent the next year and more, trying to better Oliver Cromwell for the rest of his inheritance, but a final routing at Worcester in 1651 chased the King to France to charm the ladies, to plan for the day, if it ever came, when he would be back; and meantime to leave Cromwell, Lord Protector of all he surveyed. Or almost all.

There were still pockets in Scotland loyal to the crowned King and, having dealt with Charles at Worcester, Cromwell marched his troops north and soon had his governors in every castle and great keep, except one. That was the sturdy, brooding cliff-top pile of Dunnottar Castle on the Kincardine coast. It was large enough to house a small community, with its own forge for making arms, and its bowling-green for more peaceful pursuits. The Scottish Parliament was in disarray but hurriedly sent word to the Earl Marischal, Hereditary Keeper of the Crown Jewels, to have them taken to Dunnottar, along with various documents, privy and highly dangerous to the King's party.

But that was an instruction by someone who had not seen the highways and byways of Kincardine, alive with Cromwell's soldiers moving about among the keeps of the area, and re-connoitring around Dunnottar itself to plot how best to take it. There could therefore be no triumphant entry of the Jewels to the castle, with pennants streaming and drumbeat, for the capture of the Honours, along with the letters and papers, would be a double feather in the round English helmets. While Cromwell's captains and their most trusted and alert men scoured the vaults and cellars of the castles already taken, looking for the Regalia, and searched the landscape for small troops of men secretly scurrying towards Dunnottar, others were stationed close by the castle in case such a group came to try and enter it with the treasures.

The stronghold was only under siege as yet. There was still free passage for the coming and going of old labouring servant-men, and Royalist soldiers might just try to slip in with them. But nothing untoward had excited suspicion for two or three weeks. Servants came and went from their homes in the village and besieging soldiers grew bored and disgruntled. A few had managed to entice silly young maidservants, who knew nothing of King and Parliament to daff with them in the leas of rocky outcrops in the moorland round about the castle.

Sergeant John Cady had won two of them like that and now when he saw a sonsy lass coming along the cliff path with her laundry one afternoon he wagered his companions that she would be his third. He pinched her red country cheeks and waited for the pert response which usually came, before a girl would dimple and capitulate. But with this one there was no such put-off. Instead she pulled his face down to hers, kissed him firmly on the lips and, humphing her laundry bundle, walked through a side way into the castle leaving him gaping. The others laughed and would not pay up.

'There man, you didn't get her. She took you!'

'It was as easy as that,' Mistress Drummond told her man in the manse that night. She was doffed, now, of coarse plaid and of the blush that had stained her douce cheeks when she ogled the stranger-sergeant. Her husband, the minister of the parish church, shivered, put an arm round her shoulders and was thankful that it was all over and Crown, Sceptre and Sword were out of the laundry bundle and into safe-keeping at Dunnottar with his friend Captain George Ogilvie, the Lieutenant-Governor.

But it was far from being all over. Having found no trace of the ancient treasures in the other castles, especially of the Crown which had so wilfully been placed on Charles's brow, Cromwell's officers were now the more determined to take the last remaining stronghold of Dunnottar, for surely there they would find the Regalia. The garrison inside the castle knew now that it was only a matter of time before it fell.

The siege was tightened into a blockade, those who were inside stayed there and, after a young girl cousin of the governor's wife was allowed out, without bundle or horse, her hands empty at her sides, to go home to safety with her own family, no one else was permitted to pass in or out, nor was there any food or supply let through. It was now only a matter of waiting for the castle to be taken, for the Honours of Scotland and whatever important documents were there, to fall like ripe plums into Cromwell's hands.

Meanwhile as the officers gloated at that prospect, young Miss Ogilvie, safe in the bosom of her family, was carefully unstitching the King's precious papers from the inside of her stays and passing on another plan for the minister of Kinneff nearby.

As stores in the castle dwindled, a fierce determination had grown in the Lieutenant-Governor and his wife for the Honours to be taken to safety and not allowed to go into the melting-pot as those of England had done. But Crown, Sceptre and Sword would not be taken out of Dunnottar so easily. Miss Ogilvie went to see the Kinneff minister, Master Grainger.

It was not only the besieged who were finding the blockade long-drawn-out and tedious. The soldiers, still posted outside the castle to maintain their dreich vigil and starve out the small community, were growing to hate the bleak bulk of Dunnottar and the harsh, uncivilised coastal countryside. The ordinary soldiers wished they were back at home in Warwickshire or Lincoln where their womenfolk lived, warm and friendly among their neighbours, dressed decent in Puritan grey, with good shoes and stockings and hooded cloaks, and had fine beef and ale for their tables . . . not like these Kincardine peasant-wives in rough plaids, their feet wrapped in sackings, who were to be seen every day gathering sea-weeds to make their broth.

There were some of them down there now, working slowly over the shore, singly, huddled under plaids, and either dragging sleds or leading panniered ponies. They trailed handfuls of weeding, stowed it on to the carts or into the pony-baskets, then moved to the next tangled drifts. High above them the soldiers laughed. One of them dislodged a stone with his foot, timing it to drop in front of one of the ponies to make it shy. The woman looked up angrily and shook a fist at them. Then she passed out of sight and they turned their wandering attention back to making sure that no one sneaked in or out of the castle.

The peasant beachcomber was close to the sheer cliff now, gathering her sea-dulse entirely out of sight, except there had been anyone hugging the shore in a small boat. She made sure there was not, and then gathered in a bundle hanging down over the cliff from the castle above. Carefully she untied the rope and placed the bundle into one of the panniers and covered it so that tendrils of glossy wet weed trailed from under the lid.

Slowly she came back into view of the soldiers, had they been looking. But they had finished their sport with her and were dicing with each other who would take first chance with the next likely girl who passed along the track between the hamlets. On the shore, in no apparent hurry, the peasant-woman plodded with her pony towards the manse of nearby Kinneff parish, where she was maidservant and where she presently arrived, slowly unpacked one of the baskets and carried its contents into the kitchen.

'There y'are Master Grainger, sir, and Mistress. Your parcel's safe.'

The Minister and his wife unfolded the flax wrappings and looked silently at the Crown, Sceptre and Sword of their ancient line of Kings, smuggled out to them by the Governor and Mistress Ogilvie, still captive in the castle.

The Graingers hid the Regalia in their bed and waited in an agony of suspense for the next moonless night. Then they carried the Honours into the empty, echoing church. There in front of his pulpit James Grainger scraped away the loose, dusty earth from round a paving-slab, scrabbled out a hole and laid in it the Crown and Sceptre. The scooped-out earth was brushed over it again and and the slab fell back with a thud. At the other end of the nave between two bench-seats where, if it could be seen at all for the shadows, it would look like part of the woodwork, he laid the Sword in its casing. Then he knelt down and prayed to God to keep safe the Regalia for as long or short a time as the rightful King would be in exile.

Lest that be longer than his own span, once back home in the manse he wrote and sealed a document setting out where the treasures were to be found. The letter was shown to a few trusted friends, then despatched to the Dowager Countess Marischal whose family were the Hereditary Keepers of the Crown Jewels.

Then all concerned with the adventure settled down to the long wait for Cromwell's cheerless Commonwealth to be over and Charles II to come into his own.

Many of the players in the drama had risked their very lives, the ministers and their wives, the maid at Kinneff, the Ogilvies and their young cousin, and yet, almost as soon as the bells were ringing in London to welcome back the King in 1660, it was the most marginally involved, the Dowager Countess Marischal, who fluttered south to tell the King where his Scottish Crown was hidden and to claim royal credit for its preservation. The Regalia was recovered from Kinneff kirk and delivered to Charles's representative. Minor honours and rewards eventually came the way of the others, but doubtless their satisfaction was in having the true memories of the adventure and in seeing the pieces used on all formal Scottish occasions for as many of the forty years before the Union of the Parliaments in 1707, as they lived.

Then some minion from the south had these ancient symbols, which had been used at coronations for centuries, put into a kist and locked away in Edinburgh Castle, while new English Crown Jewels were prepared in London, for, of the old, not even the Crown of Alfred the Great had survived the melting-down.

The Scottish ones lay forgotten by most people, but it was a burr in the breeks of Scots with longer memories that the Honours of Scotland, so much the more ancient Regalia, had been thrown aside while people marvelled at the shiny new ones in London. It certainly rankled with the romantic Sir Walter Scott until he arranged for a ceremonial dusting-off of the old kist. The jewels, not seen by a living soul for over a hundred years, were opened at last to the gaze of the party gathered in Edinburgh Castle for the occasion and put thereafter on public display in the Crown Room.

That may not be the true story in every particular. Some would have it that the Crown and Sceptre came out of Dunnottar, not in a dangling bundle over the cliff, but through a company of the besieging soldiers wrapped in bundles of flax with the sword disguised as a distaff to spin it. Others say that the lady carrying them was handed up into her carriage by the officer commanding

Cromwell's troops himself, and that she passed through the rest of the enemy and down the track with the package sitting on her lap.

That would have been bold and brave, but perhaps common-sense and wile were better strategy.

Glossary

Abune   Above
agley   awry
ahint   behind
an   if
Baulk   obstruct
bawbees   ha'pennies
bide   remain
bien   prosperous
biggin   building
blat   blow noisily
blether   chatter
braw   fine
breeks   trousers
brose   uncooked porridge
burr   jaggy seed-head
Cantrips   ongoings
chawner   persistent chatter
cladding   clothing
coggie   drinking bowl
corp   body
cramasie   crimson
craws   crows
cutty-stool   low stool
deave   deafen
douce   well-behaved
dugong   mythical sea-cow
dun   importune, dull-coloured
dwam   daze
Fae   from
fankle   tangle
fey   seeing beyond the natural

flit   move house
Gallused   hanged
gar'd   caused
gauger   customs officer
geegaw   trinket
girdle   iron baking plate
girnal   meal chest
glaury   muddy
glebe   patch of land, part of minister's stipend
gravat   cravat
grue   shudder
guddle   fish by hand
gude-daughter   daughter-in-law
gurlie   threatening (of weather)
Hap   wrap
hold one's wheesht   keep quiet
Ingle   fire
Jimp-kept   neatly arranged
jo   partner
jougs   punishment collar
jouk   dodge
juts (n.)   outcrops
Kail   vegetables
kain   (in) kind
kenspeckle   well-known by sight
Luckenbooth   locking stall
lum   chimney
Midden   rubbish tip
mind   remember
mort-kist   coffin

moudie	mole
mutch	head cloth tying under chin
Oxter	armpit
Partan	crab
perjink	fussy, neat
philabeg	kilt (sometimes used of sporran)
pickle	little or few
pinkie	little finger
plaid	large shawl
pother	bother
pouthered	powdered
Quern	handmill for corn
Rant	rousing music or poetry
reiving	rustling of stock
rig	narrow stretch of arable land
rile	anger
rodden	rowan
Sangster	singer
sark	shirt
sartor	tailor
sauch	willow
scart	scratch
sennight	week
shanks	legs
shauchling	shuffling
shieling	shepherd's summer shelter
skeely	skilful
smit	infection
sonsy	plump
sorner	idle beggar
sough	sigh or moan
spence	good room
spiel	discourse
spier	ask
spirtle	wooden stirring stick
staw	grudge, aversion
steerin'	restless, stirring
stoup	drinking-jug
stravaig	wander
swee	arm with chain for cooking pot
swither	dither
Tagle	tangle, hinder
targe	shield
tawse	punishment strap
teeter	balance
theekit	thatched
thirl	bind
thole	endure
thrawn	stubborn
tinkler	tinker
tirl	rattle
tocher	dowry
toft	area of land, formerly tilled
toper	drinker
Trongate	city gate close to town trone or weighing-machine
tulsie	tussle
Unco	too, overly
usque/usqueba	whisky
vittles	victuals
Wae	sad
wake	a ritual sitting-up with the dead
wersh	tasteless
whang	a cutting or slice
whiles	sometimes
wight	strong man